I0747261

Look, I'm Gone

A Novel by
James Howard Kunstler

Look, I'm Gone
First edition, published 2025

Written by James Howard Kunstler

Copyright © 2025 by James Howard Kunstler. All rights reserved.

Softcover ISBN 978-1-952685-97-2

No part of this publication may be reproduced, stored in a retrieval system, or transmitted in any form or by any means—electronic, mechanical, photocopying, recording, or otherwise—without the prior written permission of the publisher, except for brief quotations used in reviews or scholarly works.

This is a work of fiction. While it may include references to real people, including public figures, all events, dialogue, and characterizations are fictitious and created for the purpose of literary expression. The portrayal of any real person, living or deceased, is entirely fictionalized and not intended to represent factual statements about them or their actions, beliefs, or intentions.

Disclaimer Regarding Real Persons: This novel includes a fictional representation of Jerome David Salinger (J.D. Salinger), the late American author. This portrayal is a work of imagination and artistic expression, not an assertion of fact. It is not authorized, endorsed, or approved by the Salinger estate or its representatives. The use is intended as a respectful literary homage and commentary, and falls under fair use principles.

General Disclaimer: The author and publisher have made every effort to ensure the accuracy of information presented in this book. However, they assume no responsibility for errors or omissions, or for damages resulting from the use of the information contained herein.

For information, contact:

KITSAP PUBLISHING

Poulsbo, WA
www.KitsapPublishing.com

BY JAMES HOWARD KUNSTLER

Fiction

The World Made by Hand Series
The Harrows of Spring
A History of the Future
The Witch of Hebron
World Made by Hand

A Safe and Happy Place
Maggie Darling, a Modern Romance
Thunder Island
The Halloween Ball
The Hunt
Blood Solstice
An Embarrassment of Riches
The Life of Byron Jaynes
A Clown in the Moonlight
The Wampanaki Tales

Nonfiction

Young Man Blues
CrazyLand
Beauty and Catastrophe
Living in the Long Emergency
Too Much Magic
The Long Emergency
The City in Mind
Home From Nowhere
The Geography of Nowhere

This book is for my many friends lost in the vicissitudes of the 2020s.

Chapter One

Ponsonby Hall, the preparatory school for boys "thriving indifferently"—meaning, boys who had behaved badly elsewhere, or flunked out, or caused something to happen that aroused threats of the law, or perpetrated disreputable acts that engaged the law directly, or who were discarded by parents comporting themselves indifferently—loomed darkly atop an ancient drumlin formed by retreating glacial meltwaters above a thousand-acre domain of paper birch and white pine forest four miles from the mill town of Orcus, New Hampshire, on the Pompoquoddy River.

A special place for special boys, the school's ancient motto declared. "Old Poison" and "Possibly Hell," generations of boys styled the place. The Great Hall itself, a heap of red sandstone on a gray granite base in the Railroad Romanesque style, sported a variety of gables, bays, oriels, turrets, and towers with pointy finials amid steep copper roofs aged perfectly to blue-green verdigris. From a winging crow's point of view, the unbroken forest seemed to extend without limit west to the Connecticut River Valley and beyond to the Green Mountains of neighboring Vermont, rendering fugitive thoughts of escape nearly impossible among the one hundred fifty-four resident "scholars," as they were called in the school's promotional literature. (Among themselves, the scholars traditionally called themselves "inmates.")

From that same soaring crow's vantage, a few other buildings came into view behind the Great Hall: the old dairy from the days when the boys milked the school's own herd of twenty Holstein cows (said to be "character building"), discontinued after the Second World War; the field house, a US Air Force post–Korean War surplus portable field hangar with a distressed fiberglass roof that leaked in a thousand places and merely redistributed nature's own rainfall pattern within; and the handsome, original carriage house erected when Ponsonby Hall was the residence of the asbestos magnate Felix Fogelhaus, a bachelor who went down with the RMS Titanic in 1912. (Meanwhile, our crow has flown off ahead on its own urgent business.)

The property was acquired by the educational pioneer, and acolyte of William James at Harvard, Dr. Cecil Hatch, who founded the school in 1915 under the rubric: Normalizing the errant child through God's love. After Dr. Hatch died in a freak Easter vacation accident in 1938, beset by a swarm of stinging sea nettles in the surf off Jekyll Island, Georgia, Harry Raymond ("Doc") Stilgoe, PhD, chronicler of American Indian lore—including the much-loved *A Boy's Book of the Savage Nations and Their Ways*—stepped into the sachem's moccasins, so to speak, as headmaster of Ponsonby Hall, where he remained at the time of this telling, the week before Thanksgiving, 1963.

The school had just emerged that fall from a near-scandal, so far successfully contained: an unfortunate incidence of bullying that involved a clique of boys from the uppermost grades, or forms, as they were called, and which, among other abuses, entailed the systematic extortion of money from the younger boys. It could have been worse. There were three expulsions. Unknown to all concerned, most particularly the parents of the mistreated boys, was that the ringleader, one John C. ("Jack") Hannon, seventeen, was the illegitimate son of Doc Stilgoe, who, in a weak moment during the war, got a young cleaning woman with child. He did not marry the girl but provided full support, allowing her to retire from her labors to a spacious apartment on the fourth floor of the Orcus Bank building, with a splendid view of the town's rooftops and steeples—until her tragic drowning (1952) in the Pompoquoddy under murky circumstances involving a car and an alcoholic foreman named LeBrun from the blanket mill.

The downfall of Hannon's gang, who called themselves the Ancients, was sparked by their persecution of a new boy named Jeffrey Greenaway, a first former, lately turned twelve, of New York City. The boy had behaved badly enough in the final year of his primary school, P.S. 6, on Madison Avenue and 81st Street, so that something had to be done. He'd run away from home two days before Christmas upon hearing, mistakenly, that he was an orphan found in a willow basket on the doorstep by his supposed parents, Robert and Evelyn; he'd gone amok at a penthouse birthday party for a classmate enemy (actually a rival in love) and destroyed a lot of personal property (the boy's presents, the cake); he'd taken to sneaking out of the 79th Street apartment on Friday nights to the Channel 5 TV studio on 67th Street to consort with the demented actor who played Count Zackuloff, host of the midnight horror movie; and there was the recent matter of his prematurely terminated season at the suddenly defunct Camp Timahoe—not Jeff's fault, really, but another dark thread of misadventure in a childhood career that had come to seem oddly accursed.

That is all in the way of a concise history, raising the curtain on events that began to unspool on the night of Thursday, November 21, 1963.

*

Scene: the loft of the carriage house behind the Great Hall, a spacious room of fine post-and beam joinery executed in now extinct American chestnut, marinated in the fugitive, long-gone aromas of horse and hay. Five boys of various ages sat on bentwood chairs at a round table, and nine other boys sat or stood behind them, watching. The room was lit by a single sixty-watt lightbulb on a pendant cord over the table. Curls of cigarette smoke wafted above the boys' heads into the dim interstices of the rafters. In the November night chill, some of the boys kept their winter coats on.

The gathering was an informal society founded the week after the fall of the Ancients called the Knights of the Round Casino. It quickly evolved into a regular Thursday night poker game. As it happened, quite a bit of the money extorted from the boys since September was discovered among Jack Hannon's belongings. Doc Stilgoe confiscated the stash and redistributed it back among the gang's victims. The young scholars were thus flusher with cash than usual. And with few opportunities to spend their money, except at the school "canteen," which dispensed a paltry selection of candy bars, this new card-playing clique had formed of boys with a certain limbic disposition for risk. The founder, if one might be singled out, was Clarence "Dash" Fortenbaugh, fifteen, of Ridgefield, Connecticut, fourth form, consigned to Ponsonby after stealing a brand-new Sanderling eighteen-foot catboat out of the Vineyard Haven marina and sailing her clear to Block Island where the Coast Guard finally caught up with him.

Also seated at the round table were Derek Nulley, fifteen, of Cos Cob, CT (arrested for throwing snowballs filled with rocks at a commuter train), Bob "Bones" Blanding, sixteen, of Summit, NJ (charged with DUI while on his learner's permit), Derek "Tiny" Chapin, fifteen and already six-foot-two, of Muttontown, Long Island (expelled from the Taft School for punching out the geometry teacher), and the Greenaway boy, twelve by only a few weeks, the youngest player, but well acquainted with the rules of poker from his career at Camp Timahoe, and still regarded as a hero among his fellow inmates for instigating the Great Revolt against the Ancients.

It was quarter past eleven. Many pots had been won (and lost). Indeed, some of the boys spectating had run clean through their grubstakes. Jeff Greenaway had converted his initial $17 stake up to $94 early on, winning large pots on a deal of seven card stud (straight flush, seven to jack of diamonds), night baseball (four queens), and straight draw (on a bluff, holding a hand of garbage, a bold move).

"Can I try one of those," he asked Dash after raking in a pot, pointing to the pack of Kool cigarettes at the older boy's elbow.

"Didn't you hear, it'll stunt your growth?" Dash said. Chortles and titters. The Greenaway boy stood five feet, two inches tall, not abnormal for his age.

"Doesn't look like it hurt Tiny," Jeff said, observing the giant light up a Marlboro.

"It has a different effect on him," Dash said. "Turned him into a moron."

Tiny pretended to smile.

"Looks like you're normal enough," Jeff said. "I think I'll risk it."

"It'll cost you a quarter."

"Hey kid, don't you know you can buy a whole pack for a quarter in Orcus," Bones said.

"I'll give you a dime," Jeff told Dash.

"Deal," Dash said. He even struck the match for Jeff. "Hey, you gotta inhale the smoke. Like this." Dash took a drag, opened his mouth super wide to demonstrate, and sucked in a lungful of air with the smoke. Then he expelled it in a great stream from his nostrils, like a dragon in the Chinese New Year's parade on Mott Street. Jeff imitated him without hesitation, coughing only a little.

"Wow," he said. "Tastes minty."

"Yeah, Kools," Dash said. "The cigarette of champions. Whose deal is it?"

Jeff savored the smoke, coughing more, getting the feel of it in his hand, learning how to make the smoke stream out of his nose. After a few drags, it left him lightheaded. From that point on, he stayed more or less even in the game, lost some hands, won some, playing conservatively, no more bold bluffs. But then he had a run of lucky deals on stud, and follow-the-queen (in which Tiny lost everything and quit the table). There were four players left. It was Bones's deal. He called the eccentric game of Indian in which four cards are dealt down, then a fifth card is dealt and each player has to put it up to his forehead face out without looking and hold it there so all the other players at the table can see the card. Jeff was showing the four of clubs on his head. Dash showed the high card, the ace of diamonds.

"You should see what you idiots look like," said Carl ("Useless") Parmalee, who managed to lose all he had the previous Thursday by betting on a straight flush but, weirdly, mistook the two of hearts in his hand for a diamond card—the same cognitive defect that led to him flunking out of the Deerfield Academy and then Buxton—and had to fast-talk his way out of being labeled a cheat.

"Shaddup, Useless," Bones growled.

Titters.

"Hey, it's supposed to be funny, this game, you morons," Nulley informed the crowd.

"And lookit, no goddam face making or signaling from the peanut gallery, ya hear me?" Dash barked. "I'm serious. You'll get bounced out of here permanently!"

The down cards were turned over one at a time, with rounds of betting at each turn. The pot grew and grew. Bones stamped out one cigarette and asked a nearby standee, Richie ("the Master") Bayder, to light him another one, his left hand being occupied holding a card up to his head. By the third turnover, Bones was showing two kings and a ten of hearts, with the six of clubs on his head. Nulley showed two treys and a jack, with a jack of clubs on his head, two pair. Dash showed a pair of nines and the queen of hearts, plus the ace of diamonds on his head. Jeff showed two queens and a four on the table, plus the four on his head, two pair. Only the cards showing on the table counted for betting. Bones with two kings showing led the betting. Nulley raised five dollars. Bones raised that by ten. Jeff had what he could only describe later as "a feeling." He also happened to be swimming in coins at that point in the game. All his money lay in one big mixed-up mound. He saw the raises and raised another ten.

"You play poker like you're Scrooge McDuck," Dash cracked.

"Quack quack," Jeff said.

Dash had his coins neatly stacked. Nulley had his coins stacked and arranged in size-of-coin order, quarters, nickels, then dimes. It revealed something about the organization of his brain. Bones kept most of his coins in his coat pocket, hanging off the back of his chair, reaching for them only as needed.

The four remaining players kept raising on each other until there was over $160 in the pot. Finally, the other three players were all-in with no more raises. It was up to Dash, who had so few quarters left it was hardly a stack anymore. He called the table so that all hands would now have to turn over their last down card. Nulley turned up a three of hearts. He showed three threes on the table, plus the seven and then the jack on his forehead. Glances all around the table and murmuring among the layer of boys standing behind the players. Bones's forehead sweating visibly, though it was fifty-four degrees in the room, turned up his last card, the ten of clubs. He was now showing two pair, kings and tens, plus the six he now lay down from his forehead.

"Aw, crap," he said, seeing Nulley had him beat.

Dash turned up the eight of spades and then looked at his forehead card.

"Shit and damnation," he sputtered.

Jeff was showing two queens and a four on the table plus the four on his head. He turned over his last card, another four, a full house, fours and queens.

"How'd you do that, kid?" Nulley said.

"Ask Bones, he dealt 'em," Jeff explained.

"Don't look at me," Bones said. "Every deal, somebody's got to be the winner."

"You lead a charmed life," Dash told Jeff, watching him scoop the huge pile of coins to the edge of the table and then sweep them into his blue knitted watch cap, since he lacked anything else to put them in.

"Wow, that's some ball sack you got there," Nulley remarked.

"Okay, listen up everybody," Dash said, stuffing his few remaining coins in his pocket. "I'm calling this game. We'll see you morons next week, same time, same station."

"Next week's Thanksgiving," Bayder said.

"Aw, Jeezus," Tiny moaned, put in mind of his complex home life, the second stepfather in two years, whom he hadn't even met yet. "Goddam stinkin' holidays."

"Stay here, then," Nully said.

"Maybe I'll just go get lost in the city, like Holden Caulfield," Tiny said. "Get loaded. Drop in on old friends and all."

"The guy who wrote that lives near here," said Useless.

"Salinger? Where'd you hear that?"

"It was in a magazine —"

"What in the screaming, everlasting hell is going on here?" a baritone voice boomed from the top of the stairs across the big room. Standing in the shadows, hands on his hips, the boys could discern the figure of Frank Dowd, science teacher (bio and chem) and master of the third form boys on the west wing, third floor, meaning he lived on the floor and kept tabs on them. At five-foot-five he was shorter than some of the boys in his charge, but he was a devotee of the physical fitness guru Jack LaLanne and had developed himself like unto the M4 tank he rode into Caltanissetta in the Sicily campaign of the war. Dash made the cards disappear. The money was already off the table.

"Skull session," Dash said.

"Oh, really?" Dowd said. "For what?"

"Finals," Dash clarified. "We were just cramming."

"Finals aren't until the week before Christmas," Dowd said. "Jumping the gun a little, aren't you?"

"We've learned from our mistakes," said Elwin ("Eightball") Berglund.

"There's nowhere left to go after Old Poison," Nulley said, pretending to whimper. "We must excel here or become bums in the gutter."

"Yeah, yeah," Dowd sneered. "You wouldn't be smoking up here, would you?"

"Smoking's bad for you," Bones said. "Stunts the growth of your dick."

Squelched hilarity.

"Who's the ringleader here?"

"There isn't any ring," Dash said. "And therefore, no leader. *Sic probatur.*"

"We can't study after lights-out up in the castle, for godsake," Tiny said of the Great Hall. "How're you supposed to read in the dark?"

"If you want to get bounced out of here like Hannon and his bunch, just keep up the wisecracking . . . and flouting of the rules!" Dowd added, seeing that his position was untenable. "Aw, for chrissake, go back to your rooms and make it snappy. Go on! Move it!"

The boys filed down the stairs. Dowd threw the light switch.

Chapter Two

Jeff's roommate, Axel Knudsen, thirteen, of Pound Ridge, New York, known among his fellow inmates as "Stench," was fast asleep when Jeff crept into the room, which had a vivid, eye-watering odor like unto gym socks filled with Roquefort cheese and anchovies, due to Stench's disregard for common hygiene practices known to most boys. It depressed Jeff hugely to have to sleep there, but no one in the lower forms would swap places with him, so he was stuck with Stench for the semester, a grim prospect.

Even so, when he parked the woolen hat filled with silver coins in the back of his underwear and socks drawer, he enjoyed pleasant visions of the spending spree he planned to go on during the Thanksgiving break—taking in every movie currently playing on Manhattan Island, ordering sweet-and-sour pork with egg rolls at his favorite Chinese restaurant, Sing Long Low, on 59th off Third Avenue, enjoying taxi rides to the Museum of Natural History instead of waiting in the cold for the dreary crosstown bus, which took forever to arrive at the stop off Lexington Avenue, buying anything he wanted on display in Abercrombie & Fitch's first-floor game room, ordering endless hot fudge sundaes at Schrafft's, with roasted almonds on top—and soon these fantasies merged with his dreams down the slippery slope of sleep.

Friday, November 22, Jeff put on his Ponsonby blazer and baize green and crimson regimental tie as quickly as possible to get away from his fetid room as efficiently as possible, though the stink of Stench lingered on his clothes. He endured the boring fifteen minutes of chapel that all the boys, gentile and otherwise, were required to attend, with a homily on sportsmanship by philosophy and religion master Walter Lamb, who also served as Ponsonby's chaplain. He passed the hours between nine and noon agreeably in master Khan Hamdoon's English literature class discussing Upton Sinclair's *The Jungle*, about the meatpacking industry in turn-of-the-century Chicago; then on to ratio tables with math master Gerald Osmint; and then on to Cortés meets the Aztecs with the history master, the colorful Ivar Everson, who always wore a tam-o'-shanter in class. Being Friday, fish sticks were on the lunch menu, an item unknown in the Greenaway household that Jeff had adapted to with the lavish application of ketchup. The tater puffs that rode shotgun on the plate helped. He had barely begun to address his green lime Jell-O with embedded fruit cocktail chunks when headmaster Doc Stilgoe bustled into the dining hall looking drawn and visibly sweating as he hurried down the aisle between the rows of long tables to the rostrum at the head of the room reserved for ceremonial occasions.

The boys had stopped eating and jabbering of course. Doc Stilgoe surveyed the room as a hush fell over it, and he looked as if he were about to speak for a painful, silent interval but couldn't bring himself to the task. The corners of his mouth twitched. He snatched a handkerchief from his back pocket, patted his brow, each eye, his mouth, looked down at the podium, then back up, and said, "Boys, I have some terrible news," and then failed to go on.

World War Three, Jeff thought, and he was not the only one.

"A little while ago," Doc managed to continue, "President Kennedy was shot in Texas."

Gasps, moans, curses, erupted into a blob of tortured noise.

"He may be dead."

Groans, shouts, and a few loud sobs.

"I have no further information, but I'm sure we'll learn more in the hours ahead. Classes are canceled for the afternoon. The senior masters and I will confer about what happens next here at Ponsonby. You may go outside, use the trails, the ball fields. We'll all convene in the chapel directly after supper." Doc glared up at the neo-medieval exposed beams on the ceiling, his lips trembling. "Oh, dreadful day," he blurted out, wiped the moisture from his eyes again, and marched with military stiffness back down the aisle, out of the room.

Jeff felt as if some terrible beast had snatched out his innards through his throat. The other boys milled around with faces still frozen in shock, many with their mouths gaping, before drifting out of the big room. Jeff rode the tide of his classmates into the grand foyer with its many trophy heads of assassinated elk and bighorn sheep adorning the walls. Returning to the room he shared with Stench was out of the question. Then, he remembered that Carl ("Monk" for monkey) Andelthorn had a radio and charged up the stairs to the room on floor Three-West that Andelthorn shared with Craig ("Sparky") Veach. Soon, he was jammed in the small room with eleven other boys of the first and second forms. Monk was busy tuning in the gigantic Zenith Trans-Oceanic Royal radio to WBZ out of Boston. The feeling of history-in-the-making electrified the room.

The boys learned that President John F. Kennedy was shot in the head while riding in an open limousine through downtown Dallas. At one-thirty, a White House press officer announced from Parkland Hospital in Dallas that the president had died of "a gunshot wound to the brain." Vice President Lyndon B. Johnson would be sworn in as president. CBS newsman Walter Cronkite was quoted saying that Dallas was a hotbed of political extremism. A month earlier US ambassador to the United Nations Adlai Stevenson had been booed and heckled at a speech he gave on UN Day. There was much ill-feeling in Texas over civil rights agitation. Back in April, someone had taken a shot at retired general Edwin Walker, a rabid anticommunist. The would-be bushwhacker had not been apprehended.

Meanwhile, in the hours after the president's death, a mysterious culprit, identified as a white man in his twenties, shot a Dallas police officer named Tippit dead on a downtown street. Just before two o'clock, Dallas police apprehended the cop killer in a nearby movie theater. Radio newsmen speculated that he could well be the assassin. By then Jeff had heard enough. Plus, he was nearly passing out from the lack of oxygen in the packed room.

He threaded his way out and downstairs, across the great foyer, and into the bracing autumn air. The sun rode so low at four o'clock that it flared through the bare treetops and threw long, stark shadows across the great lawn where a dozen middle form boys were playing a game of touch football. Jeff skirted them down to the margin of the woods, where he entered a wide, well-groomed path that led a quarter mile down to the Great Pond. Here, Ponsonby's handsome red-and-green crew shells were stored in a graceful boathouse beside a long dock. Jeff had been hoping to try out for a position on the JV rowing crew when he advanced into the second form next year. In his few idle hours back in September and October, he had often come down here to watch the varsity crew practice. He admired how they manned their sweeps with such precision, skating neatly across the water in the sleek boat like a many-legged insect.

There were several milk crates on the dock, and another boy was sitting on one: Sheldon ("Trotsky") Perlmutter, sixteen, of Brookline, Mass, whose only crime, according to his parents, was "spending far too much time in his room, alone, reading." He had been reading Karl Marx's *Das Kapital* at the time. His father, Barney, having become New England's leading supplier of institutional cooking equipment to schools and prisons, hoped that Ponsonby Hall would wring the communism out of Sheldon and turn him into a normal American boy with healthy interests such as business, girls, and baseball. He was widely regarded among his fellow scholars as "a genius." Jeff went out to the end of the dock.

"Hey," he said.

"Hey," Trotsky answered.

"Mind if I sit here too?"

"Go ahead, Ace," he said. Trotsky knew who Jeff was: the new kid who had brought down the hated Ancients. The older boys were not sad to see the Hannon gang get kicked out of Ponsonby. "Rough day, huh?" Trotsky said.

"Yeah. I still can't believe it," Jeff said.

"It's for real, apparently."

"Walter Cronkite said it. It must be true."

They watched a pair of mallards take off and fly low across the steel-gray water.

"They caught some mutt named Oswald," Trotsky said.

"Yeah, we heard. Oswald Rabbit. His name will live in infamy."

"There's got to be others behind it, though."

"Yeah? What others?"

Trotsky mulled a moment. "The bankers," he said.

"What'd they have against JFK?"

"Cuba."

"What do the bankers have against Cuba?"

"Not against Cuba."

"What, then?"

"Castro. The Bay of Pigs, remember? Maybe you were in your stroller then."

"I remember the Bay of Pigs. It was only a coupla years ago."

"Yeah, well, it pissed Castro off, royally, that little caper."

"So, where do the bankers fit in?"

"The bankers," Trotsky said, "they run everything."

"But Cuba's communist. They don't even have banks."

"Exactly. Guess where all the money goes."

"I don't know."

"To the international bankers. Rothschilds, Bilderbergers, and their evil spawn."

"What?"

"Not directly, of course. It's more complicated than that."

"How could anything be more complicated?"

"Calculus," Trotsky said. "That's complicated,"

"They said on the radio that this Oswald guy spent time in Russia," Jeff said after a silent spell. "Do you think he was working for the Russians, or maybe the Cubans?"

"Well, connect the dots!"

"I'm trying to. Believe me. Are you saying the Russians killed Kennedy?"

"You ask too many questions," Trotsky said. "It's exhausting." Just then, the sun blinked down over nearby Sentinel Hill (elevation 1,068 feet) to the west. "Well, old Lyndon Johnson's president now, the bankers' pet. Right now, it's a big dirty mystery what actually happened. Just wait. In five years, maybe, we'll know the whole, true story of this dark day."

"Five years," Jeff said. "Gawd, 1968. That's a long way off. There'll be flying cars by then."

"More likely they'll just start another war," Trotsky said wearily and lifted his long spidery frame off the milk crate. "They're crazy for war, those bankers. Come on, I'll walk back with you."

Dinner that night matched Ponsonby's melancholy mood: liver and onions with parsnips, with rice pudding to follow. Jeff swapped his dessert to Tiny Chapin for a Marlboro cigarette, which he stashed in the breast pocket of his blazer. Afterward, the boys moved en masse to the chapel, where Doc Stilgoe announced that he and the masters had decided to send all the scholars home Saturday to be with their families for President Kennedy's funeral on Sunday, extending the Thanksgiving break an extra three days. The headmaster had chartered a train that would leave White River Junction, Vermont, at eleven o'clock in the morning and arrive in New York City by suppertime. Some parents, notified of the situation, had elected to drive to Ponsonby, and Doc read out these boys' names. Everybody else was told to pack for the week ahead and sent back to their rooms to get a good night's rest. Jeff was among everybody else.

*

The next morning after breakfast, Ponsonby's two rickety buses and the cars of the masters who owned one were enlisted to convey the boys twenty minutes to the station at White River Junction, where the sleek, silver chartered train sat on the tracks waiting for them. Riding the train always thrilled Jeff. He was more concerned about getting a window seat than about who he might sit next to so he scrambled aboard and found one. Before long, the aisle seat next to him was occupied by Paul ("Psycho") Burnham, fifteen, third form, of Old Brookville, Long Island. Burnham had put a classmate at the Pomfret School into the hospital with a blow to the throat from a lacrosse stick, deemed by witnesses to have been on purpose. He was expelled, of course. Litigation was still ongoing. Burnham was notoriously taciturn. As soon as he sat down next to Jeff, he whipped out a paperback of *The Catcher in the Rye* from his blazer pocket and commenced reading with intense concentration. The train just sat idling on the tracks while the buses and cars returned to Ponsonby to fetch the remaining forty-three scholars in a second convoy. Jeff could see the book's cover, which depicted a teenager in a winter coat wearing a red hunting hat backwards, carrying a suitcase on a city street. He could not figure out what the story might be, except that the boy on the cover was traveling somewhere.

"How's that book," Jeff asked.

"Goddam interesting," Burnham said.

"I haven't read it yet. I keep hearing about it."

Burnham didn't respond. Jeff waited a while, then turned to the window, surveying the dusty rail yard where nothing moved. He tried to wipe off some of the grime on the window with his blazer sleeve, but the dirt was all on the outside.

"What's it about, anyway?" he eventually asked.

"Huh . . . ? Burnham said, roused from a transport.

"The book."

"You know, this sentence I'm trying to read is really fascinating," Burnham finally said.

"Just wondering," Jeff said.

Burnham finally looked up at Jeff.

"Do they have bookstores where you live?" he said.

"Manhattan? You kidding? There's a million of 'em."

"Do me a favor and buy yourself a copy when we get there."

"Maybe I will."

Burnham turned a page and returned to his reading.

By and by, the rest of boys came aboard, the engineer pulled two blasts of his whistle, and the train slowly pulled out of the station.

The mood in the car was subdued as though the shock of President Kennedy's assassination had informed the boys that horsing around would be indecent. Jeff had overlooked bringing a book to read on the train. Next up in Khan Hamdoon's lit class after *The Jungle* would be *Uncle Tom's Cabin*, which Jeff had already started and found monumentally boring. So he just gazed out the window at the Connecticut River, and the little towns that flashed by, and the seemingly endless stretches of sepia autumn woods in between them. The scenery had a soothing, hypnotic rhythm. This was the first time since he'd entered Ponsonby Hall in September that he'd had the mental leisure to reflect on his own affairs. It occurred to him that for three months he had not thought that much about New York City, and he wondered if he actually missed the place. Same for his parents. Aside from sticking him in Ponsonby, they were pretty good parents, but he just hadn't thought about them a whole lot. He wasn't homesick like some boys, for instance, Alex ("Weepy") Bertrand twelve, down the hall from him in Two-West-Six, whose pitiful wailing sometimes woke Jeff up at night.

What really got Jeff was realizing that if he stayed at Ponsonby for the rest of his school career, as many of the boys there did, he'd never have a room of his own again, never see any of his friends from his old life, except at holidays, and maybe never live in New York City again if he happened to go straight into some college after prep school. Between his summers at Camp Timahoe up in the town of Lost Indian, Vermont, and his fall semester so far at Ponsonby Hall, Jeff began to suspect that he actually preferred the backwaters of New England to the hurly-burly of the big city.

Jeff was an only child—It was just how things worked out, his father once told him. But virtually all his friends had brothers or sisters, and it was sometimes a little lonely, such as on the family trip to the nation's capital the previous spring when they tramped from one museum to another for days on end. At camp and at boarding school, you were always around other kids like you. In both places, he'd found kindred spirits, though the screwups at Ponsonby with their garish histories were a bit harder to make friends with than the kids at camp. He adored being out in the country, though. You could see the stars at night, and steal into the woods and explore when you had a free hour, and you could get into a ball game any old afternoon on the playing fields behind the Great Hall.

In Manhattan after school, you couldn't just drop into any ball game. The ball fields of Central Park were monopolized by Puerto Ricans for some reason, and they didn't want to let anybody else on the field, even if you brought your own mitt. Of course, you could go to the movies anytime you wanted in New York if you had some money, and there was nothing like the Museum of Natural History anywhere near the town of Orcus. But, Jeff realized, he'd seen the blue whale exhibit and the glass case with three shrunken heads a hundred times, and the dinosaur skeletons, ditto, and the dioramas of the Serengeti Plains too, and there was rarely anything new to see there. Maybe, he mused, he'd end up living in a place like Orcus when he became a grown-up, be a lawyer like his father, or better still a doctor, who went from house to house on snowy days with his black bag of medicine, curing the sick.

After that, his mind drifted to the assassination. He was a big fan of President Kennedy. After school back at P.S. 6, he'd tuned in to JFK's late afternoon press conferences on TV, and he admired the president's suave way with the reporters. JFK could really crack a joke. He didn't remember Eisenhower ever cracking a joke, and he was too young when Harry Truman was around. All he knew so far about the assassination was reported on the radio yesterday. Who was this Oswald character that shot Kennedy and the governor of Texas, Connally, from a sixth-floor window in downtown Dallas, he wondered? Was he a trigger man for some shadowy group, the Russians, the Cubans, as Trotsky had intimated? Kennedy getting killed in Texas sure didn't make Lyndon Johnson look good. Was Johnson part of a plot to rub out Kennedy and take over? He didn't know much about Johnson besides that he was the Senate's majority leader before the election in 1960. He knew because during the 1960 election year he'd gotten into the habit of reading the Time magazine that came to the apartment every week. He wished he had a newspaper to read on the train. But the masters had shoved the boys directly onto the train on the sidetrack without going through the little station at White River.

*

Jeff's parents, Bob and Evelyn, were waiting on the platform at Track 18 in Grand Central Station when the train pulled in at quarter after five. His mother swept him into her arms and began to blubber, saying, "Isn't it just horrible, what's happened, Pussycat?"

"He was a great president," Jeff said, getting teary-eyed himself. "What's the latest? We didn't get any news all day sitting on the train."

"He's lying in state in the White House," Jeff's father said. "It all happened so fast. I think they're figuring out the procedure on the fly. They say the funeral's on Sunday."

"Who do you think was behind it? This kid I know at school thinks it's the Russians and the Cubans. Do you think we're gonna bomb Cuba now?"

"Nobody's going to bomb anyone," Evelyn said. "Shall we go?"

As soon as they had all climbed into the Checker cab on Vanderbilt Avenue, Jeff's parents lit a couple of cigarettes.

"Mind if I join you?" Jeff said, extracting the Marlboro he'd grubbed off Tiny and plugging it into his mouth.

"Since when are you smoking?" his father inquired.

"I'm thinking of taking it up."

"Give me that thing!" He snatched it out of Jeff's mouth and threw it out the window. "Where'd you get it?"

"Another kid?"

"Do they allow smoking at Ponsonby Hall?"

"Of course not," Jeff said. "But some kids do anyway."

"Really, Pussycat," his mother said conclusively, expelling a stream of smoke from her nose and mouth, like the giant billboard on Times Square that advertised the Camel brand.

Nobody spoke the rest of the way home to 139 East 79th Street, off Lexington Avenue.

*

Evelyn had a pot roast waiting when they got home. It was her own mother's recipe with sour cream gravy, one of Jeff's favorites, and buttery mashed potatoes that were so different from the lumpy, flavorless spuds that Mrs. Dinsmoor served up at school. For dessert, she'd acquired a Sacher torte from Greenberg's bakery, another of Jeff's favorites. They ate the meal on their laps before the TV in the living room, since it happened to be time for the Huntley-Brinkley evening news report and, considering events of the past forty-eight hours, it could not be missed.

Lee Harvey Oswald had been formally charged with the murder of President Kennedy and police officer Tippit, and was cooling his heels in the Dallas lockup. Viewers learned of his background as a former US Marine and then a traitor who had defected to Russia for a couple of years. He had married a Russian gal named Marina, quit Russia, and was let back into the USA. The couple moved around between Dallas and New Orleans. Huntley and Brinkley showed a sinister photograph of Oswald in his yard, holding the very rifle, an Italian Mannlicher-Carcano, that he shot the president with. He is wearing a pistol in a holster on his hip and, in his right hand, displaying two newspapers said to be "communist."

"There's the little bum himself," Jeff's father muttered between bites of pot roast.

"He doesn't look like much of anything," Evelyn observed. "A worm of a man. A nebbish."

"How long before he goes to the electric chair?" Jeff asked.

"They have to hold a trial," Jeff's father said. "This is still America."

No one had anything further to say about that. The evening news bled into more special programming on the assassination, the usual sitcoms and variety shows banished on account of the tragic events. It was as though nothing else had happened all day. All three TV networks showed President Kennedy's coffin reposed in the East Room of the White House. All ran quickly cobbled-together biographies of JFK, photos of the whole giant Kennedy clan when it was still intact before World War Two, photos of young Jack the war hero rescued from the Pacific after his PT boat (number 109) got sunk, then as a skinny young congressman, the iconic shots of Jack and Jackie sailing at Hyannisport, shots of the 1960 campaign trail, JFK shaking hands with West Virginia coal miners, of the inauguration and his inspiring speech, of the three Kennedy brothers Jack, Bobby, and Teddy conferring gravely on a lawn somewhere, video clips of his witty press conferences, film of little Caroline and John-John playing on the rug before the president's desk. . . . It was hard to imagine such a vibrant young president dead in that black box, Jeff thought. Throughout the evening, all three Greenaways were reaching for the Kleenex box.

The newsmen endlessly repeated the little bits so far known of Oswald's biography. The new president, Johnson, declared Monday, the actual day of the funeral, a National Day of Mourning. At nine o'clock, Jeff asked to be excused and went to his room. It was supernaturally tidy, since he'd been away for three months. The unnerving thought passed through his head that it was like the room of someone who had died. And in a way, he realized, it was true.

The wall over his bed was papered over with photos of ghouls, blood beasts, vampires, and werewolves cut out of the *Famous Monsters of Filmland* magazines he'd been obsessed with back in his old life, his life before Ponsonby. He was a different person now. He wore a tie and blazer every day like a miniature grown-up. He played poker for money and was learning how to smoke. He glanced up at the shelves next to his old desk where his childhood books stood, the Landmark series of biographies of famous Americans, *John Paul Jones, Fighting Sailor; Geronimo, Wolf of the Warpath; The Pony Express; Custer's Last Stand.* His beloved *Winnie-the-Pooh* books with tattered spines had belonged to his mother long ago. There was *Black Beauty,* the book about the horse that went from owner to owner through his life of travail, and made Jeff cry at the end when he came, at last, to a happy retirement under the apple trees. Jeff's eyes moistened just remembering it.

When his mind turned back to President Kennedy and the image shown on TV of his casket lying so lonely in the East Room of the White House, it occurred to him that something in the life of America had died with JFK, that we were a different country now than a few days ago, just as Jeff was a different person than the scamp who'd cut out all those pictures of misbegotten horror movie fiends from the magazines. He quickly changed into his pajamas and crawled in between the crisp, fresh sheets crying for the dead president and the country.

Chapter Three

Sunday morning, it was back to the television for more of the grim, ongoing national ceremony. Jeff didn't need to be instructed why all the ritual was necessary. But since he'd had no TV at Ponsonby for three months prior, the proceedings as viewed through the boob tube grew increasingly surreal to him. A military guard of honor bustled JFK's coffin out of the White House East Room onto a caisson drawn by six gray horses for its journey to the Capitol rotunda, where it would repose for another day before the funeral. Behind the caisson strode a riderless black horse named Black Jack, saddled up with a pair of empty boots fixed backwards in the stirrups to signify the death of a commander. The surviving brothers, Bobby and Ted, and other dignitaries followed behind the caisson on foot, all the way up Pennsylvania Avenue. Then, just before lunch, the broadcast switched over to Dallas where the authorities were about to move Lee Harvey Oswald from the Dallas city jail to the county jail. It was the public's first opportunity to actually see the alleged assassin on live TV. When they brought Oswald down from his fourth-floor cell to an armored car waiting in the basement garage, a thuggish figure in an overcoat and gangster fedora stepped forward a few feet from the killer and shot Oswald right in the guts. Oswald groaned and crumpled. Jeff was not sure he actually saw that happen. The newsmen on camera seemed equally astonished.

When the ensuing commotion died down, it came out that the assassin of JFK's assassin was known to some of the police officials on hand. He was a local nightclub owner named Jack Ruby. Oswald was stuffed into an ambulance and Ruby, in custody, was briskly whisked off the scene. What followed for another hour was video replay after replay of the horrendous act, intercut with scenes of citizens filing through the Capitol rotunda around JFK's flag-draped coffin. Jeff felt trapped in a malevolent trance watching it all. Evelyn's tuna fish sandwiches went uneaten. Just after one o'clock, the TV announced that Oswald was pronounced dead in the same hospital where the president had died two days earlier around exactly the same time of day. At two o'clock, Jeff said he couldn't take it anymore and asked if he could go outside for a while and get some air.

"Where would you go?" his mother asked.

"I dunno. Over to the park or something."

It is a fact that for some years Jeff had been at liberty to go about Manhattan as he pleased after school or on weekends when his parents had planned nothing else in particular, no ball games at the stadium, no visits to Grandma in Connecticut.

"Let him go, Evie," Jeff's father said.

"All this stuff on TV is making me suicidal," Jeff said.

"Hey, if you have to wisecrack, at least think of something funny," his father said as Jeff went to fetch his school blazer from the bedroom, along with a fistful of coins from his trove of poker winnings.

On his way out, his mother ambushed him in the foyer, enfolding him in her nimbus of cashmere and Chanel No. 5. "Don't be late for supper, Pussycat."

"I won't," he assured her and wriggled away.

The heavy front door closed behind him with its familiar reassuring thunk.

*

He marched directly three blocks west to the Central Park entrance on 79th and Fifth Avenue, past the great faux chateaux of bygone robber barons. Traffic was sparse. Inside the park, a few oldsters occupied the benches that lined the walks, taking in the weak fall sunshine. Jeff attempted to read their thoughts behind their fallen, wrinkled faces: *Oy vay, now this, after Auschwitz and all . . . God, why don't you just let me die . . . This world stinks. . . .* He realized almost instantly that these dark thoughts reflected his own melancholy state of mind, that the old folks might have been thinking: *I sure could go for some chopped liver on rye, or I wonder who's on Ed Sullivan tonight. . . .* He stole south past the Conservatory Pond, all but drained for the winter, with a skirt of plastic trash in the exposed shallows. A few solitary moms pushed prams and strollers on the way down to the zoo at 64th Street. Most every Sunday it would be open, but not this Sunday. The door to the monkey house was locked, though he could hear them screeching and howling inside. The seals were disporting themselves in the large central pool that was their home surrounded by a waist-high cast-iron fence. He watched them for a while, envying their playful obliviousness to events in the news.

Jeff exited the park at 59th Street and stopped to pet a horse hitched to one of the carriages lined up there awaiting tourists. The driver up on his bench said the mare's name was Ruby, after a nip from a half-pint bottle of Old Overholt stashed in the pocket of his grimy greatcoat.

"Ruby!" Jeff squawked. "Gawd."

"Yeah, she's a gem," the driver said.

"Didn't you hear? The guy who shot Oswald, his name is Ruby."

"What! Oswald got shot now?"

"Yeah. Just an hour ago."

"What in the Jeezus Christ . . . ?"

"At police headquarters in Texas. It was a mob guy named Ruby, they said."

"This country's gone bananas."

"You're telling me," Jeff said. "They showed it right on TV, live. Oswald's dead."

"Dead, fer chrissake!"

"Anyway, she's a nice horse."

"Yeah," the driver said, reaching for his bottle again. "She's a gem. Jeezus."

Jeff bought a paper sack of roasted chestnuts for a quarter from the pushcart in front of the Pulitzer Fountain, vacant this fateful afternoon of the young lovers and shutterbugging tourists usually found there.

"Didja hear? They shot Oswald now," he informed the vendor, a shriveled figure with a wrinkled, sooty face stuffed into a hat with three furry flaps on it. Jeff was puzzled as to how the front flap worked. How were you supposed to see? The vendor mumbled something back in an incomprehensible dialect from the Carpathian outlands of Europe.

Jeff moved on, munching the chestnuts. They tasted like little potatoes with a sweet edge. He remembered years ago when he thought they were revolting, but with age he'd acquired a liking for them. The great emporiums along Fifth Avenue were closed: Bonwit, Tiffany's, Saks. The Christmas tree at Rockefeller Center was already up on the little alley between 49th and 50th, decked out in gigantic, shiny red and gold glass balls, but the golden statue of Prometheus looked down on the empty ice-skating rink. Jeff had never seen the city so desolate. Surely there must be some signs of life over on Times Square, he thought.

He was right, it turned out. No sense of decorum came between the president's casket on view in the Capitol Rotunda two hundred miles south and the many businesses avid for dollars in what was politely known as New York's Theater District. The blush had come off that rose in the decades since the archetypal sailor boy gave a Hollywood kiss to a young gal he hadn't even been introduced to there on V-J Day. These days, the district's seediness was a kind of attraction in and of itself.

A joke shop that Jeff had patronized many times when he still resided at home was open for business at 49th Street and Seventh Avenue, next to the Skee-Ball parlor. He went in and perused the various practical joke offerings: plastic ice cubes with insects embedded inside, the whoopie cushion, joy buzzers, disappearing ink. Being frugal, like his father, he made only one purchase: a "disguise kit" that contained several fake mustaches, fake scars with gory stitch holes, and black plastic eyeglass frames without any lenses. He paid the dollar-ninety-five entirely in coins, immediately broke open the cellophane, and selected a bushy brown droopy mustache styled in the manner of Grover Cleveland.

"Have you got a mirror?" he asked the cashier, a small, round-shouldered, middle-aged gent who reminded him of Mr. Mole in *The Wind in the Willows*.

"Naw," the man said. "You want it on? Gimme. I'll put it on ya."

Jeff leaned in over the counter. The cashier peeled off the backing and stuck it on Jeff's upper lip. "There. You're all set."

"How's it look?" Jeff asked.

"I'd never know it was you," the man said.

"How about now?" Jeff said, putting on the eyeglass frames.

"Now especially. I wouldn't guess in a million years."

"Hey, did you hear? Oswald got shot."

"Yeah, yeah. I heard. Couple of bums, both of 'em. I see bums like them day in and day out here. This country is turning into Bum Central. Sometimes lately I'm a little sorry I fought for our side in the war."

"Whose side would you fight for then? The Nazis or the Japs?"

"Neither. They was both bum outfits. I'da gone on the lam. I'da took off for the North Woods or something."

"I'm on the lam," Jeff said.

"Yeah, what from?"

"From the North Woods," Jeff said.

"Waita minnit . . . What were you doing up there?"

"I can't tell you. You might turn me in."

"Naw. Not me. I ain't a snitch. C'mon."

"I was at a reform school in New Hampshire."

"Jeezus, that really is the North Woods. What'd you do to get sent?"

"Nothing. I mean, it's a long, boring story."

"Anyway, they'll never find you now, kid, the way you look. I can hardly recognize you."

"Yeah, well, I better get going."

"Good luck out there. It's a jungle."

Once outside, Jeff checked himself in the window of the Skee-Ball parlor. Indeed, he looked like an entirely different person: a mature midget, a somewhat sinister presentation, he thought, having acquired a horror of midgets and other misbegotten persons that one encountered not infrequently on Manhattan Island. The temperature was dropping and a stiff wind blew uptown on Seventh Avenue. Jeff clutched the lapels of his blazer together. He wished he'd remembered to bring a muffler.

The famous lights of Times Square blazed in the late autumn afternoon's crepuscular gloom. *It's a Mad, Mad, Mad, Mad World* was playing at the Criterion. He had no desire to see a comedy that was obviously trying too hard to sound funny. Smoke rings billowed out of the Camel cigarette billboard a couple of blocks down. The giant piggybacked signs for Castro convertibles and Beefeater gin pulsated like electric tombstones across Seventh Avenue. He turned the corner on 47th seventh Street to get out of the wind for a little while and at once confronted a door with a strangely enticing sign behind the glass. "Dreamboat Landing," it read. "Girls, Girls, Girls . . . 25 cents a dance. 2nd Floor. Gentlemen welcome."

He went inside the vestibule. Music emanated from somewhere upstairs. The stairway was wallpapered with movie posters from before the war featuring men kissing women. The stairs creaked as he ventured up. The only door on the second floor was wide open. Inside was a large room that had started its life decades ago as a rehearsal studio with a sprung hardwood floor for Flo Ziegfeld's chorus girls. A mural on the longest side wall with no windows depicted a night scene of a steamboat landing framed by live oaks dripping Spanish moss, with fresh-faced beauties dressed in antebellum crinolines, carrying parasols, sashaying down the gangway to waiting gentlemen.

The actual live human scene within the room was a bit more prosaic: three couples danced listlessly to a recording of Bing Crosby singing "Cabin in the Cotton." Four other women sat in attitudes of boredom in chairs along the wall under the steamboat mural, smoking cigarettes, filing their nails, reading a paperback. As Jeff stepped in, one of them bestirred herself to put down her book and come over to him. At five-foot-one, she was almost his own size. She wore a shimmery gray-green shift that made Jeff think of a mermaid. Her brown hair was a short bob, with bangs.

"Dance fella?" she said with a cockeyed smile, more pronounced on the left side.

It hadn't occurred to Jeff that he'd be put on the spot like that. He had no idea what to do.

"That's a quarter in advance," she said.

"Can I just watch for while?"

"This ain't the Polo Grounds," she said, referring to the home of the brand-new New York Mets baseball club. One thought rang through Jeff's mind: get with a girl. That was the phrase that the older boys at Ponsonby used incessantly in their bull sessions: get with a girl. He'd gotten with a girl only once before, and only slightly, Wendy Waldbaum, a classmate at Public School Number 6, whom he stole a kiss from deep in the mummy's tomb exhibit at the Metropolitan Museum of Art one spring lunch hour before school ended for the year. That was before he turned twelve the following fall and got shipped off to Ponsonby.

"You ever dance with a girl?" she asked.

"No."

"Gimme a quarter. I'll teach you. You gotta learn sometime. Might as well be now. Come on."

He dug a quarter out of his pocket and she put it in a little sequined purse on a long string over her shoulder.

"Okay, here's how you do it. This is called the box step. Real simple."

She put his right hand behind her back and seized his left.

"How's that feel?"

"Okay," Jeff said. In fact, it felt better than just okay. Her back was warm and the flesh of her flank area was yielding beneath the dress. She smelled good, too. It electrified him. She began slowly swaying, just side to side, easily.

"See, we're dancin'," she said, and snapped her gum. "Okay, now do the same thing forward and back. There you go."

"Am I doing it right?"

"Perfect. Now make the steps like you're outlining a square box on the floor. Great! You got it! You're a quick learner. How old are ya?"

"Uh, sixteen."

"The heck you are."

"Sure I am."

They went around the box without speaking.

"If you're sixteen, you're gonna grow up to be a midget," she said.

"All right. I'm twelve," he admitted.

"Whatcha doing in disguise?"

"How can you tell?"

"Those glasses you're wearing don't have any glass in 'em, and I'd say the mustache is fake, too."

"They're probably not meant to be seen up this close."

Her face was indeed quite close to his. He could feel her breath, which also smelled sweet, like lilacs. She was rather pretty, he thought.

"How old are you then, if I may ask?" he inquired.

She smacked his shoulder with the hand that had been reposing on it.

"No, you may not. You're not supposed to ask a lady that, silly."

The song ended. She dropped his left hand. Almost immediately another number came up. Artie Shaw's version of "All the Things You Are," a foxtrot.

"'Nother dance?" she said. "You really need more lessons."

"In a jukebox you get three plays for a quarter," Jeff said.

"Yeah, but this ain't a jukebox. You get a live girl here. So, pony up. Anyway, your pocket's jinglin' and janglin' like the Good Humor truck. Whaddaya doing with all that change?"

"I won quite a bit of money in a poker game," Jeff said.

"Where'd you do that?"

"At school."

"They allow gambling? What kind of school is that?"

"Kind of a reform school. They don't call it that, but everybody there is a screwup."

"What'd you do to deserve that?"

"Bunch of things."

"Like what?"

"You're not supposed to ask a kid that," Jeff said. "It's embarrassing."

"Well, you look like a high-class kid, suit jacket an' all. It must be a high-class reform school. Say, that book I'm reading is about a screwup kid who runs away from school."

"Sounds like the story of my life," Jeff said.

"Yeah? You should read it. I'm bored with it. All this kid does is complain and screw up. I'll give it to you. Now, come on, pony up another quarter and I'll show you the foxtrot. Every young man should learn the foxtrot."

That dance was a bit more complex for Jeff. Step, step, side, stop, and so on. In the process of looking down at his feet, he could not fail to notice the twin mounds of her bosom jiggle and heave at the neckline of her shift. She was quite developed, he noticed.

"Are you payin' attention," she asked as he misstepped for a third time."

"Sorry. I was thinking about President Kennedy."

"Ain't it tragic," she said. "Who would want to kill such a nice man. And handsome too! Talk about your dreamboat."

"The Russians," Jeff said.

"The Russians are the worst," she said. "The landlord of this joint is always coming in looking for free dances with us and we have to show him a good time. Mr. Kokokavich. They call him Koko. It fits. He's like a gorilla. He has BO and his breath stinks. He don't even tip. My boyfriend, Angelo, says one day he's gonna shove him down the stairs."

"Jeez, he could kill the guy. They could send him to the chair."

"I know. He's got a terrible temper, Angie. He busted me in the kisser once."

"What for?"

"I was mouthin' off. I mouth off a lot, can't you tell?"

"What's he do, this Angelo?"

"Grown-up stuff," she said. "You wouldn't want to know."

"You could get a better boyfriend. You're real pretty."

"Aw, you're real sweet," she said and pulled Jeff so close to herself that he could feel her bosom on his breastbone. "If you weren't a child, I'd take you home with me, show you what makes the world go 'round."

"Want to go out for dinner? I can take you out for dinner. I'm loaded. We could go to Lindy's. It's just up the street."

"What do you know about Lindy's?"

"My parents go there all the time."

"They must be well-off, your parents. They bring you along?"

"Sure, a million times. My father's an attorney? They have corned beef and turkey à la king. Come on, I'll take you."

Meanwhile, the song ended and another came right on: Ella Fitzgerald singing "A-Tisket, A-Tasket."

"Naw, you're sweet, kid, but I'm on until eight and then Angie's pickin' me up. He ain't all bad. But you're right, I could probably do better. Well, now you're officially an expert dancer. Want to try another one?"

"They're expecting me home," Jeff said. "I have to go."

"Come back another time, kid. I'll teach you the jitterbug. Then you'll be all set for life."

"Okay. What's your name?"

"Uh, Yvonne," she said.

"Really?"

"Yeah, sure. What's yours?"

"Uh, Elston Howard," Jeff said, borrowing the name of the Yankees' MVP catcher.

"Well, a pleasure dancin' with you, Elston. Hey, wait a second!" She tripped lightly across the room and returned with the book she had been reading. "Here, the story of your life." It was a paperback copy of *The Catcher in the Rye*.

Jeff was stunned. "Jeez, I've been meaning to get this. All the guys at school are reading it. Hey, thanks."

"I like you better than him, the kid in the book," she said. "And you're a good learner, too. Now lemme give you one more lesson before you go. In a joint like this you're supposed to tip a lady at the end."

"Oh, Jeez, excuse me." He dug into his pants and handed over five more quarters, which, he had noticed, was exactly the retail price printed on the book's back cover.

She beamed her cockeyed smile and said, "You're a real gentleman, for sure, Elston. Come back again some time."

*

When he got home at six o'clock, Jeff's mother was only minutes away from presenting the family's spaghetti and meatball supper. She was out of view in the kitchen.

"Is that you, Pussycat?" she called to the foyer.

"It's me, all right. Meow."

"I was worried to death."

"You worry too much."

His father was on the living room sofa, nursing a scotch on the rocks, watching a round table of intellectuals on channel 13 gabbing about the future of the nation with JFK out of the picture.

"Where you been, sport?" his father asked, minus any tinge of reproach.

"All over the place," Jeff said. He stepped into the arc of his father's vision.

"What's with the disguise? Are you undercover or something?"

Jeff had forgotten all about it. He reached up and felt the fuzz on his upper lip.

"It's just for fun," he said.

"Where'd you get it?"

"That joke shop in Times Square. Where they have the fly in the ice cube and all."

"How are things in the outside world?"

"The city's deserted. The zoo's all closed up. No skaters at Rockefeller Center. It's eerie . . ."

"You really get around, don't you?"

"I'm a rambler and a gambler," Jeff cracked, a line he'd heard on a Kingston Trio record back at Ponsonby. Sparky Veach was crazy about them and had all their records.

"Hey, what'd I say about wisecracks?"

"Sorry."

He omitted to report on his adventure with Yvonne at the Dreamboat Landing dance hall and excused himself to go to the bathroom where he carefully removed his fake mustache and stashed it away for future use.

Dinner was a glum affair, despite the excellence of Evelyn Greenaway's veal meatballs (her mother's recipe) and homemade sauce that had simmered all day. Afterward, they had bowls of chocolate ice cream in the living room, watching more film footage of President Kennedy's biography cobbled together by the TV networks. (Ed Sullivan and all the other regular Sunday night programs were suspended for the occasion.) Everybody shed a tear at the scenes of Jack and Jackie on the sailboat in Hyannisport, the debates with Nixon, the inaugural address, Jack and brother Bobby in the Oval Office during the Cuban Missile Crisis, and the stirring moment when the president spoke in Berlin: "Ich bin ein Berliner!"

The network had taken to playing music from the Broadway musical *Camelot*, as a sort of Kennedy theme song over the film footage. It clearly signified that a brief, heroic, romantic interlude of history had passed and the nation hardly realized how wonderful it had been until it was gone.

The whole family turned in early to prepare for the state funeral on TV Monday. Jeff was too exhausted from the day's ramblings to crack open the book that Yvonne had given him. They were all back in the living room the next morning for the solemn marathon of the funeral. It was an all-day affair. Charles de Gaulle of France and Haile Selassie, emperor of Ethiopia, both splendid in their military uniforms, led the parade of foreign dignitaries along with Bobby and Teddy, as the president's casket was transported by the horse-drawn caisson to St. Matthew's Cathedral, the spirited, riderless horse with backward boots in the stirrups following. In every phase of the complex set of rituals and ceremonies, the military bands played somber music in a minor key. In the big crowds of ordinary citizens along the complex route of the ceremonies, nearly everyone was weeping. The precision of the military honor guard at every step spoke of a republic presenting itself with the utmost decorum and order in the face of the awful presence of chaos. The splendor of the Catholic church and its ancient funeral rites amazed Jeff, who had never been to a mass, and had only ever stepped inside St. Patrick's Cathedral on Fifth Avenue for a few minutes now and again when it swarmed with rubbernecking tourists, hoping to catch a glimpse of Cardinal Spellman.

When the service in the cathedral ended, First Lady Jackie stood outside with her two little children. She bent over and whispered something in her son John-John's ear. He brought his little hand up to his brow in a salute as the caisson bearing his father's coffin rolled off toward Arlington Cemetery with a military drum corps behind and a band of Scottish pipers in kilts behind them. By then it was noon. Evelyn served the tuna sandwiches that had gone uneaten the day before when Ruby shot Oswald at lunchtime.

It took an hour for the funeral procession to cross the Memorial Bridge on the Potomac into Arlington. Finally, the cortège arrived at the gravesite. The flag that had draped the dead president's coffin was ritually folded into a triangular bundle and presented to the widow. Then the long, shiny black box went down into the grave. Jackie and Bobby lit a gas jet that was said to be an eternal flame. The TV cameras lingered on the scene until the murky November twilight descended, and that was the end of John F. Kennedy, America's thirty-fifth president.

Jeff felt a distinct weird sense of vacancy, as if there was no way to restart the stopped time of the past three days and return to normality.

"I need a drink," his father said and moved to switch off the TV that had come to seem like a domineering extra member of the family who wouldn't shut up. Evelyn pulled a long-playing record out of shelf above the built-in phonograph. It was the music to *My Fair Lady*, also by Lerner and Loewe, who wrote *Camelot*.

"That's a relief," Bob Greenaway muttered as he hoisted his scotch on the rocks.

After a decent interval, Evelyn announced that dinner was served.

Chapter Four

When he woke up Tuesday morning rather late at quarter to ten, Jeff realized that he was on Thanksgiving vacation with no school and no obligations. He remembered the huge cache of coins he'd brought home and that put him in mind of a substantial agenda of things he intended to do. His mother was in the foyer, all dolled up and putting her winter coat on.

"Oh, you're finally up, Pussycat."

"Meow," Jeff replied. His father had already left for the office in midtown. Life was normal again, except being back in the city was no longer normal for Jeff.

"Are you going to go see your little friends?" she said, meaning his old pals from P.S. 6. His best friend, Bobby Schindler, was now enrolled at the Collegiate School on the West Side. He hadn't heard from him in months, despite writing several letters from Ponsonby.

"I might give them a ring. Where are you off to?"

"Getting my teeth cleaned at Dr. Krajak's. Then I'm meeting Joyce and Franny at the Met for lunch by the fountain. Want to join us?"

Are you crazy? Jeff thought. "No thanks. I have things to do," he said.

"What things?"

"This and that. Where's Thanksgiving this year, anyway?"

"Uncle Ira's," she said. Ira Kooperman made sports documentaries for TV. He was Bob Greenaway's roommate at Colgate, 1948. Ira's wife, Joan, was Evelyn's little sister, a successful actress in the soap opera *All Our Days*. They put on excellent holiday parties, with all the shrimp you could eat. They lived in a huge, rambling apartment on Park Avenue and 83rd Street the size of a Connecticut country house. "Thank God it wasn't us this year. It would have killed me," Evelyn added. "And what are your plans for today, young man?"

"I dunno. Go the movies maybe."

Evelyn dove into her pocketbook and withdrew a five-dollar bill.

"Get yourself some popcorn too," she said, sweeping Jeff into her arms and kissing him goodbye. "I'm so glad to see you, Pussycat. Well, off I go! Be good!"

When she was out the door on a cloud of Chanel No. 5, Jeff went to the phone in the guest room that doubled as the den and dialed up Wendy Waldbaum, the former classmate he'd managed to kiss in the mummy's tomb one lunch hour the previous June. Her mother got her on the line.

"It's me, Jeff."

"Huh? Jeff Rosen?"

"No, Jeff Greenaway?"

"I didn't think so."

"You didn't think . . . what?"

"That it was Jeff Rosen. You don't sound like him."

"Who the hell is Jeff Rosen. I don't remember any Jeff Rosen from P.S. Six."

"A boy. I met him at camp. His voice is deeper than yours. He's fourteen."

"Oh . . . ?"

"He's very . . . mature."

"Isn't that wonderful."

"He goes to Trinity."

"You remember me, don't you?" Jeff said.

"Sure I do. You were the funny one!"

"Yeah, I'm a riot. And I'm back in town."

"From where?"

"They sent me off to sleepaway school up in New Hampshire."

"That's where our camp is. Near Dartmouth."

"My school's near Orcus."

"I never heard of Orcus."

"It's in the middle of nowhere."

"What'd you do to get sent away?"

"Nothing. Say, want to go out for lunch with me? I know this Chinese place around the corner from Bloomingdale's. It's got swastikas on the floor and—"

"Swastikas? Like the Nazis had?"

"The building's from the eighteen hundreds. Before the Nazis. They're tiles in the floor. It's hilarious."

"Why would I go to a Chinese restaurant with Nazi swastikas on the floor?"

"It's funny. And the food's pretty good."

"The Nazis weren't funny."

"Of course. You're right. But—"

"Do you go there a lot?"

"Not lately. I'm stuck way the hell up in the North Woods."

"Anyway, I can't go. I'm going to see *It's a Mad, Mad, Mad, Mad World.*"

"Really? Can I come along?"

"I'm going with Jeff Rosen."

"Just with him? The two of you?"

"It's a date."

"A date?"

"Yeah. A date. Like you just asked me on a date for lunch just now."

"I thought you might want to meet up and say hello."

"That would be . . . a date."

"Oh. Well, I didn't mean to be pushy or anything. Have you been on many dates with this Jeff Rosen?"

"Yeah, a few."

"So, you're, uh, dating him?"

"We go on dates. Yeah."

"Do you remember the mummy's tomb at the museum last year?"

"Yes. You were funny."

"I wasn't trying to be funny."

"Let's just say it was cute. Did you try that with other girls?"

"No. Just you. I was crazy about you."

"I have to go, Jeff. It's been really nice hearing from you. Good luck up at that school."

"Thanks. Good luck wherever you're going now."

"Brearley."

"Where's this Jeff Rosen go?"

"I told you. Trinity. I've got to go."

"I hope the two of you are happy together."

Among the various emotions roiling him, Jeff felt most keenly and directly a desire to get out of the apartment after three days glued to the TV watching President Kennedy's funeral. But he felt guilty, too, being so anxious to get past the grotesque event, to leave it behind, forget about it. How could you forget President Kennedy? And there was something about the new president, Lyndon Johnson, that continued to bug him. JFK was dashing, witty, and heroic. Johnson just seemed like any other politician, a plodding old schemer in a cowboy hat. He felt sad that President Kennedy would not be in the news anymore, that America would just get on with its business and the memory of JFK would get absorbed into the colossal cosmic amoeba of history, as everything eventually is.

The thought gave Jeff a distinct chill. It put him in mind of what the genius Trotsky Perlmutter had said about the Russians being behind JFK's assassination: that in five years, maybe, they'd know what really happened. What really did happen? he wondered. Oswald had been in Russia for a whole year after the army and married a Russian girl. Walter Cronkite must have mentioned it a hundred times since Friday. Didn't they suspect anything? And now Oswald the killer was dead, and no one would ever be able to give him the third degree. Who was this Ruby character, anyway? Was there some kind of plot afoot? All of it made Jeff uncomfortable.

He knew that the Russians had an embassy on 68th Street and Park Avenue because a few years earlier that was where Nikita

Khrushchev stayed when he visited New York and famously banged his shoe on the table at the United Nations General Assembly. Jeff and his classmates had gone down to 68th and Park after school more than once hoping to catch a glimpse of the famous commie tyrant, who had made a few appearances from the second-floor balcony that week, but there were police barriers along the sidewalk and about a dozen officers patrolling in front of the building and Khrushchev never did come out. He made a mental note to stop by the Russian embassy later that day just to see if there was anything unusual going on. In the meantime, he really did have things to do.

*

First, he had to get to a bank to change all those coins into paper money so he wouldn't have to go around with them sloshing in his pockets and weighing him down. He was used to putting on a tie for school so he dressed accordingly for the bank. He had a rock collection in a cigar box on the bookshelf in his room and he switched out the rocks with the coins. Then he wrapped several orbits of masking tape around the box to keep the lid closed.

This time, when he went out into the world, he remembered to wear a muffler. The city had come back to life. The sidewalks were bustling again. There was a Franklin National Bank up at 79th and Madison. When it was his turn on line, he went up to the teller's window, put the cigar box on the counter, and opened the lid by sawing open the masking tape with his house key. The teller's eyes bugged out just slightly. He was a young man, sharply dressed, with a red carnation boutonniere on his lapel, but with noticeably bad skin and very weak chin that suggested no matter how sharply he dressed he'd never get anywhere in life. Jeff felt sorry for him.

"That's quite a lot of coin," the teller said. "Is it your life savings?"

"I won it in a poker game."

"Really?" He gave a snort of disapproval. "Since when do they let kids like you gamble?"

"We play poker at my school."

"Must be some school."

"It's way up in New Hampshire, in the North Woods. Frankly, it's for juvenile delinquents."

The teller snorted again and looked down on Jeff with a crooked smile of opprobrium.

"Is that what you are, kid, a JD?"

"You have to be to get into the place."

"What'd you do?"

"I'd rather not discuss it."

"How do I know you didn't break open a bunch of parking meters or rob a cigarette machine?"

"Can I just trade these coins in for regular paper money? Please."

"There, you said the magic word!"

The teller grinned and reached under his counter, bringing forth a wad of paper coin-wrapper sleeves and dumped them in Jeff's open cigar box. "You have to put 'em in rolls first. Have fun."

"I don't know how . . ."

"Really, a card sharp like you? You'll figure it out. It's easy. Just make sure you count 'em correctly," he said. "Next!"

Jeff slunk away from his cage and out of the bank. There was a Soup Burg lunch joint just down Madison on 76th. He got a stool at the counter and ordered a slab of Dutch apple pie and a cherry coke and commenced figuring out how to stuff quarters into the paper tubes. Printed on each roll were instructions that said "$10 Quarters." He did the math to determine each roll held forty quarters. He came up with a system to load five quarters at a time to help him keep count. But when his order arrived he lost count and had to start all over again. Then, when he was satisfied that he had loaded a roll properly, he just loaded additional rolls to match the length of the first one. And so it went with the rest of the quarters, dimes, and nickels. The entire procedure took nearly a half hour. The waitress asked him twice if he wanted to order anything else, and Jeff had been in such establishments enough times to get the drift that she wanted him to vacate the stool. So he ordered another piece of pie (lemon meringue) and a refill on the cherry coke. When he was finished, he had sixteen rolls of quarters, six rolls of dimes, and ten rolls of nickels: $210, with $2.95 in loose change left over, more than enough for the $1.10 check and a generous fifty-cent tip.

He headed downtown on Madison with the cigar box to find a different bank, and came across the New Amsterdam Bank for Savings at 73rd Street, where a teller briskly exchanged his rolls of coins for paper money with no wisecracks: five twenties, ten tens, a five, and five singles, plus the five his mother gave him. It was quite a wad. Jeff felt suddenly as though he had magic powers in his pocket. He could do anything. He deposited the cigar box in a city trash basket on the corner.

From there, he walked a block east to Park Avenue where, on 68th Street, stood Russia's Permanent Mission to the United Nations housed in a redbrick and limestone neoclassical gem of a building so perfectly American it might have been copied from Colonial Williamsburg, Virginia. Unlike the days of Khrushchev's visit, this November day there was absolutely no police presence, no barriers, no officers, no picket line of protesters, just two young KGB agents in boxy suits at each side of the portico. Jeff considered asking them if they were aware that President Kennedy was dead and maybe their own country was behind it, but he lost his nerve at the last moment and moved on.

From there, it was a quick journey over to Third Avenue where five movie theaters stood in a row across from Bloomingdale's department store. *Lord of the Flies* was playing in Cinema One. He'd heard the kids in the third form at Ponsonby talking about the novel by William Golding they were required to read. It was about a bunch of British schoolboys marooned after an airplane crash on a desert island who turn into savages before they are rescued by the British navy. But the first showing had been on for more than half an hour and he wanted to see it from the beginning. So instead he bought a ticket for the 12:15 showing of *The Victors* at the Baronet Theater, a World War Two drama about a squad of young American soldiers who battle their way across Europe, becoming increasingly demoralized by the wicked acts they engage in and witness. To Jeff, the soldiers were a lot like his classmates at Ponsonby Hall.

He was hungry again when the movie was over and it happened that his favorite Chinese restaurant, Sing Long Low, was right around the corner on 59th Street, upstairs on the second floor. He was disappointed to see that the swastika pattern in black-and-white tiles was gone. In its place was grayish-beige linoleum that could not have held less interest for the human eye. When the waiter came over, a cadaverous-looking young man in a stained apron, Jeff asked what happened to the old floor.

"Old floor gone," the waiter said.

"Yeah, I see. Why'd you change it?"

"City. They no like."

"It was a great floor."

"City no like it. Sonofabitches say they shut us down."

"I used to come here just for the floor."

"Yeah? You wan' order o' whu?" he asked impatiently, tapping a pen on his pad. There was some yelling in from the kitchen down the narrow dining room. "Hold you horses," the waiter hollered back.

Jeff ordered wonton soup and spare ribs and ate them disconsolately. A small pot of tea came with the food. He poured a packet of sugar in the pot. Without the swastikas the place just seemed seedy. He was glad that Wendy Waldbaum had not accepted his invitation to eat lunch here. It would have embarrassed him. The few other patrons at that hour, midafternoon, seemed a rather low order of New Yorkers, a man alone wearing socks that sagged down to his ankle bones, an old lady with an obviously cheap wig, another man in a jumpsuit printed with Midtown Exterminators—and Jeff understood that this was not a sports team. He got out of there in a hurry, leaving a couple of uneaten ribs on the plate.

His next stop was Schrafft's, a block down on 58th Street, where he bought a hot fudge sundae with roasted almonds for fifty cents. It was wonderful. The hot fudge got semihardened where it met the frozen ice cream, and it took some work to dig into it with the spoon. Wendy would certainly like one of these, he reflected. Schrafft's was full of normal, prosperous-looking people, the kind you would call ladies and gentlemen.

It happened that the Sutton Theater was right around the corner from Schrafft's and the 3:30 showing of *The Great Escape* was about to start. More World War Two. Allied prisoners of war scheme to break out of the Nazi camp they're stuck in. Jeff bought a ticket and went in. After all that food, the smell of popcorn was nauseating. But the movie entertained him hugely. It made him wish that there was a fence and a deadman's line around Ponsonby Hall so that he and his fellow inmates could scheme heroically to bust out of there. As it was, you could just walk out of Ponsonby. But there was nothing but woods for miles around. His favorite part of the movie was Steve McQueen racing a motorcycle across the German countryside, trying desperately to make it to the Swiss border and freedom. Sadly, Steve couldn't make that final jump over the barbed-wire fence. The Nazis captured him there, but unlike his fellow British and American escapees who got rounded up and machine-gunned, Steve was just returned to the same jolly prison camp that he broke out of.

The whole day's adventures and entertainments had cost Jeff little more than ten dollars. He splurged on a taxi home to 79th and Lexington. His mother was roasting a chicken.

Chapter Five

At the dinner table, Jeff revealed only that he'd gone to see *The Great Escape* that day, but nothing more about his spending spree around town. His parents chattered about the day's news: President Johnson met with Charles de Gaulle and promised to press civil rights for Negroes; Jack Ruby's ties to the Chicago mob were revealed; Oswald got buried in a Texas cemetery in a plain pine box. "The world is slowly returning to normal," Bob Greenaway declared when Evelyn slid the dessert plates on the table: Sara Lee brand banana cake.

Jeff retired to his room after the meal, saying he was sick of TV. It had been on his mind to start reading the book that Yvonne had given him, *The Catcher in the Rye*, which had so engrossed his fellow inmates back at school, so he lay back on his bed, propped the pillow up behind his neck, and cracked it open. Before he got to page two he was completely spellbound by the voice of Holden Caulfield. He especially liked Holden's artful use of the word goddam. It was a word you didn't encounter in works such as *Bartleby, the Scrivener* or *Uncle Tom's Cabin*.

Holden is a few years older than Jeff and seems to know a thing or two about the world, and he has very strong opinions about everything. He's apparently telling the story of what happened to him the previous Christmastime from a loony bin in Los Angeles where he's recovering from a nervous breakdown. Holden's big brother D.B. is a literary writer who has sold out to Hollywood and made a bundle. Holden says he hates the movies. That was all just the first paragraph.

Holden talked just like Jeff and every other boy he knew talked. It amazed him how the author captured that. What hooked Jeff most of all, though, was the second paragraph where Holden takes the reader back to Pencey Prep, a private boys' school that was a ringer for Ponsonby Hall, except it wasn't for boys who had behaved badly, just normal kids who were no less screwed-up, as far as Jeff could tell. The story starts on Saturday just before Christmas vacation, after the last football game of the year with Pencey's rival school. Holden is watching the field from a distance on a hilltop. It bugs him that there are no girls at Pencey. He tells of a conversation he had on a bus with the headmaster's daughter who had a big nose and "bleedy-looking" bitten-down fingernails, and how he felt sorry for her—just like Jeff felt sorry for the pimply-faced bank teller with the weak chin and the dapper suit who gave him a hard time about the coins he brought in. Jeff realized how you often feel sorry for the disagreeable people in your life. Most of them can't help it. They are who they are. He admired Holden for admitting it.

You soon find out, though, that Holden is a screwup. He has been tossed out of several other prep schools before landing at Pencey. He'd just come back that day from a fencing team trip to New York where he managed to lose all the equipment he was in charge of on the "goddam subway." Jeff hated the subway. He avoided it at all costs. But New York buses were agonizingly slow. Unless you could walk to where you were going, New York was a colossal pain in the ass to get around, he thought. He was glad he happened to have enough money to take cabs while he was home for Thanksgiving.

Next you learn that Holden is flunking four subjects and has actually been expelled from Pencey Prep now, too. Jeff wondered how he managed to do that. Holden is obviously smart and very observant. For all the problems Jeff had caused for himself, he at least never fell behind in his schoolwork. It wasn't a struggle. He enjoyed reading and wanted to learn about the world. Holden apparently likes literature—he mentions several classic books that he's been reading—and his roommate, Stradlater, considers him a good enough writer that he cons Holden into writing a term paper for him while he's out on a date with a girl Holden used to know. Jeff really wanted to know what was eating Holden, and soon finds out that his younger brother died of leukemia a couple of years before and Holden is still deeply upset about it. Jeff could imagine himself being Holden's dead little brother, and that in the book Holden is speaking directly to him in heaven, telling him all about his life and his problems in the most personal way.

Holden says he plans to leave school early to be on his own for three days in New York without notifying his parents, but for the next several chapters he is still at Pencey as night falls on Saturday. He's hanging around his dorm room, squabbling with the disgusting kid next door, Ackley—a boy, Jeff noted, rather like Stench back at Ponsonby—and with his glamour-boy roommate Stradlater. Holden is all torn up about having to leave the place. He remembers some good times there: chucking a football around on a fall afternoon with friends and going into the nearby little town to get hamburgers and play pinball. All that made Jeff likewise appreciate his own feelings about being at Ponsonby Hall: that despite being sent away from home—banished!—to a school for screwups, and despite the annoying things he was subject to at the hands of the Ancients when he first got to Ponsonby that fall, there was a lot about the place that appealed to him too—touch football on a beautiful October afternoon, with the air crisp and the trees all scarlet and orange. around you, and the camaraderie of the dorms, and the trips to the ancient broken-down opera house in Orcus where they showed movies on Saturday nights, and playing poker with the guys up in the old carriage house . . .

Just after ten o'clock Jeff's father peered into his room.

"How's it going, kiddo?" he asked "You still up?"

"Uh-huh."

His father stepped in.

"Reading Salinger, are you?"

"Yeah. Ever read this?" He held up the paperback.

"Catcher? No. I hear it's sensational. I've read some of his stories in *The New Yorker*. Salinger's their pet writer, you might say."

His father sat at the end of Jeff's bed.

"This is the best book I ever read," Jeff said. "It's like real life."

"You reading it for school?"

"No, a girl gave it to me."

"Really, what girl? Where do you meet girls?"

"Around town," Jeff said. "New York's full of girls."

"I guess it is," Bob reflected. "Tell me, what's it about, this Catcher?"

"It's about a kid like me, only a little older, sixteen. At a boarding school. He flunks out."

"Oh, dear . . ."

"It's so real you can't believe it. I mean, the main character is like an actual person you might know."

"Well, you're not flunking out, at least. They sent us your midterm grades, you know. You seem to be doing quite well."

"There's no TV there. You might as well do the assigned reading. Otherwise, you'd go out of your mind."

"We're glad you're doing well up there. But we miss you. Your mother and I have been thinking. If you have a good year, maybe we can find a school for you here, back home, next year."

"Oh?"

"Trinity. Collegiate. McBurney . . ."

"The thing is, I kind of like it up there, at Ponsonby."

"But we miss you. Don't you miss us? Being a family?"

"Sure. But it's nice up there in the country. There's a lake. I'm gonna be on the rowing crew next year."

"Is that so?"

"Well, you have to try out, but I plan to. I bet there's no crew at Trinity or McBurney. Where would you row? The goddam East River?"

"Hey—"

"And there's no woods here except Central Park, which is a phony, fake woods with a phony lake filled with old potato chip bags and crap. The lake at Ponsonby has real fish in it. The woods there are real. You could get lost in them."

"Do us a favor. Don't get lost."

"I won't, Dad. I'm just sayin,' you know, really, I like it up in the country."

Bob Greenaway had been raised in New Canaan, Connecticut, before the war, when it was still very much a rural corner of New England. His was a boyhood of meadows and frog ponds. His father, a surgeon at Norwalk Hospital, gave him a .22-caliber rifle when he was Jeff's age.

"Of course, New York has its advantages," Bob said.

"I've been to every museum a thousand times. And now, there's no more Camp Timahoe to go to in the summer," Jeff said.

Jeff's camp had unexpectedly gone out of business halfway through the past season, in an unfortunate series of events involving the owner, one Murray Horvath, who had taken out some irregular loans with the wrong sort of lenders.

"Here's the good news," Bob said. "You know that place we rented on Nantucket for two weeks last August?"

"Yeah, I liked it there. The ocean and all."

"We're taking it for the whole month of August this summer."

"Great. But what am I going to do in July? Hang around here and watch TV, waiting for it to be August?"

"It just so happens your mother is looking into an outfit that takes kids on a monthlong group bike trip around France."

"France?" Jeff said. "What's in France?"

"You'll be amazed. And it's coed."

"With girls?"

"Yeah."

"Jeez. Where do you stay at night?"

"They have these accommodations called hostels. Like an inn for young travelers. With bunk beds."

"All mixed together, girls and boys?"

"Separate quarters, I'm sure. There's counselors, just like at camp. You'll love it. Then you come back here and go to Nantucket. You can spend every day at the beach. If I was a kid that'd sound ideal to me."

"I guess. Girls. Jeez . . ."

"Everything in France is beautiful. You'll be out in the country. And you're already taking French at school so . . ."

"Oui," Jeff said. "C'est vrai."

"Hey! Nice! So, there you are. Nothing to worry about."

"The kid in this book," Jeff said. "He's got a lot to worry about. I'm worried about him."

"It must be a great book, then. Maybe you can lend it to me when you're done."

"I'm taking it back with me. I'm gonna read it again. You can get your own copy."

"Maybe I will."

"Salinger could probably use the money."

"I doubt it," Bob said.

"They say Salinger lives up in New Hampshire somewhere near my school. One of the guys mentioned it."

"Oh? Do you remember Dave Hodge, my colleague at the office? Rather short guy with a bum arm from the war. He came to a Yankee game with us last year."

"Yeah, sort of."

"Well, one of his clients is Little, Brown, the publisher who puts out Salinger's books."

"No kidding."

"I'll ask Dave if he can get Salinger's phone number. Maybe you can drop in on him, say hello, tell him you love his book."

"That'd be great. I'd love to meet him."

"You going to stay up late? It's half past ten."

"I might read a bit more. I don't have anything pressing tomorrow, seeing as it's the day before Thanksgiving and all."

"Think about coming home next year."

"Sure. Sure I will. Yeah, that'd be terrific, being back home, I guess."

"See you tomorrow, son."

"Not if I see you first," Jeff cracked.

A mock stern look from his father.

"Just kidding," Jeff said. "Ha ha . . ."

His father shut the door. Jeff continued reading and he didn't stop until two-thirty in the morning, when he finished the book, and set it on the night table with profound regret that it was over. Holden was right at the end of his story, Jeff thought, when he said: after a tale is told you'll miss everybody who was in it, and Jeff was going to miss Holden Caulfield especially. In some ways, he could see himself becoming Holden Caulfield.

Chapter Six

When he woke up a little groggy at nine-thirty the next morning, there was a note from his mother on the dining room table on a legal pad in her characteristic green ink and curvy cursive, saying: Must run Pussycat. Eye doctor and then lunch with Dottie Kovacs. There's a lovely coffee cake in the kitch. I know you love movies, so take yourself to one. Love, Mom." There was another five-dollar bill tucked under the legal pad.

Jeff took a shower and put on khakis and his Ponsonby blazer, with a green crew-neck sweater under it for walking outside on a cold day. After consulting that day's *New York Times* movie page, he cut a large chunk of the pecan cinnamon coffee cake lying on the kitchen sideboard and headed out the door for the 10:45 showing of *Lord of the Flies* at Cinema One on 59th and Third Avenue. At the newsstand outside Hunter College on 68th and Lexington, he stopped to buy a pack of Marlboro cigarettes, the preferred brand of the upper form boys at Ponsonby. When he asked for a pack of matches, the old man inside the kiosk grunted and said, "I thought you said they was for ya mudder."

"Yeah, well, she needs to light 'em, doesn't she?" Jeff said.

Inside the cinema, Jeff sat in a loge seat, the smoking section, and broke open the Marlboro pack while the previews were on. Since Holden smoked ("like a fiend"), Jeff was determined to learn how to smoke like someone who does it all the time. The first few inhales made him cough, but he soon got the hang of it, and enjoyed the lightheaded buzz it produced. He was also getting good at making the smoke stream out of his nostrils. There were only a few other people scattered around the loge section for the early show, most with plumes of cigarette smoke rising in the projector light above their shadowy figures.

The movie started off promisingly enough with the castaway British schoolboys reconnoitering their tropical island still wearing their school neckties and beanies. Their British-inflected speech made them appear more intelligent and capable than American boys. Jeff hoped that they'd organize themselves smartly, in short order, and create a Robinson Crusoe–type castaway community that would keep them safe and sound and allow them to have gallant adventures until someone rescued them. But the boys rapidly degenerated into savagery, the strong ones persecuting and finally hunting down the weak. The most picked-on boy, called "Piggy," is killed when someone pushes a boulder off a cliff on him. Finally, the British navy shows up on the beach. But you can tell from the looks on their faces that the rescued boys have been irretrievably soul damaged and will never be the same. Jeff had to conclude that elegant British speech did not mean the boys were all that intelligent. If a bunch of Ponsonby Hall kids got shipwrecked, he brooded, surely the older ones would look after the younger ones, and that they'd organize themselves like Seabees in the South Pacific during the war, which America had won by pulling together, even if they spoke crudely like southern hillbillies and Brooklyn mugs. At least, he hoped so.

The movie left him in a such a dark frame of mind that he decided against getting another lunch around the corner at Sing Long Low. Outside, the temperature had barely risen above freezing, so Jeff ducked into Bloomingdale's at the Third Avenue entrance and bought a pair of wool knit gloves with leather palms for seven-fifty. The whole afternoon lay before him. The last thing Jeff wanted to do was see another movie. What would Holden do? he asked himself. Holden would go back to Dreamboat Landing on Times Square, Jeff decided, and see if Yvonne would have lunch with him at Lindy's. That's what Holden would do.

That's exactly what Jeff did. He came out the Lexington Avenue side of Bloomingdale's and made his way over to Times Square in under twenty minutes. Upstairs in the Dreamboat Landing studio, Fred Astaire crooned "Beginner's Luck" over the loudspeaker. Yvonne was not among the six ladies working the dance floor, four of them with sailors who wore the uniform of Her Majesty's Royal Navy, including the goofy mushroom hats. A seventh young lady was unoccupied, buffing her nails on a comfortable couch under the mural of the steamboat landing on the far wall. Jeff threaded his way over to her through the dancers. She was dark-haired and plump with eyebrows painted on and rolls of blubber leaking over the arm holes of her red cocktail dress.

"I'm on break," she said, barely glancing up at him.

"That's okay. I'm looking for Yvonne."

"There's no Yvonne here."

"Sure, there is. I danced with her here just the other day. Green dress. About my height. Big mouth, but a good heart."

The dancer finally looked up at him.

"Oh . . . her. A good heart. That's rich."

"She told me her name was Yvonne."

"Yeah, well, we don't give out our real names to any gentlemen. I'm sure you can figure out why."

"Do you know when she's coming in?"

"She ain't coming in anytime soon."

"What? Did she quit?"

"Not exactly."

"Get fired?"

"Who wants to know? What're you, some midget detective from the vice squad?"

"Just a friend."

"A friend!" the dancer laughed. "That's rich."

Jeff took out his pack of Marlboros and stuck one in his mouth under the theory that it would make him look more like a person to be taken seriously.

"Since when're you smokin'?" the dancer said indignantly. "A kid like you."

"Since forever," Jeff said. "I smoke like a fiend." It took him three matches to get it lit. The dancer watched the operation with a look of disapproval.

"Looks like you just started smokin' the other day. It's terrible for you. You'll end up a midget your whole life."

The first drag sent Jeff into another coughing spasm. When he got over it, he ventured a fresh attack: "Is Yvonne, or whatever her real name is, ever coming back here?"

"Look, kid. I hate to tell you. That bum she shacks up with pushed her down a flight of stairs."

"What! That guy Angie?"

"How do you know Angie?"

"She told me about him."

"Yeah, that mouth of hers—"

"Is she dead? Did he kill her?"

"Naw. She's in Bellevue."

"Is she hurt bad?"

"There ain't nothin good about it. But I think she's gonna live. Her career in dance might be over for a while. You can take a spin on the dance floor with me, if you like."

"Some other time, maybe. Say, did you happen to visit her at Bellevue?"

"Yeah, a few of us went down. She's pretty banged up."

"Can you tell me where Bellevue is located exactly?"

"It's down around Twenty-sixth off Foist Avenue. But I wouldn't bother going down there."

"Why not?"

"Who're you gonna ask for?"

"And you won't tell me her real name?"

"Nuh-uh."

Jeff could see the futility of the situation and had to wonder why he would involve himself further.

"If you go down there again, tell her I said to get well soon," he said, and made for the door just as Artie Shaw's band started playing "Star Dust."

It was one-thirty when he got back out on 47th Street. A small crowd of people caught Jeff's attention, moiling under the grand marquee of the Barrymore Theater across the street and down a little. The hit musical *The Wayward Family Singers*, by the team of Tibbets (music) and Marmelstein (lyrics), had been there for almost a year. Jeff's mother played the original cast album frequently on the hi-fi at home, and Jeff rather liked the catchy songs. He strolled down to the theater and discovered that the Wednesday matinee would be starting at two o'clock. Across the street from the theater was the Hotel Edison. It seemed like just the sort of hotel that Holden Caulfield had stayed in his first night back in New York after he left Pencey Prep. Holden had often mentioned going to Broadway shows starring a famous acting couple called the Lunts, whoever they were. Jeff was suddenly inspired and hurried down to a pay phone booth in the middle of the block. He put in a dime and dialed Wendy Waldbaum's number. By some miracle, Wendy actually picked up the phone herself.

"Hey Wendy, It's me, Jeff Greenaway."

"Oh, hi. Where are you? It's awfully noisy there."

"I'm down here on Forty-seventh Street at a pay phone. You want to meet me and go see a Broadway show? The matinee's starting in half an hour. You could make it easily if you catch a cab."

"What show is that?"

"*The Wayward Family Singers.*"

"Oh. We went last year."

"Want to see it again?"

"Like, right now? Today?"

"Yeah."

"I don't think so."

"Are you just hanging around the house, or what?"

"I'm not hanging. As a matter of fact, I was just getting ready to go down to Saks when you called."

"You want to meet me for dinner at Lindy's later on?"

"No. I have to help my mom with Thanksgiving. Tomorrow's Thanksgiving, you know."

"I forgot."

"Well, it is."

"Yeah, I guess. How are things going with old Jeff Rosen? We saw *It's a Mad, Mad World*."

"Yeah, I know. You told me. By the way, there's two more mads in it. Mad mad mad mad."

"It's boring to say them all. I'm sure people get it after the first two mads."

"Yeah, that's why it's not really funny. How was it?"

"Funny."

"I bet. So what are you doing the day after Thanksgiving? Want to go skating at the rink in Central Park or Rockefeller Center?"

"I'm going to see *Under the Yum Yum Tree* with Jeff R."

"Rosen? So you two are still hanging out?"

"Yeah. He's kind of my boyfriend now."

"Oh. Do you let him kiss you?"

"That's none of your business."

"Are you gonna marry him?"

"I really have to go."

"Remember when you kissed me in the mummy's tomb back in June?"

"The way I remember it, you kissed me."

"Well, it was nice, wasn't it?"

"I have to go. Have a happy Thanksgiving. Please stop calling me," she said and hung up.

Jeff exited the phone booth and strolled back to the theater, vibrating with rage. Since he had nothing better to do, and wanted to leave the real world behind for a while, and had a wad of cash in his pocket, he decided to take in the matinee. The box office was open and the lady inside sold him a ticket at the back of the middle mezzanine for four-fifty. He followed the crowd of mostly suburban matrons with children in tow through the lobby and trudged upstairs to his seat. In the palpable preshow excitement, his consternation dissipated as he took in the splendid neoclassical details of the Barrymore and the orchestra tuned their instruments below. Before long, they launched the overture and the houselights dimmed. The curtain went up exactly on time, the stage lights blazed, and the audience was thrust back to the spring of 1940, just as Hitler and the Nazis were about to launch their invasion of Norway, Operation Weserübung.

You are introduced to the household of Captain Magnus Nordhall, a punctilious retired naval officer recently widowed, left with a disorderly pack of children ranging from ages eight to eighteen. Into their midst comes a new governess, Anna Lund, a country girl from the little village of Tengesdal. Captain Nordhall has grave doubts about Anna's ability to manage the brood. But it turns out the she is a musical genius and soon has the children organized into a chorus, singing the favorite folk anthems of the old Viking land.

As Jeff watched the proceedings his attention was drawn to the middle child, called "Ingrid," approximately his own age, as far as he could tell, a blonde beauty in a sailor's middy blouse who leads her brothers and sisters in the ebullient number "Alpha, Beta, What's the Matter," sung in a woodland setting above the fjord. By the end of Act 2 the household is thrown into chaos as the Nazis invade and the Nordhalls are forced to flee their homeland for America. Jeff studied the playbill in the dim light, trying to find the name of the actress playing Ingrid, one Kathy Kaine, it turned out.

He tried to imagine where such a radiant creature might have come from. Kathy Kaine, child star, an angelic confection sent to earth by a god of romance to astonish boys just beginning to sense the strange stirrings of interest in that otherwise bewildering subdivision of the human race known as female. Was she a New York schoolgirl who somehow got plucked from a mass audition of a hundred other aspiring actresses . . . or was she spotted, as they say, by a Broadway producer while eating a sundae at Schrafft's—beyond that, Jeff realized he could not conceive of the mechanism that put a kid in a Broadway show. Was it not part of the magic of showbiz that stars just burst on the scene, propelled by their own talent and magnetism?—and Kathy Kaine sure had it! Was there some way he could meet her? Maybe stand out on 47th Street after the show and wait until she finally came out of the theater? She had to come out of there at some point. The kids in the cast couldn't live there.

At the intermission, Jeff followed the crowd out to the mezzanine lobby where sodas and candy bars were dispensed from a little counter and the children were squealing around it. He pulled out a cigarette and lit up, attracting the censorious glares of not a few suburban matrons, many of them smokers themselves. For a change the smoke didn't make him cough, but he now recognized the subtle buzz of the nicotine. Soon the whole upstairs lobby area was enveloped in a haze of tobacco smoke. He noticed an usher in her quasi-military blue uniform beside the curtained entranceway and approached her.

"Can I ask you a question?" he said.

"Sure." She seemed amused by Jeff, and she wasn't especially busy between acts since the audience already knew where their seats were.

"Is there any way I could get a message to someone in the play?"

"You can go to the stage door."

"Really? Where's this stage door?"

"On the left side of the entrance out front. You go down, like, a little alley. The stage door is up some steps at the far end. Who're you interested in visiting with?"

"Oh . . . I'd like to maybe meet . . . the guy who plays the captain," Jeff confabulated.

"Viktor Dannenberg? He's quite a character. Be careful around him."

"How come?"

"He's a little funny with kids."

"Like how?"

"Handsy."

"Oh?" Jeff said. He was stumped about what that meant, exactly, but it didn't sound good. "How about the kids who play his kids in the play?"

"What about them?"

"Do they ever meet with fans from the audience?"

"Sure, they have their admirers. Which one do you like?"

"I like the one who plays Ingrid."

"Kathy Kaine? Sweet kid. Say, how old are you?"

"Thirteen," Jeff lied.

"I believe that's her age, too. But, say, aren't you a little young to be smoking?"

"Hey, you gotta start sometime. Everybody in the whole goddam country smokes," Jeff said, thinking how Holden would put it. "You might as well start early and get good at it."

"I guess," the usher said. "But what have you got against our country?"

"America? Nothing."

"So why are you cursing it?"

"Well, they let President Kennedy get shot."

"Nobody let anything. It was that nut Oswald."

"I think the goddam Russians—"

"I hope you don't talk that way around Kathy Kaine. She's a nice girl," the usher said. "Maybe I should go backstage and warn her about you."

"Please, don't do that. I'll be a complete gentleman. I swear."

"You better."

The usher relaxed and let a smile creep over her mouth. Even her eyes seemed to smile. She was pretty enough, Jeff thought, to be an actress herself.

"Say, can I bum a smoke off you?" she said.

"Sure." Jeff shook one up from the pack. She took it out and stashed it inside her hussar's tunic.

"For when the third act starts," she said, patting it.

The overhead lights flashed, signaling the audience to return to their seats.

"Hey, thanks for the tip on the stage door," Jeff said. He stabbed his own smoke out in the fine, white sand of a cylindrical ashtray and headed back inside.

In the third act, the Nordhall family has come to America and taken up residence in the little city of Duluth, Minnesota, on Lake Superior, among many fellow Norwegians, where the Captain has found a job as chief of port operations, with all the able-bodied American men joining the armed forces. Meanwhile, the oldest Nordhall girl, Dagney, falls for a young Minnesota lumberjack who has just enlisted. They try to elope but are foiled by a storm on the lake, saved by Captain Nordhall's port detectives. The Captain blames Anna, the governess. But then the remaining Nordhall Wayward Singers, as the children's chorus is known, puts together a heartwarming medley of American folk songs and their fame spreads all over the radio. When the USA goes off to fight against the Nazis, the Nordhall kids are invited to sing at the White House to honor the alliance of European nations against Hitler—with an actor, one Leland DuBois—appearing in cameo as Franklin D.

Roosevelt in an uncanny impersonation. As it happens, Captain Nordhall finally recognizes Anna's genius and begs her to marry him, and FDR presides over a double marriage right there in the Oval Office, including Dagney and her beloved lumberjack, while the rest of the children sing "The Wedding Song of the Lakes"—Jeg Elsker Deg Aå Mye—in Norwegian, which just happened to be a current number-six hit on the US pop charts in the fall of 1963, covered by Bobby Vinton. Actual tears are shed in the audience of the Barrymore Theater, as had been so for the previous three hundred and seventy-seven prior performances.

Jeff barely noticed any of the action on stage, he was so lost in a transport over Kathy Kaine and, most particularly, torn over whether to risk going backstage after the show. What would Holden do? he repeatedly asked himself. Act 3 seemed to last a mere five minutes, with FDR hoofing along with the entire Nordhall family in the finale, as though he'd never gotten polio. Then the cast took the last of three curtain calls and the houselights went up. But then, it seemed to take forever for the ladies and children in the mezzanine to debouch downstairs and out into the four-thirty autumn darkness on 47th Street. Jeff feared there would be a half dozen other boys his age, Jeff Rosen types, trying to get in and woo Kathy Kaine ahead of him. But when he made it into the little alley, he was the only one there. He climbed the five steps to the stage door and found it unlocked.

Just inside, an old duffer in shirtsleeves, suspenders, and a battered old fedora, with an unfiltered Chesterfield hanging from the corner of his mouth, sat on a stool, a clipboard on his lap.

"Who ya here for?" he asked in a gravelly voice.

"Uh, Kathy Kaine," Jeff croaked.

"What's your name?"

"Uh, Caulfield."

He wrote it onto the form on his clipboard. "Wait here, Cawffle."

The old duffer waddled off and returned a minute later.

"This way," he said and ushered Jeff down a dreary hall painted in dingy seafoam green. An attractive woman with flaming red hair steered a bubbly, eight-year-old, red-headed child down the corridor and past them—Jeff recognized the kid who played the youngest Nordhall child, Astrid. Eventually, they came to a door with a cardboard sign that said Nordhall Girls on it. The old duffer knocked and threw the door open when a voice called, "Come in."

"Mr. Cawffle for Miss Kaine," he said.

Kathy Kaine turned in her seat to see Jeff. She was swaddled in a terry-cloth robe and wore a headband that drew her golden hair completely away from her face, which was slathered with cold cream. Her expression, mouth open, looked at once full of expectation along with something that denoted sadness. Beside her, bending to the lighted mirror to put the final touches on her lipstick, was the young lady who played eighteen-year-old Dagney, in jeans and a black turtleneck sweater.

"Don't look at me," Kathy said, and swiveled back around.

"It's okay," Jeff said. "My mom puts that crap on her face all the time."

"See ya on Friday night, Kath," the older girl said as she pulled on a wool poncho. "Have a great Thanksgiving."

"Yeah, you too, Carol," Kathy said as the older girl bustled out past Jeff, leaving him and Kathy the only ones left in the dressing room.

"Hey, it's really you," Jeff said.

"It's me, all right," Kathy said with a sigh. "Have a seat." She pointed to a battered armchair next to a rack of costumes.

"Hey, you were great out there. Boy, can you sing—"

"Thank you. You're very kind. Okay," she went on, as if going through a routine she'd rehearsed a hundred times before, "what's your name?"

"Uh, Holden, uh—" Jeff stopped himself.

"I'm holding," she said, a little impatiently, and mopped the cold cream off her face with tissue.

"I mean, it's, uh, Jeff—"

Just then, the door opened and suddenly there was Captain Nordhall himself, the actor Viktor Dannenberg, in a knee-length leather jacket, eyeglasses with lenses oddly tinted violet, and black velvet loafers with gold insignia embroidered on the toes.

"How's my little girl," he said, approaching Kathy and crouching down so he could see his head beside hers in the mirror. He proceeded to give her a theatrically loud smooch on the cheek.

"Cut it out, Viktor," she said, batting him away with her Kleenex.

"Whussamatter?"

Kathy made a pistol of her left hand and pointed in the mirror toward Jeff in the battered armchair.

Viktor stood up at once as his eyes locked on Jeff. Next, he took a dozen tiny mincing steps toward Jeff, a bit he'd developed on his

TV variety show, which ran for five years on NBC (1956–60) and in which he played a recurring set of comic characters in the skits cooked up for him. This bit was for the character he called Mr. Plumrose, an effeminate buffoon always getting fired from one job after another. Jeff dimly remembered seeing it once or twice. He pretended to smile as Viktor approached and squatted down to Jeff's level. He could smell something yeasty on the guy's breath.

"Hello dere, kid!" he said, with a slight trace of his Viennese accent. "How'd you like the show?"

"It was heartwarming," Jeff said.

"Listen to him," Viktor said. "A critic!"

"I'm not criticizing," Jeff said.

"What a cheeky little fellow!" Viktor said. "I like you!" He proceeded to pinch Jeff's cheek while placing a hand on Jeff's thigh for leverage, leaning in toward him. Jeff recoiled.

"Leave him alone and bug off, will ya, Viktor?" Kathy said.

Viktor stood up and backed off.

"Where're you going for the Thanksgiving, my love," he said, twirling back around toward Kathy.

"None of your business," Kathy said.

"You could be with us and a dozen fascinating people. Schatze is roasting a goose, he says. It will be divine."

"I don't eat goose."

"Bet you never tried it. It's full of fat and lovely, lovely . . . juice!"

"Viktor, please! Get lost."

"Now you have hurt my very sensitive feelings," he pretended to start weeping, as his Mr. Plumrose always did, and just as quickly dropped the act. "Watch out for her," he said to Jeff, winking and pointing at Kathy with his thumb. "A regular femme fatale. An American Dietrich in the making. Auf wiedersehen, little gooses," he concluded and strode actorishly out the door.

"What's with him," Jeff said when the door closed behind Viktor.

"He's a perv."

"He was all over me."

"Yeah, like I said."

Jeff stared at the door Viktor had just exited. He had never encountered an actual pervert before.

"Anyway," he eventually said, "I was wondering if you might be in the mood to go out for dinner with me?"

Kathy turned to face Jeff. She'd removed all the goop from her face and now took the headband off so that her golden hair fell naturally back into place. For the first time, a smile lifted the corners of her mouth.

"Tonight?" she said.

"Yeah, tonight. Why not?"

"Why, that's very nice of you. Yeah, why not?"

"Have you ever been to Lindy's?"

"Yes, many times. It's just up the street from here, you know."

"Well, yes, I guess it is. Want to go?"

"It's corny. Turkey à la king. Uccchhh."

"Oh? Well, sure," Jeff agreed. "We can go anywhere you want. I'm paying."

She squinted at him. "How old are you, anyway?"

"Thirteen. Just."

"You look a little younger. Your voice hasn't cracked."

"I'm a slow developer. I'll catch up soon."

She giggled. "You're amusing. Do you live here in the city?"

"Yeah. Seventy-ninth and Lex."

"With parents, I suppose."

"Of course."

"Don't you have to be home for supper?"

"I'll call and say I'm busy. Is there a phone around here?"

"There's a pay phone in the hall."

"Okay, I'll check in with them," Jeff explained. "Where do you live?"

"Normally? Glen Oaks, Wisconsin. It's in the burbs, outside Milwaukee. But while I'm in the show I stay at the Bomoseen Hotel. On Seventy-first and Broadway."

"With your parents?"

"No, silly. My mom is back in Glen Oaks. The Bomoseen is a grand place. We can go up there, I'll show you."

"Is there anywhere to get dinner near there?"

"Plenty. I know them all. I've been here since September. I replaced Bobbie Singletree, you know."

"I didn't know that."

"Original cast. She got pregnant."

"Jeez. With, like . . . a baby?"

"What else with? A pumpkin? Of course a baby. She was older, though. Fourteen."

"God," Jeff said. "A goddam baby."

"Yeah, a goddam baby," Kathy said. "Uccchhh. Now, lookit. I have to put my normal clothes on so would you mind going out in the hall for a few minutes while I change? The phone's there and you can call."

Jeff exited the dressing room. He saw the phone on the wall and popped in a dime. His mother picked up at her end on the first ring.

"Where are you?" Evelyn said with a tinge of irritation.

"I'm down at Times Square, in a theater."

"What movie?"

"Not a movie, a show, on stage. *The Wayward Family Singers*."

"You took yourself to a Broadway play?"

"Yeah, the matinee. I'm going out for dinner with a girl."

"What? What girl?"

"Kathy Kaine. She's in the show."

"How do you know her?"

"I went backstage to meet her."

"Are you crazy?"

"What's crazy about that, Mom? You just go to the stage door. She's a doll."

"Yeah, and you're Nathan Detroit all of a sudden. Believe me, it's crazy. How old is this girl?"

"My age. She plays the middle kid in the show."

"And now you two are going out for dinner? Two twelve-year-old kids?"

"Yeah. I don't think there's any law against it."

"That's not the point. Since when are you dating girls?"

"Since now, I guess. I asked her out for dinner and she said okay."

"Where did you get money to take a girl out for dinner?"

"At school."

"Doing what?"

"Mom, it's okay. I have enough money."

"That's not the point. It'll cost you twenty bucks to take two people out."

"I've been saving all fall. There's nowhere to spend it up at Old Poison."

"Old what?"

"Ponsonby Hall, that school I go to."

There was a dead spell on the line.

"I don't know about this . . . this . . . About you all of a sudden dating girls. When did this start?"

"I dunno. I'm developing an interest."

"Did she ask her mom and dad if she could go out on a dinner date with a boy?"

"No. She lives in a hotel. She doesn't have to."

"What? Where are her parents?"

"Outside Milwaukee. In some goddam suburb."

"Don't you swear at me."

"Sorry—"

"She lives in a hotel? By herself?"

"Mom, she acts in a Broadway show. She can't go home to Milwaukee every night."

"Well, doesn't someone look after her? There must be some adult who's responsible for her."

"I don't know. I just met her. I'm sure I'll find out."

"How come she's not going home for Thanksgiving?"

"I have no idea. I'll ask."

Just then, Kathy stepped out the dressing room door. She was radiant in a red jumper over dark green tights and she carried a black wool coat with a rabbit-fur collar over one arm and a hobo-style sack-like shoulder bag in the other.

"I have to go now, Mom."

"Wait!"

"Don't worry about me. I'll take a cab home. Nine o'clock at the latest. Everything's just fine."

He hung up.

Chapter Seven

Jeff was a little discouraged to see that, standing up, Kathy was about two inches taller than he was, but then he noticed that her shoes had two-inch heels. They walked over to Eighth Avenue in the nippy evening air and caught a cab uptown. In the cab, whizzing past the lights of the city, he couldn't fail to detect Kathy's flowery perfume. It seemed to summarize everything he was trying to understand about a girl's entrance into adulthood.

"You two goin' out on the town?" the cabbie cracked, cheerfully.

"Yes, I guess we are," Kathy said and grinned at Jeff, who loved being in on the joke and loved being in a cab with Kathy Kaine more than anything in his life lately.

"I was nineteen when I got married," the cabbie volunteered. "You should see what she turned into."

"We all turn into something," Jeff said.

"There's a nugget of wisdom," the cabbie said.

"Looks like you turned into a cabdriver," Jeff said.

"Yeah, but I'm a great cabdriver." He took a hard left off Eighth Avenue onto 71st and Jeff was thrown against Kathy so hard it was like being on the Tilt-a-Whirl ride at the Lamoille County fair in Vermont, where Camp Timahoe was.

"Here we are, the Bomoseen Hotel," the cabbie said with a flourish. "You better be a gentleman, kid. She's some tomato!"

Jeff gave him two dollars, including a fifty-cent tip.

"How am I a tomato?" Kathy said out on the sidewalk.

"I think that was a compliment," Jeff said gazing up to take in the building. "Wow! This place looks like my goddam school!"

The Bomoseen, built in 1897, was a fantastic twelve-story eclectic heap of redbrick and limestone featuring stacked bays of oriel windows, gargoyle-bedizened brackets, statuary, cherubs, medallions, escutcheons, swags, a turreted copper mansard roof, balustrades with stone urns, and a light-court entrance with a bridge looming high above at the eighth story.

"It's a fairy-tale castle," Kathy said. "Come on, let's go in."

The lobby, all wainscoted and coffered in chestnut, plushily furnished, was bustling at this hour of the day with visitors checking in for the holiday weekend. It was a renowned custom of the hotel to set out a sherry decanter on a side table at five in the afternoon each day. Kathy made a beeline for it and poured two stemmed clipper glasses of the brown liquid. She handed one to Jeff, who had naturally followed right behind her.

"Hey, this is booze!" he said.

"Yes, it's sherry. Very tasty and light. Try it."

Jeff took a sip. He'd had wine before, many times, at the Passover seders which were his family's only bow in the direction of religion, usually at the homes of relatives and friends, like "Uncle" Ira, who was holding this year's Thanksgiving.

"It's delicious," Jeff said.

Kathy swallowed hers in a couple of gulps.

"Quick, finish it up and put your glass down before somebody sees us."

Jeff knocked back the rest. His belly glowed.

"C'mon, let's go up."

He followed Kathy to an elevator. It was very grand, with mirrors on all sides and gold-leafed appointments and a human operator in a uniform.

"Hello, Leroy," she said to him.

"Evenin' Miss Kaine."

They got off at the seventh floor and passed many doors to the very end of the hall. Kathy fished out the key from her shoulder bag and threw open the door. It was a modest suite: sitting room, bedroom, and bath, in fact, one of the smallest in the entire hotel, but luxurious in Jeff's eyes, especially as he harked back to the stuffy little dorm room he shared with Stench at school.

"Wow, this is real nice!" he said.

"Have a seat," Kathy said, tossing her coat on a chair beside a small writing desk. "Make yourself at home."

Jeff plopped down in a chintz wing chair catty-corner from a matching sofa. There was a potted amaryllis on the coffee table with a big swelling bud coming on. Kathy poked around in a cabinet console, which included a small refrigerator that a twenty-three-inch TV sat on. She produced two glasses with ice cubes and two miniature vodka bottles, which she conveyed across the room, giving one of each to Jeff.

"Wow. This is a cute little bottle," he said.

"It's the real stuff," she said. "Go ahead, pour yourself one. We'll have a cocktail before dinner."

Now, Jeff had witnessed hundreds of cocktail hours since he'd become a sentient person living with two adults in a Manhattan apartment, so it wasn't as if he didn't know how to proceed. Of course, he hadn't been a participant until now.

"Where do you get these tiny little bottles?" he said.

"A bellboy named Sammy. He's sweet. He'll do anything for me."

"You're way underage, though."

Kathy laughed.

"Go ahead," she said. "Pour yourself one."

Jeff wondered, What would Holden do? He was feeling enough of a zing from the two ounces of sherry he'd downed minutes ago to arrive at the conclusion that Holden would say, *Go ahead, ya moron, and have a goddam cocktail.* He emptied his mini into the glass and took a sip.

"Whoa! This has got some kick," he said.

"Is this your first real drink of the hard stuff?"

"Naw. My mom gave me some scotch last year when I had a toothache and told me to swirl it around in my mouth. It was like fire."

"But it made you feel better, right?"

"Yeah, actually, it did."

"Vodka's made out of potatoes," she said. "The Russians invented it."

Jeff almost choked on his second sip when she said that.

"Goddam Russians," he said when he finished coughing. "You know, they might have been behind Oswald, the guy who shot Kennedy."

"What do you mean 'behind'?"

"Like . . . part of a plot."

"Where'd you hear that?"

"Guy at my school. Older kid. Genius. They call him 'Trotsky.'"

"What's a Trotsky?"

"Some guy in Russia, back in the revolution, I think. Goddam communist. I might go over to the Russian embassy one of these days and see what I can find out about it."

"Find out what?"

"If the Russians helped Oswald kill Kennedy."

"Well, I hope you'll be careful. Russians are no one to mess around with."

"Goddam Russians . . ."

"How's your cocktail?"

"Goddam good," Jeff said. "Makes you feel all right. Hey, you mind if I smoke?"

"You got some ciggies?"

"Oh, yeah."

"Can I have one?"

"Sure."

He pulled out his pack of Marlboros, struck a match for himself, and then leaned toward the sofa to light hers. They smoked quietly for a minute. She looked like she had some experience with it, the way she held it in her hand, like his mother did. He demonstrated his own skill blowing the smoke out through his nostrils.

"Does that bellboy who gets the liquor also get you cigarettes?" he said.

"Actually, I have to watch it with the ciggies," Kathy said. "I don't want to wreck my voice for the show, you know, so I only have them occasionally."

"Of course," Jeff said, taking another slug from his glass. He noticed that all his nervousness had vanished. He felt completely at ease with the stunning Kathy Kaine in her beautiful hotel suite. He felt confident that he could talk about anything.

"So," he began, expelling a stream of smoke, "I get the feeling you're not going home for Thanksgiving."

"No, I'm not."

"How come?"

"It'd be crazy for me to fly halfway across the country for one night. I have to be in the show Friday evening. I talked to my mom about it. But I think the real reason is she's got this new boyfriend."

"Boyfriend? What happened to your father?"

"He's not in the picture."

"What does that mean, not in the picture?"

"He walked out on us when I was hardly six years old."

"Oh, jeez. Where is he now?"

"I don't know. I haven't seen him in many years." Kathy squeezed her eyes shut and shook her head. Soon Jeff could see tears on her cheeks.

"Oh, jeez, I'm sorry about that."

Kathy began to shake and sob.

Jeff got out of his chair and bent down to her, petting her shoulder, saying, "It's okay. I'm sorry. Don't cry." He didn't know what else to do. And then Kathy stood up abruptly and threw her arms around Jeff, with her head on his shoulder, and she was all the scents of perfume, tears, tobacco smoke, and vodka. Jeff let her hug him until she stopped shaking and sobbing. Eventually she let go and slid back into her seat on the sofa. Jeff returned to his wing chair.

"Look, you should come to our Thanksgiving," he said. She lifted her head, sniffled, and wiped her tears away with the hand not occupied by a cigarette.

"Oh, I don't know . . ."

"Really, you should. You're not going over to Viktor's with all those pervs, right?"

"God, no."

"And nobody else invited you, right?"

"They're all scattering to the winds," Kathy said, recovering her self-possession. "Carol, who plays my big sister, she's going up to Connecticut, where her current boyfriend's from. I can't stand Larry, who plays Anders, the next older kid in the show. And Betty Bridges, who plays Anna the governess, is a goddam bitch on wheels—"

That cracked Jeff up.

"I gotta remember that one," he said. "A bitch on wheels. That's goddam rich."

"She is," Kathy said, laughing along with Jeff now. "She's so mean. She calls Viktor 'Miss Vicious' behind his back. Anyway, she didn't invite me to whatever she's doing. I don't think she likes me."

"Well, we're going over to Uncle Ira's tomorrow. He was my dad's college roommate. He married my mom's kid sister. She acts in a soap opera."

"Really, which one?"

"I have no idea. They're all the same to me. You can ask her tomorrow. They live in this huge penthouse and there'll be a million people there. Nobody will notice you."

"A girl likes to be noticed."

"Okay, they'll probably notice you. You're such a tomato. I mean, you really are attractive."

"Awwww . . ." Kathy got up from the sofa, went over to Jeff, bent down, and kissed him moistly on the cheek. Feeling her so close, Jeff felt his blood rise and the hair on his neck tingle. "You're so sweet," she said, and turned to snuff out her cigarette in the ashtray next to the budding amaryllis. "I'd love to come tomorrow. Wait here a minute. I'll be right out."

When Kathy emerged from the bedroom, she had applied lipstick and mascara, changed into a clingy cashmere sweater that revealed her developing curves, and looked easily a couple of years older.

"Wow," Jeff said. "You kill me."

Kathy beamed.

"Bang, you're dead," she said, making a pistol of her hand. "Come on, let's go get some dinner. I'm starving."

"Yeah," Jeff said, knocking back what remained of his drink. "Let's go get some goddam dinner."

*

On Kathy's recommendation, they went two blocks up Amsterdam Avenue to a bistro called the Gay Hussar. It was plush and dim in there. The walls were covered with tapestries depicting scenes along the Danube, and the ceiling was upholstered in blood-red pleated satin, like being inside a capacious tent. Each table had a little lamp with a shade. Behind the bar hung a large gold-framed oil portrait of the legendary Major János Ferenczy in his splendid green and gold hussar's tunic, plumed bearskin busby, and leopard-skin cape worn on one shoulder, famous for his daring charge against Marshal Joachim Murat's field headquarters at the Battle of Donauwörth in the opening of Bonaparte's 1805 Austrian campaign. Gypsy violin music played lowly in the background.

Jeff had been in many Manhattan restaurants, but never one quite as posh. It was like stepping into a jewel box. Kathy seemed to glow as warmly as the lamp on their table. When they were seated, a waiter with a grave Magyar face in a spotless white apron approached.

"Good evening, László."

"Good evening, Madame. So nice to see you again."

"I'll have a martini, straight up," Kathy said. "Twist of lemon."

"Very well. Something for the boy?"

Jeff attempted to sit up straighter. "I'll have what she's having."

"I'm afraid that's impossible, young fellow. You are a boy."

Jeff decided not to argue. "I'll have a ginger ale," he said.

László departed.

"You can have some of mine," Kathy said.

"How do you get to order booze here?"

"I take care of László, and he takes care of me."

"Jeez, you seem to know all the angles. What I don't get is, who takes care of you, being in the city all by yourself and all?"

"I take care of myself."

"You don't have any, I don't know, counselor or guardian or someone who checks in on you?"

"There's Mrs. Warneke. She tutors us kids in the show. She holds what they call 'school' backstage two hours every day, one session for the little kids and one for us older ones. It's not much but we do learn a few things."

"But nobody checks in on you at the hotel?"

"The first two months, there was a Miss Atkinson who used to come backstage after each show and take me uptown in a cab. Then she just stopped coming. They must have figured I learned how to get there myself. Carol says they didn't want to pay her anymore."

Their drinks arrived. Jeff studied the menu.

"I wish they had pictures of these dishes. How are you supposed to know what Szkely Tlttt Kposzta is?" he said. "I can't even pronounce it."

"Stuffed cabbage rolls," she said and poured about half her martini into Jeff's ginger ale.

"You must have been here a million times," he said.

"At least once a week since I got into the show."

"Jeezus," he said. "What the hell's headcheese?"

"Don't order it, it's gross," she said. "For a starter, get the little meatballs in dill sauce. And you can't go wrong with the chicken paprikash with the potato dumplings for a main dish."

"Goddam headcheese. I can't get over it. What are you getting?"

"I like the cold cherry soup and I think I'll have the duck leg."

So it went for the next hour as they worked their way through their sumptuous dishes. Jeff regaled Kathy with the tribulations that led to his getting sent away to Ponsonby Hall, and his subsequent adventures there in the New Hampshire woods, and how he had been reading *The Catcher in the Rye*, which was the best book ever, except maybe boys would appreciate it more than girls, and how he was now able to see how much phoniness there is in so much of modern life, and how he really wanted to go meet the author, J. D. Salinger, who supposedly lived not that far from Ponsonby Hall in the Granite State.

Kathy allowed that life in the Milwaukee suburbs was unspeakable unto a death by boredom, but she loved being in New York and doing the show, notwithstanding her nutty and self-centered fellow cast members. She'd done a TV commercial at age eleven for Kohler bathtubs, a Wisconsin-based company, that went national and led to an audition for the Excelsior Talent Agency for professional children, which led to the audition to replace pregnant Bobbie Singletree in the show, and now her agent, Dottie Dabney, got her a role in a horror movie about a family that moves into a house possessed by demons, with filming to start in June in Los Angeles. She was going to get paid twenty thousand dollars.

"That's a lot of moolah," Jeff observed.

"I know. And it all goes to my mom."

"What!"

"Yeah, supposedly she puts it in a trust fund."

"You don't get any of it?"

"I get an allowance. Until I'm eighteen. In the meantime, I'm sure she's spending my money on her goddam new boyfriend."

"That's goddam unfair. My dad's a lawyer. Maybe he can fix that."

"They've got a lawyer at the Excelsior Agency. He told me that's how it works."

"Jeez."

They finished with slices of chocolate Dobos torte (he) and the almond Eszterházy torte (she), and then the bill came. It was thirty-four dollars and change. Jeff left two twenties on the table and then walked Kathy back to the hotel. Both of them were a little wobbly, and at one point, Kathy said she might barf, but it passed and they entered the hotel. As they made their way to the Bomoseen's elevator, Jeff glanced at the handsome clock above the front desk.

"Jeezus," he said. "It's eight goddam thirty. I'd better get home."

"What time is this Thanksgiving get-together tomorrow?" Kathy said. "And where should I go?"

"It's more than a get-together. It's a big party. Middle of the afternoon. Don't worry, I'll come over and pick you up and we can take a cab there."

"That'd be lovely," she said. "Just call the Bomoseen's desk in the morning after ten. They'll ring my room. Thanks, Jeff. I really had a nice time tonight."

"Me too," Jeff said. "You're amazingly . . . uh . . . normal . . . for a Broadway star."

Kathy leaned in and gave him a kiss right on the lips just as Leroy threw open the elevator door. Every cell in his body tingled.

"'Night," she said, and stepped inside with all the mirrors reflecting countless images of her bright blonde hair floating above the dark coat with its fur collar.

Leroy closed the door right in Jeff's face.

Chapter Eight

Bob and Evelyn were on the living room sofa when Jeff came through the doorway at five minutes to nine. The credits were rolling on *The Dick Powell Show* on the television but neither of them had been watching. Bob lowered the *New Yorker* magazine he'd been reading and Evelyn stopped scribbling in that day's *New York Times* crossword puzzle.

"Wow, kiddo," she said, glancing at her Cartier tank watch. "You made it by a cat's whisker. Eight fifty-seven."

Jeff unwound the muffler from his neck.

"Well, here I am," he said. "Home safe and sound after all."

His parents appeared slightly miffed, unable to nail him on being late.

"What's with this sudden interest in girls?" Bob inquired.

"I dunno. Getting ready to be a teenager, I guess."

"But you're not a teenager yet," Evelyn said.

"It's like spring training in baseball, Mom," Jeff said. "You have to get into shape for the regular season."

"Your mom tells me you went backstage on Broadway and met this gal."

"I did. She's a doll. You'll be crazy about her."

"Oh?" Evelyn said. "Are you bringing her over soon?"

"Well, not exactly. I invited her to come for Thanksgiving."

"What?"

"Without asking us?"

"Aw, come on, Mom. There'll be a million people at Uncle Ira and Aunt Joanie's. You know what it's like. Nobody'll notice. She's stuck in the city with nowhere to go for Thanksgiving. Her mom's way the hell out in Milwaukee and she's got to be in the show Friday, so she can't fly home. Plus, her goddam father's out of the picture. She was all sad about it."

"Out of the picture?" Evelyn said.

"She hasn't seen him in years, she says."

"Oh, dear . . ."

"That's a tough break," Bob said.

"I had to invite her on the spot. There wasn't time to check with you. She was weeping, for chrissake."

Bob got up and glided over to a reproduction Hepplewhite tea table, where various liquor bottles were deployed on a large silver tray, and refreshed his scotch. Evelyn adjusted herself on the sofa.

"Does she even know where Uncle Ira lives?" she said.

"No. I'm going to pick her up at her hotel and bring her there."

"Oh . . . okay. Points for being the gentleman," Evelyn said. "Where's her hotel?"

"Over on the West Side. The Bomoseen."

"That's rather swell."

"It's quite swell," Jeff said.

"Did you go there?"

"Just for a little while, after the show."

Bob and Evelyn shared another glance.

"Who looks after her there?"

"I'm not sure. The people who run the hotel, I think."

"That doesn't sound right."

"Well, I can't tell you. I really don't know."

Evelyn took a fresh tack: "What'd you two do there?"

"Nothing. She just changed her clothes. You know, coming home from the theater after a hard day's work and all. I just sat there."

"In her room? While she changed?"

"It's a suite. There's, like, a separate living room."

"So, where did you go on this date?" Bob asked.

"The Gay Hussar. Hungarian joint on Seventy-fourth and Amsterdam."

"Oh," Evelyn said to Bob. "We were there once. With the Sturgeons, remember?"

"Yeah, I guess so. Comfortable place. Good chow."

"Pricey," Evelyn said. "How much was it?"

"Forty bucks." Jeff said. "With the tip."

"And you paid for the whole thing?"

"Of course. Isn't the guy supposed to pay?"

Bob gave a little whistle.

"Well, she's performing in a Broadway show," Evelyn said. "She must be getting a very nice paycheck every week."

"It didn't occur to me to ask," Jeff said.

"Where do you get that kind of money to blow on dates," Evelyn said, her voice raised slightly.

"I told you. I saved up the last three months. Plus, I won a little money playing poker at school the night before President Kennedy got shot."

"They allow poker games at Ponsonby Hall?"

"Not really."

"But you play. You say there was a game?"

"Yeah, we play sometimes. For godsake, Mom, it's a bunch of guys in the middle of nowhere. We do things that guys do, like play cards. They can't stifle everything."

"He's got a point, dear," Bob said.

"Well, I don't approve of you throwing money away on gambling," Evelyn said. "That's what Edgar Allan Poe did at West Point. It ruined him for life. That and all the drinking."

"Hey, I won. I didn't throw anything away. And I'm not ruined. And why are you giving me the third degree like Perry Mason? I'm home from vacation. I went out for dinner with my own goddam money. And I came home when I said I would. What rules did I break?"

Bob and Evelyn exchanged faces of consternation. A silence ensued. Jeff almost reached for his pack of Marlboros he was so annoyed.

"Well, are you going to let her come to Thanksgiving or what?" he finally asked.

"I don't see why not," Bob said. "Poor thing. Alone for the holiday."

"Doesn't she have any friends in the cast of her play?" Evelyn asked. "Some adult who can roast a turkey?"

"They're all creeps, she says. I met one of them backstage when I was there. Viktor, the guy who plays the father."

"Yes . . . ? What about him?"

"Well . . . he kind of squatted down in front of the chair I was in and put his hands on my leg and squeezed it."

"What!" Bob said.

"Kathy kicked him out. She says he's a perv."

"We'll come with you in the cab to pick her up at the Bomoseen," Evelyn said.

"I can go get her myself."

"It's not up for discussion. Anyway, I haven't seen the inside of that place in years."

"Okay, whatever you say," Jeff said. "I'm goddam bushed. I'm going to bed."

"What's with all the cursing all of a sudden?" Bob said.

Jeff didn't try to explain.

*

Jeff reached Kathy Kaine easily by phone at ten-fifteen the next morning and arranged to rendezvous at the Bomoseen at three o'clock for the trip to Uncle Ira's and apprised his parents of the plan. At that hour, Evelyn was busy baking her "famous" chocolate pecan pie to bring to the Thanksgiving feast. Bob was holed up in the den composing a brief for Hunsinger Properties v. Beasley Construction, a liability case concerning the explosion of several propane tanks and ensuing fire that badly damaged a new twenty-story luxury apartment tower just then being built at 64th Street and Second Avenue.

Jeff learned in the *New York Times* that the new president Lyndon Johnson proclaimed that the Cape Canaveral space center would be renamed Cape Kennedy, after the dead president. Also that day, Mr. Johnson appointed Chief Justice Earl Warren as chairman of a commission to investigate the assassination of Mr. Kennedy. Mr. Dulles of the Central Intelligence Agency was a member. Surely, those G-men would get to the bottom of it. So much about it was obviously fishy, especially the murder of Oswald by Ruby. Jeff recalled Trotsky, back at the school dock on Great Pond, saying it might be five years before they figured out what really happened, and that was before Ruby had entered the picture. Five years. By then, Jeff realized, he'd be in college—unless he chucked it all, as Holden constantly suggested, and went off to live in the woods like a hermit.

He killed an hour rereading parts of *Catcher in the Rye*, amazed at how much Holden's world was like his own, feeling as if the story had been written specifically for him, sent like a message in a bottle fated to be found washed up at his feet on the beach. Holden himself had said that if you're really crazy about a book, you'd wish that the author was your close friend, and you could call him on the phone and talk to him whenever you wanted. So, Salinger they said lived in New Hampshire, not very far from Ponsonby Hall. Was he a hermit, hiding out in some kind of a hermit hut? More likely he lived in a regular house of some kind, even if it was off in the woods somewhere, perhaps even a very nice house. After all, his book was a sensation, apparently being read by every kid in America. He must have made enough money to live well. Jeff was dying to know what Salinger might think about the Kennedy assassination.

By eleven o'clock, awaiting the holiday's late afternoon festivities, he was sick of being cooped up in his room. Evelyn had moved on from making her pie to making a platter of her "famous" deviled eggs with their "secret" ingredient (English hot mustard). His father was still consumed with legal matters in the den. So, considering he had several hours before picking up Kathy, Jeff decided to go out and get some air.

The city was unusually quiet again Thanksgiving morning as it was the day of the president's funeral. Jeff hiked over to Fifth Avenue and entered Central Park just south of the great art museum, wending his way into the wooded Ramble area beside the boating lake. The thirty-six acres of winding paths, rocky promontories overlooking the water, and little footbridges in the rustic peeled logs style was intended to evoke a Catskill forest. The trees were bare now, the boathouse closed for the holiday, and the lake unusually still. He settled on an outcrop of New York schist beside the Gill, an artificial stream fed by a man-made pipe under a rock ledge. Seated on the rock, with the titanic, thrumming engine of Manhattan partially blotted out, he yearned for the real thing, the vast genuine woods around Ponsonby Hall, and felt some comfort knowing he would return there soon. He did not want to hurt his parents' feelings, but he also did not want to return to Manhattan to go to school here. Difficult as boarding school could be sometimes, he much preferred it to the city. Even though Holden disparaged Pencey Prep, Jeff thought he seemed more relaxed there than anywhere else, especially New York. And though Holden was crazy about his sister Phoebe, and his tragically deceased brother Allie, and talked about them a lot, he hardly ever mentioned his parents, except to say that his father, Mr. Caulfield, was a lawyer. Maybe this was just how it was as you got older, Jeff thought. And anyway, he was an only child, with no siblings to care about.

After a while, Jeff grew chilly sitting on the rock under the clotted gray sky and wended his way back out of the park, emerging onto Fifth Avenue around 76th, north of the zoo. His route home happened to take him by the elegant brick and limestone, Federalist revival–style mansion known as the Percy Rivington Pyne House on the northwest corner of 68th Street and Park Avenue, constructed in 1909, and designed by the renowned firm McKim, Mead & White, which happened at this time to serve as the Soviet Mission to the United Nations, well known to Jeff who had waited there that October day in 1960 hoping for a glimpse of Khrushchev.

A pair of plainclothes KGB agents, sturdy young men in crew cuts and boxy brown suits, stood by each side of the door under the handsome neoclassical portico that fronted Park Avenue. Jeff lurked on the sidewalk glaring at them for several minutes. At first the two agents pretended to ignore him, clutching their hands at their belt buckles, glancing this way and that way along Park Avenue, with its holiday stream of yellow taxicabs southbound toward Grand Central Station. By and by, though, while Jeff remained fixed in place beside the "No Standing" sign at the curb, the two agents decided to return his gaze until something like a stare-down was underway. Finally, the two agents exchanged some words in Russian, and then one barked at Jeff: "What you are wanting here, boy?"

Jeff shrugged his shoulders but continued gawking at the two big men.

"Maybe you get lost, hey," the other agent suggested. "Go! Beat it!"

Jeff continued to give them the hairy eyeball, as if sizing them up for something. After a few more minutes of this, one of the agents slipped inside the embassy and returned shortly with a middle-aged gentleman much better dressed in a pinstriped suit, who stepped briskly toward Jeff with a smile on his face that was meant to convey wry amusement. He was not so tall as the two KGB guards, slender and quite polished-looking, a veteran of the Russian diplomatic corp. He was, in fact, an attaché.

"What do you want, young fellow," he inquired, taking a French Gauloises cigarette from a pack and lighting it. Jeff likewise took out his pack of Marlboros, extracted a smoke, and lit up. "Ah, I see, you are comedian," the attaché said. "This is not Ed Sullivan theater. Can I ask you please to move along, go home, or wherever you are supposed to be."

"This is a free sidewalk," Jeff said.

"Is that so?"

"It is so," Jeff said. "In a free country."

The attaché's smile turned slightly scowlish.

"May I ask, what is your name, boy?"

"Mooski Toffski Offski," Jeff said.

"Is that so?"

"It is so," Jeff said, and flicked the ash off the tip of his cigarette.

"Sounds Russian, a little bit," the attaché said. "But not really. As if I pretend to be American and tell you my name is Mickey Mantlemouse. Now, why are you hanging around bothering my men?"

"I want to know why you guys killed President Kennedy," Jeff said.

The attaché flinched at that.

"Did you not read papers, young Mr. Mooski Tootski? Do you not watch Walter Cronkite? Do you not know the assassin is your own Oswald, pride of Texas, ride 'em cowboy . . . yippie."

"You bastards put him up to it," Jeff said, becoming strangely overcome with emotion, as if suddenly all the accumulated grief and horror of the week past was trying to pour out of him.

"How do you know this?" the attaché said.

"Everybody knows."

"No, that is not true," the attaché said calmly and diplomatically. "Who told you this?"

"A very smart person."

"I see. Well, this genius is not correct. I am sincerely sorry for tragedy of your country. I will tell you, we felt great improvement in relations after Cuba affair. Believe me, we did not want Mr. President Kennedy removed from scene. It was not in our interest. A smart person would understand this."

"Oswald went to Russia for a whole year. You must've done something to him. Messed with his brain."

"No," the attaché said with lips pursed. "He left Soviet Union with same brain he come in with. You know what he did in Soviet Union?"

"Did?"

"Did," the attaché said, "with his days. Occupied himself."

Jeff had to ponder a moment. "Not really."

"Oswald worked in radio factory. That is all. It appears he did not like this work. He did not like Soviet Union. He went home. Now, you should go home. Please, go home. Pretend you are Oswald and this is Soviet Union. Go home."

"I'm not Oswald."

"That's true. You look like you come from bourgeois family, clean, nice clothings. It is your holiday feast today, yes? Give thanking. Go home. Eat a turkey. I don't want to call police."

Jeff didn't want to tangle with the police either, and he took the hint, but not before dashing his cigarette to the sidewalk and grinding it out under his heel like it was Khrushchev's face.

Chapter Nine

They rode across Central Park in the cab at three o'clock in silence, so fraught were the family's relations these strange six days after the president's murder, with the emerging tensions between a boy leaving childhood behind and his exasperated parents. But entering the Bomoseen's magnificent lobby, Evelyn exclaimed, "Oh, my! They've really kept the old place up! Why I had drinks here in the bar on V-J Day with Betty Fishman and Myra Segal."

Jeff went straight to the front desk and asked the clerk to call Kathy Kaine's suite and tell her he was in the lobby. Then he took a position beside a pillar of Vermont green marble facing the elevator, and waited. Bob and Evelyn had been circling the large room admiring the paintings and the bronze figurines on display, and drifted over to stand beside Jeff just in time to see the elevator door slide open and Kathy Kaine stride confidently out in her black coat with the rabbit-fur collar and three-inch-high heels. She was also wearing lipstick and eye makeup, including false eyelashes, with her blonde hair coiffed into a golden sweep across the left side of her head, revealing an impressive double-drop earring with a rhinestone the size of a Jordan almond in it. Altogether, she looked at least five years older than she had the night before, throwing Jeff into a strange panicky rapture while Bob and Evelyn looked on in amazement.

Kathy strode up to them, kissed Jeff politely on the cheek, and turned directly to Bob and Evelyn, saying, "You must be his mom and dad. It's so nice to meet you."

Utterly disarmed and flustered, they each took a turn with Kathy's hand and said how pleased they were to meet her.

"Well, we might as well get going," Bob said, without further formalities. "There are plenty of cabs out today. Maybe we can get a Checker." The Checker cab was famous for its spaciousness and its jump seats in the passenger compartment. Out on Broadway, Bob promptly flagged a Checker down. They all piled in the rear and Jeff pulled up the jump seat for himself. Bob, Evelyn, and Kathy sat on the cushy back seat.

"Eighty-third and Park," Bob told the driver.

"It's so nice of you to invite me along," Kathy said as the cab took off. "I'm from the Midwest. There wasn't time to go all the way home and make the Friday show."

"Yes, we heard. Milwaukee, was it?"

"That's right. Actually, a little nowheresville outside it. Glen Oaks, Wisconsin. Rah, rah."

"Well, we're delighted to have you along. Jeff's an only child, you know. Suddenly it's like he's got a big sister."

"For godsake, Mom."

"I believe we saw the show just after it opened . . . When was that, Bob? Last winter some time—"

"March," Bob said.

"Were you in the original cast?"

"You probably saw Bobbie Singletree."

"Ah. So you replaced her?"

"Yes, in June."

"Oh? She wasn't with the show very long."

"She had problems," Kathy said.

"What sort of problems?"

"She got knocked up," Kathy said, just as the cab swerved so sharply off Central Park West into the transverse drive that Jeff almost fell off the jump seat.

"Oh, dear," Evelyn said. Conversation stopped dead until they emerged from the sunken transverse onto Fifth Avenue and minutes later arrived at their destination. Kathy got out first.

"Can you take this a second?" Evelyn said handing Kathy the basket that contained the goodies she brought. "I hope you like chocolate pecan pie. It's Jeff's favorite."

"Sounds yummy," Kathy said.

Jeff was last to get out. Evelyn stuck closely to Kathy, yakking away all the way to elevator, while Jeff and his father took up the rear.

"So, that was your date last night," Bob whispered, marveling at the idea. "Since when do you get to meet a bombshell like her?"

"I just went backstage to say hello, and things developed from there."

"Kudos to you, kid."

There were only two apartments on the fourteenth floor, Penthouse East and West, and Uncle Ira Kooperman, his wife, Aunt Joan, and twin daughters, Jeff's cousins, Zoe and Chloe, age eight, were in PH West. It was ideally suited for entertaining, with a deep foyer entrance, a spacious dining room set up for the buffet yet to come, a large living room twenty-five feet long that communicated in a direct line to a library, and doors in several places to the broad penthouse terrace beyond with its planting boxes and outdoor furnishings. The Koopermans made good use of it, Uncle Ira being in the sports documentary business, with the need for frequently schmoozing up clients and customers from the television world.

At three-thirty this Thanksgiving, fifty guests already circulated in the elegant rooms decorated in the English country style, all overstuffed with cabbage roses, wing chairs, club chairs strangely offset by contemporary art on the walls, including a painting of primary color squares by Hans Hofmann, a black inky blob by Robert Motherwell, and a squiggly drawing by Arshile Gorky. Through the windows, the last of Thanksgiving's daylight lingered among the rooftops of Manhattan while candles twinkled festively all around the many rooms. Laughter rang through the apartment and behind it the recorded jazz piano music of Erroll Garner laid a relaxing cushion of sound.

"Wow," Kathy said, as a valet took her coat. "Look at this place! It's like heaven!"

"Wow," Bob said to himself reflexively as he beheld Kathy Kaine, coat off, suddenly revealed in her clingy black velvet bias-cut cocktail dress with a deep neckline that displayed her developing décolletage to excellent effect.

"Jeez," Jeff said to no one in particular.

"Don't you look grown-up!" Evelyn said as she surrendered her own vintage sealskin coat (once her mother's) to Bob.

Then Joan Kooperman was upon them with kisses and greetings and the Greenaways' introduction of surprise guest Kathy Kaine, star of *The Wayward Family Singers* on Broadway, and the instant bonding with Kathy on account of Joan being a veteran actress herself in the long-running CBS soap opera *All Our Days*. In fact, there were several other television actors and actresses on the premises, as well as a raft of TV writers, directors, and agents—denizens of the Koopermans' glamorous world—and Joan decisively took Kathy by the elbow to show her off while advising the Greenaways to head for the bar in the library and have a drink.

Jeff watched Kathy vanish into the crowd like a shimmering particle absorbed into a great amoeba, wondering if he would ever get to spend a few precious moments in her company that evening, or if she would be hopelessly monopolized by all the grown-ups fawning over her. Indeed, while Bob and Evelyn made their way to the bar back in the library, Jeff, who had barely gotten a thing to eat all day, turned his attention to the several waiters who were circulating through the crowd with trays of edibles—"angels on horseback" (scallop and bacon tidbits), cheese puffs, jumbo shrimp, chicken liver pâté on toast, and those deviled eggs Evelyn insisted on bringing—and intercepted them inbound and outbound from the kitchen until by happenstance he found himself bumped up against the back of Uncle Ira himself, who wheeled around, hoisting his rocks glass of Dewar's scotch whisky deftly over a young redhead who worked at ABC Sports, seemingly delighted to find his nephew standing there.

"Hey, Jeff, when did your gang get here?" Ira said.

"A little while ago," Jeff said.

"Where's your old man?"

"The bar, I think."

"Good for him! Didja see Koufax in the Series?"

It was a little hard to hear amid all the chatter and the tinkling piano music.

"There's no TV where I am," Jeff said.

"Huh? No TV?"

"I'm not home anymore. They sent me to this sleepaway school in the middle of nowhere."

"Oh, yeah, I think Joanie mentioned it. Up in New England somewhere?"

"New Hampshire. Ponsonby Hall. Way up in the North Woods. It's a special school for screwups. We call it Old Poison."

"What'd you do to deserve that?"

"Nothing," Jeff said. "Just some kid trouble. You know."

"Yeah, I know. I was kind of like that myself. They must have good sports there, though. Those prep schools are crazy for athletics."

"I'm going to try out for the rowing crew this spring."

"Thataboy!" Uncle Ira said. He was a large man with a barrel chest, and a halo of curly gray hair. Smiling expansively as if remembering something from his own youth, he tousled Jeff's hair with the hand that wasn't holding a drink.

"You'll turn out fine," he said. "You should have seen Koufax. He was magnificent."

"Hey, Ira," Jeff said. "How come everybody's all happy and laughing it up and President Kennedy has been moldering in the grave for only a few days?"

Uncle Ira's mouth turned down. "Life has got to go on, kid," he said, gravely.

"They should at least be a little sad."

"Hey, it's Thanksgiving. The living have to live."

"I think the Russians were behind it."

"What? Killing Kennedy?"

"You know Oswald was over in Russia a whole year."

"Yeah, I heard. it's a little screwy, this story. Our boys'll find out. Don't you worry. Mr. Dulles is on the new commission. CIA. They have their ways . . ."

Just then Ira spied new arrival Zane McClachy nearby, a producer with ABC's *Wide World of Sports*, with whom he had a pending deal to film an Oklahoma rattlesnake hunt, and excused himself, telling Jeff they'd catch up later on. On his own again, Jeff ricocheted from one hors d'oeuvre tray to another through the living room and eventually landed in the library. A young bartender in a white apron stood behind a trolly of bottles there with a wall of books behind him.

"My mom asked me to get a scotch and soda for her," he told the bartender.

"You eighteen?"

"Of course not. I'm a kid."

"We can't serve kids."

"It's for my mom."

"I heard you the first time. She'll have to get it herself."

"She's in there," Jeff pointed to the crowded living room. "In a wheelchair."

"What?"

"You know that plane crash over in Jersey last year?"

"Yeah . . ."

"She was in it."

"What? Oh, gosh . . . I'm sorry to hear that."

"She can't possibly get through this crowd in that wheelchair."

"All right, kid. Calm down."

The bartender fixed a scotch and soda and handed it over.

"I hope she gets better," he said.

Jeff took the highball glass and plunged back into the crowd in the living room. When he was out of sight of the library entrance, he sampled the drink. He found the smoky-bubbly taste quite pleasing. Then, he spied Kathy through two conversational groups and wended his way toward her. A young man with slicked-back hair, horn-rimmed glasses, and a pink button-down shirt had been chatting her up.

"I got something for you," Jeff said, and put the drink in her hand.

"Why, thank you, sweetie," she said and took a big gulp. "This is Judson. He writes for Candid Camera."

"Is that so?" Jeff said. "What's there to write on that show?"

"The gags," Judson said. "You know, the stuff that happens."

"Why do you have to write it? The camera tells the whole story."

"You have to set up the gag, you know, that the camera catches people doing."

"Must take you about thirty seconds to write one of those."

"Well, you have to constantly set up new gags that haven't been done before."

"How much do they pay you to do that?"

"Jeff!" Kathy said. "Don't be rude."

"Who's this kid?" Judson said. "Your little brother?"

"I'm her attorney," Jeff said.

"Oh, really? You should write comedy, kid."

"What if I told you that you were on Candid Camera right now, and you've been caught trying to put the moves on a thirteen-year-old girl?"

"You're thirteen?" Judson said, turning a shade of red that complemented his pink shirt.

"I'll be fourteen in March," Kathy said.

"Jeezus," Judson said. "You don't look thirteen."

"Oh, she is," Jeff said.

"Are you?"

Kathy made a moue and took a gulp of her drink.

"Well, anyway, it's been a pleasure," Judson said. "And you," Judson turned to Jeff. "You better be careful someone doesn't knock your teeth down your throat one of these days, you little shit." He smiled and peeled off.

"What'd you do that for?" Kathy said when he was gone.

"That slimy bastard was trouble. I could tell."

"He was all right."

"He just wants to give you the time," Jeff said.

"The time? What's that supposed to mean?"

"You know."

Kathy made another face, chugged down the rest of her drink, and stuck the glass against Jeff's sternum.

"Would you please get me a refill."

"That's right," Jeff said, taking the glass. "You stick with me. I'll take care of you."

Jeff headed back to the bar in the library.

"Mom needs another one," he said, presenting the glass. The bartender looked him up and down.

"What was that?"

"Scotch and soda."

"You better not be drinking these yourself."

"Why would I do that?"

"To get plastered," the bartender said. "You think I never worked a bar mitzvah?"

"This isn't a bar mitzvah."

"Yeah, well, I'm not pouring you another one after this, so don't come back. Tell her to send your dad."

"My dad got killed in the Korean War," Jeff said.

The bartender turned red and just stared at Jeff for a long moment.

"Jeezus, you're the unluckiest family I ever heard of. Stay out of the army, kid, if you can."

Jeff took the drink and went looking for Kathy, but she had vanished from the place in the living room where he'd left her. What would Holden do now, he asked himself. Why, go out on the terrace and have a smoke and enjoy the drink in peace and quiet. So he stepped through the iron and glass door beside the baby grand piano and out into the evening. He found a cast iron chair beside a little table, put down his highball glass, and lit up a Marlboro. It was so chilly out that his breath was visible before he even exhaled any smoke. The scotch and soda went down easily. Between the nicotine rush and the alcohol, he was enjoying the scintillating lightness in his brain. He began to imagine how he would regale the other screwups back at Old Poison about how he met the glamorous Kathy Kaine when someone else stepped out on the terrace. It was Uncle Ira's little brother, Artie Kooperman, who was an agent, representing a list of soap opera stars and writers. Jeff had seen him several times a year his whole life at family gatherings like this. They'd always enjoyed a jocular relationship.

"Who's that over there?" Artie said, squinting. "Oh, whaddaya know. Hey kid. How you been?"

Feeling the artificial confidence that liquor brings on, Jeff decided not to hide the fact that he was smoking a cigarette. He was in the mood to show off.

"Lousy," Jeff said (because Holden surely would have said that if someone happened to ask).

"Yeah?" Artie said. "What's lousy?"

"You know, life. This goddam world is full of phonies."

"Yeah, there's sure a lot of them out there. But, hey, you think it's lousy now? Wait until you grow up and you get to enjoy a divorce from a really stupid, vicious actress. Say, are you smoking?"

"Yeah. I'm a regular fiend about it."

"It'll cut your wind."

"I got all the wind I need."

"Yeah, you think so? I'd quit now if I was you."

At that, Artie took out a pack of Newports and lit one up himself. Jeff could tell that Artie had been drinking, too.

"Are you really getting a divorce from Aunt Barb, Artie?"

"Ex-aunt," Artie said. "Yeah. She's taking me to the cleaners, kid."

"Jeez, that's a tough break," Jeff said and exhaled a cloud of smoke that wafted over the parapet of the terrace and vanished into the surrounding Manhattan roofscape of water towers looming darkly above similar penthouses. He didn't know what it meant to be taken to the cleaners, but it didn't sound good.

"Do yourself a favor, kid," Artie said. "Stay away from actresses. They're nothing but trouble. Boy, it's freezing out here."

"Yeah," Jeff said. "It's colder than a witch's tit." (Holden liked to say that.)

"A witch's tit! Ha!" Artie said. "Where'd you hear that one?"

"Nowhere," Jeff said.

"You know what's colder than that?" Artie said. "Your ex–Aunt Barb's heart. It's a regular Frigidaire. I gotta go back in."

He peeled off, chuckling at his own joke, and made for the door.

Jeff lasted only a few minutes more himself out there and went back inside.

Before long, news filtered through the rooms that the buffet was laid out in the dining room and everyone should come and get a plate. Jeff spotted Kathy by the big Motherwell painting (the black blob), chatting with an all-American-type young man in chinos, baggy sport coat, a tie with the knot almost the size of an apple turnover, and a brush cut with the front waxed up. She had another drink in her hand, with a napkin around the glass. The young man was leaning in on her. Jeff battled his way through the throng that was headed in the other direction to the buffet in the big adjoining dining room.

"I wondered where you were," Jeff said.

"I'm here," Kathy said. "With . . . Chuck?"

"Todd," the young man said.

"Sorry," Kathy said. "Todd."

"Yeah, I see. What are you two yakking about?"

Todd recoiled slightly, a big smile on his face, the dimples in his muscular cheeks so conspicuous they seemed to be winking. "We were talking showbiz," he said.

"Yeah?" Jeff said. "Are you in showbiz?"

"I'm in sports," Todd said.

"Which one?"

"Baseball. The big leagues."

"Oh. Like . . . a batboy?"

"Who is this kid?" Todd asked Kathy.

"A friend."

"I'm her date," Jeff said.

"That so?" Todd asked. "You're a riot, kid."

"Todd plays for the New York Mets," Kathy said.

"Huh? Jeez, really . . . ?"

"It's the God's truth. Todd Merritt, second base. Left field sometimes." The ballplayer held out his hand to shake and Jeff obliged. "Sounds like you don't follow the Mets."

"I don't, actually."

"Why not?"

"That's a good question." Jeff knew the answer, but he didn't want to say. The 1963 Mets—their second season since their entry into the National League—were the worst team in baseball with a record of 51 wins and 111 losses. "What do you do now that the season's over?"

"Yeah, what do you do?" Kathy chimed in and knocked back what remained in her glass.

"Little of this, little of that," Todd said.

"Mostly what, though?"

"I'm learning how to sell Corvettes. Dealer out in Syosset, DeLauro Chevrolet."

"Are you any good at it?" Jeff asked.

"Hey, I'm just learning the racket. I could coast, you know, likes some guys do. Go down to Mexico, play some beanerball maybe, sit on the beach. I signed a two-year contract with the Mets for twenty-three Ks a year. I figure I'll be able to buy my own dealership by 1968, when I'm smack in the middle of my career. Then, when I got to go to the glue factory, like we all do, I'll be set up in a great business."

"That sounds very promising," Kathy said. "Could you get me another drink?" She held up the empty glass.

"Sure, baby," Todd said. "What was it?"

"Scotch and soda."

Todd departed obediently for the bar.

"You sure are a popular girl tonight," Jeff said.

"I can't help it," Kathy said.

"You should tell 'em you're thirteen, at least."

"Why should I do that?"

"You know why."

"I'm just practicing for later on in life."

"Aren't you hungry? There's all kinds of food in there. Come on, let's get some turkey."

"You go ahead. Todd's bringing me my drink."

"You better not drink too much. You'll be vomiting all over the place. I know how you get."

"I'll be fine. Don't worry 'bout me. Go on. Get yourself some turkey and stuffing."

Jeff reluctantly headed into the dining room. As it happened, he found himself in line right behind his parents.

"Hi, Pussycat," Evelyn said. "Having a grand time?"

"Yeah, grand," Jeff said. "Old Uncle Ira sure knows how to throw a party."

"It's all Joanie," Evelyn said.

Bob slung an arm over Jeff's shoulder and drew him closer.

"Hey, Ace," he said. "I notice your girlfriend has been pounding down the booze."

"She is?"

"I've been keeping my eye on her."

"How do you know it's not ginger ale."

" 'Cause these young guys keep on bringing her drinks. I've got half a mind to read her the riot act."

"Don't do that, Dad!"

"Then you tell her to cut it out. We'd could end up being liable for her."

"What's that mean?"

"Her parents could sue us if anything happens to her. We're in loco parentis tonight."

"What's that mean?"

"Nominally in charge of her welfare. She's still a kid, you know."

"Okay, I'll tell her what you said."

Just then, Evelyn, who'd had a couple of Old-fashioneds herself and was a bit wobbly, stuck a plate into Jeff's chest.

"Try the Brussels sprouts with chestnuts, Pussycat. They're divine."

They went through the chow line with its magnificent traditional offerings. Jeff took his loaded plate back out and found a side chair in a corner under a pink blob painting by Jack Tworkov and next to a large potted ficus tree where he could survey the big room and especially surveil Kathy Kaine, who was now seated on one of several sofas distributed around the big room with the ballplayer Todd. The couple's conversation seemed animated. Kathy kept reaching for a highball glass on the adjacent side table, and, in gales of laughter from what were apparently hilarious stories Todd was spinning about life in the big leagues, she kept touching him about the shoulders and pectorals with the hand not occupied by her glass, as if saying, *Stop it, you're too funny*. Jeff understood now how Holden felt just thinking about his old flame Jane Gallagher out on a date with his sleazy roommate Ward Stradlater. After a while, Jeff couldn't watch it anymore.

He ditched his plate under the chair and made his way around the room. He began to notice various drink glasses that had been abandoned by the drinkers and decide to sample them. The adults in the room were too busy schmoozing to notice. Some of the drinks were still quite strong. The warm sensation in his belly made its way to his head and amplified the lightness he was enjoying. He wended his way back to the dining room where many desserts were laid out, cut himself a wedge of his mother's renowned chocolate pecan pie, and brought it out to Kathy.

"Try this," he said. "My mom made it."

"Hey, where's my piece?" Todd said.

"You can get your own. You're a big boy," Jeff said.

Kathy and Todd looked at Jeff a moment and then both cracked up.

"Your date," Todd said. "He's a crack-up."

They cracked up again.

"Lemme try some," Todd said.

Kathy loaded a fork and fed it to Todd.

"Damn," he said. "That's some A-one boss knockout pie, kid."

"Say, Jeff," Kathy said. "Would you be a dear and get me 'nother drinkie-winkie?"

"No. I think you're getting bombed."

"Naw. Coupla few drinkies. I can handle it."

"Anyway, the bartender cut me off," Jeff said.

"Sit tight," Todd said, rising. "I'll get you something. Don't let Junior here sweep you off your feet."

When he was gone, Jeff took Todd's place on the sofa next to Kathy and watched her finish the pie.

"What a party! Whew!" she said. "They don't have 'em like this in Glen Oaks."

"My dad's been watching you," Jeff said. "He's worried about your drinking."

"Watching me! That's a little creepy."

"He says he could be held responsible if anything happens to you."

"What could happen to me? Hey, that was some pie!"

"Yeah, she makes a great pie. I'm just telling you what he said."

"Is your dad a perv, watching me?"

"What! Of course not."

"Just kidding," she said, giving his shoulder a little shove. "Relax, I'm doin' fine."

Her million-dollar smile lit her up. It was obvious to Jeff why she got picked to be in a Broadway show.

"Look, Kathy, I have to go back to school on Monday," Jeff said. "Way the hell up in New Hampshire."

"Oh?" Kathy said. "How come?"

"Because vacation'll be over. We might not meet again for a while."

"It was great getting to know you," Kathy said.

"Can we stay in touch?"

"Tell you what. I'll send you the record of the show. It's the original cast with Bobbie Singletree, but you can pretend it's me. We sound a lot alike. It'll be just like me being there with you at school."

"No, it won't. Anyway, I don't have a goddam record player up there. Can I write you letters?"

"Sure, I love to get letters."

"Do you get a lot of them?"

"I get some. Not a lot. You can write to me. I'll write back. I'll tell you what all the perverts in the show are up to."

"That'd be great," Jeff said. "I'll be back in the city at Christmastime. Maybe we can get together then. Go out to some nice place. Just the two of us. Like before."

"Sure," Kathy said. "Just give me a ringding at the ol' Bomoseen."

Along about that time, Ted Schifreen, the music coordinator for ABC television, sat down at the baby grand piano and began dipping into his deep repertory of Gershwin and Cole Porter tunes, starting with the former's "He Loves and She Loves." He was a delicate stylist.

"I'm just worried about you," Jeff said.

"I know. Don't worry. I can take care of myself."

"If you let all these guys try to give you the time, you could get in trouble, you know, like what's-her-name."

"Bobbie Singletree is a dumb bunny. I'm not like her. I've got a career ahead of me."

Just then, Todd returned and proffered Kathy a martini glass filled with a pastel green cocktail.

"What's that!" Kathy said.

"A grasshopper. You'll love it," Todd said. "Buzz off, kid."

"Yum," Kathy said. "It's delicious."

"I'm serious, Kathy. Don't drink that thing. It'll make you barf."

"Kid," Todd said. "Be a gentleman and please get lost."

Jeff reluctantly yielded his place on the sofa.

"I'll let you know when it's time to go," Jeff said.

With the piano tinkling out Gershwin poignantly in the background, and his mind roiling, Jeff wandered back into the dining room. Maybe Artie was right about actresses, he thought. The help had set out a tray of chocolate mints. The centerpiece on the table remained in place, an array of gourds, small pumpkins, oranges studded with cloves, and fall foliage executed in wire and silk. Jeff stuffed several gourds and an orange in his jacket pocket, snatched up a mini-pumpkin the size of a softball, and headed back outside to the terrace.

It was even colder than before and a few snow flurries fell softly in the ambient light emanating from the party within. Jeff lit a Marlboro and reclined on a chaise with a backrest. He practiced blowing smoke rings for a while until he heard someone singing above the piano stylings of Ted Schifreen. The song was Cole Porter's "Anything Goes." This was the usual routine at Uncle Ira's holiday parties. As things wound down, Aunt Joanie or one of her showbiz pals would start belting out the great standards of their youth.

It took a few moments for Jeff to realize that he recognized a more youthful voice this time: Kathy Kaine's. He twisted around on the chaise and saw through the window between the fronds of a potted palm within that Kathy was seated on the piano. Ted was playing the song torch-style, slowly. She could really belt it out, he realized. By the end of the intro, all conversation had stopped, and everyone around the big room was riveted on her. Jeff was so rapt himself that he forgot he was holding a cigarette between his fingers until it began to burn his knuckle. He flicked it away and stood up.

Kathy finished to wild applause and whistles. Jeff moved closer to the window and peered in. Kathy leaned over toward Ted at the keyboard, confabbed briefly, and then they launched into another tune, the plaintive "Someone to Watch Over Me," by Gershwin. Jeff could not fail to notice that the ballplayer Todd Merritt was watching Kathy from right up front in the crowd, and not ten feet away from him the TV writer Judson was also watching her. Both of them had the look of slavering predators, like wolves from the storybooks. Yet, Jeff thought, he was the one truly watching over her, if only she'd realize it. When she finished the song, and everyone was clapping, cheering, and whistling again, Kathy reached for her drink, the grasshopper, and polished it off, then dramatically slipped one puffy sleeve of her velvet dress down off the shoulder, provocatively exposing more tender flesh. Todd stuck his fingers in his mouth and did a wolf whistle. Jeff couldn't stand to watch anymore.

He lurched over to the chest-high brick wall that edged the terrace. Planting boxes stood all along the wall, filled now with dead flowers. Jeff climbed up on one of the boxes allowing him to peer over the wall at the sidewalk twelve floors below. The building's elegant gray canopy jutted out to his left. Just then, the doorman emerged from it and helped an elderly lady out of her cab. Jeff reached into his pocket, brought out the orange studded with cloves, kissed it, and tossed it over the side like a hand grenade. He watched it land with a splat a few feet in front of the doorman and the elderly lady, and then quickly ducked behind the brick wall before they could look up and see him. He waited several minutes, stood up, and peered over the edge again. The coast was clear. More applause, cheers, whistles came from within. Ted Schifreen segued directly into "The Man I Love," another Gershwin number, the quintessential torch song.

Jeff retrieved the small pumpkin he'd left on the chaise and then returned to his post on the planting box overlooking the parapet. The doorman was no longer around. Traffic was sparse this Thanksgiving evening. Eighty-third Street was still. Jeff kissed the pumpkin and tossed it, grenade style, in a lofty arc, off the terrace and out into the street, hoping to see it detonate with spectacular force on the asphalt. By a stroke of ill fortune, however, at exactly the moment he released it, a bottle green English Bentley S3 turned the corner at Park Avenue and glided directly under the vectoring pumpkin, which landed square on its roof with a resounding metallic thud, followed by the screech of brakes and squealing rubber. Not a moment later, Bob Greenaway stepped out onto the terrace and barked, "What the hell are you doing?"

"Nothing," Jeff said, stepping down from the planting box.

"I heard that racket down there," Bob said. "You're throwing stuff off the roof, aren't you?"

"No."

Jeff was visibly shuddering, and not from the cold.

Just then as Kathy Kaine completed the lyric ". . . maybe Tuesday will be my good news day," a sharp gasp from the crowd could be heard inside the penthouse. The music had stopped abruptly, followed by a commotion. Then, some groans and a woman's screech penetrated through the fenestrations to the terrace. Bob whirled around and bolted back inside. Jeff waited a few seconds and followed. Kathy Kaine no longer sat demurely on the piano. Rather, she was on all fours like a large dog on the silk Persian carpet with its sickle-leaf and vine scroll motif, heaving up the contents of her stomach, tinted pastel green from her final cocktail of the evening. Ted knelt beside her, his hand patting her back. The help rushed into the room with towels, a bucket, and a mop as the partygoers peeled away from the scene in embarrassment and disgust.

Kathy raised herself up to a kneeling position. She looked shell-shocked, glassy-eyed. A sympathetic costar from Joanie's TV show gave Kathy a wet napkin to wipe her mouth and then helped her swab some blobs of vomit from her dress. Evelyn Greenaway swooped in and knelt beside her. Whatever Evelyn said was lost in the rhubarb of the other guests milling about, some with their coats on heading for the door. Jeff watched the gruesome spectacle from beside the potted palm, which afforded little to hide behind. Kathy began sobbing quietly. Bob stooped down and, together with Evelyn, helped Kathy to her feet while the help moved in with their towels and mop, and Joanie yelled at them to be careful and "blot up the mess. Blot, don't rub!" She had paid three thousand dollars for the carpet. It was a two-hundred-year-old antique.

Evelyn stood beside Kathy while Bob went to get her coat. Kathy was weaving slightly on her feet, so Evelyn steadied her. When Bob returned and helped Kathy into her coat, Evelyn ducked into a bedroom and emerged with her sealskin coat and Bob's glen plaid Brooks Brothers overcoat. Bob spun around and discerned Jeff lurking beside the potted palm. Many of the guests had lined up at the door and were saying goodnight to Uncle Ira when the doorman from down below appeared with a policeman in tow and began interrogating the owner of the penthouse, who just shook his head in bewilderment.

"Get over here," Bob barked at Jeff. "Now."

Jeff shuffled over to his father and the others.

"Follow me," Bob said. By now, the doorman and the cop had backed Uncle Ira to a corner of the foyer, leaving an opening at the front door. Bob led his family and Kathy Kaine out to the hall where other departing couples waited. Almost immediately, an elevator arrived and they all piled in. "In spite of it all, you sang beautifully," one of the women said as the elevator lurched down. Kathy was still crying when they exited the building. A little way down the street, the Bentley had pulled over with a New York City police cruiser behind it, its single revolving gumball light painting the street with garish red streaks.

"You two go home," Bob said to Evelyn and Jeff. "I'll take her back to the hotel." He slipped Evelyn a five-dollar bill for a cab, and flagged down one for himself and Kathy. Jeff watched helplessly as his father and Kathy drove off.

In the next cab, with his mother, in the short ride back to 139 East 79th Steet, Evelyn said. "Apparently, she was drinking up a storm. How do you let a thirteen-year-old kid live on its own in this city? It just baffles me."

Jeff didn't say a word.

*

Bob returned about an hour later. The Thanksgiving party had started in midafternoon, of course, so it was still pretty early, eight-thirty. He found Jeff in his room, holding up *The Catcher in the Rye*, which he was halfway through reading for the second time.

"Nice going, Ace," Bob began. "I called Ira from the Bomoseen. They found pieces of pumpkin all over the street, of course, and there's a nice dent in the roof of that Bentley. Ira's going to have to pay for it and I'm going to have to pay Ira back. Probably cost me five hundred bucks." He pulled Jeff's desk chair out and sat down beside the bed. "What's the matter with you, anyway?"

"I don't know."

"Why can't you stay out of trouble?"

"I don't know."

"Then you admit you tossed that pumpkin off the roof?"

"I don't know."

"You don't know? What do you know?"

"I don't know."

"We know you're not retarded. It must be something else. Some defect of character. But honest to God I can't figure out how we raised you wrong. You have a nice home here. Your own room. An allowance. I didn't have any allowance when I was your age. I had to mow lawns and clean out people's stables. I'll tell you one thing, though. That little chat we had the other night about you maybe staying home next year and finding a school here in New York. You can forget about that. You're going to have to stay up at Ponsonby Hall. Maybe they can straighten you out. What do you have to say about that?"

"I like it up there."

"That's nice. It'll go easier on you then."

"And I'm sorry you hate me."

"I don't hate you. You're my kid. I love you. I just don't know what to do about you."

Bob stared down at Jeff until Jeff had to look away.

"I guess I was upset about things," Jeff finally said to the wall.

"Yeah, what things, exactly?"

"President Kennedy."

"You're not the only one."

"Everybody's just laughing and singing and having parties and President Kennedy's moldering in his grave. It makes me sick."

"They have this commission now. The chief justice of the Supreme Court of the United States, Mr. Warren, is in charge. They'll figure it out, I'm sure."

"Yeah, maybe in five years."

"I know. It kind of stinks. This Jack Ruby fellow . . . But we just live here in the USA. We can't control everything that happens in it. Life is tragic."

"What do you mean by that."

"There aren't always happy endings."

Jeff let that sink in.

"What happened with Kathy?"

"You know what happened. She drank too much. She's a kid. Those grown men were getting her sloshed."

"I mean, what happened when you got her home, back to the hotel?"

"Nothing. She went to bed. I waited ten minutes until I was sure she was asleep. Then I left."

"Uncle Artie says that actresses are crazy."

"He oughta know. That Barb's a piece of work."

"He says she's taking him to the cleaners. What's that mean?"

"Taking him for all he's got in the divorce. Cleaning him out. He told you that?"

"Yeah, he mentioned it."

"Kathy's a little fast for you. I advise you to move on. Meet a nice prep school gal. They take you to dances there occasionally, don't they, over at girls' schools? They did for us when I went to Kent."

"Yeah, for the upper forms. Not for us in the lowers."

"Well . . . you'll be far away from Broadway, up at school, anyway. If I were you, I'd concentrate on sports for now. It's a good outlet for all these . . . feelings you get at your age. Now, here's the tough part, kiddo. There's got to be some consequence for you throwing stuff off the roof. You realize, if that thing clobbered a person in the street, it could have broken his neck, killed him."

"It was a tiny pumpkin."

"Please. It put a dent in the steel roof of a car. So I've decided you're grounded here until that train goes back up to New Hampshire Sunday morning. You don't leave the apartment Friday and Saturday. Got it?"

"What am I supposed to do around here?"

"Get some reading done. I recommend *Catch-22* by Heller, or Shirer's *Rise and Fall of the Third Reich*. They're on the shelf out in the living room. That ought to keep you occupied."

"Got any other books by Salinger, by any chance?"

"Your mother might know. Anyway, tomorrow's just another working day for the old man. Nighty-night, son."

Jeff felt lucky that two days of house arrest was his only punishment. He was beginning to understand that throwing large objects out of tall buildings might be a foolish and reckless pastime. But he couldn't stand the idea of not seeing Kathy Kaine one more time before he left town. What would Holden do?

Chapter Ten

Jeff finished *The Catcher in the Rye* for a second time at around one in the morning and fell asleep thinking that J. D. Salinger could write a book about his, Jeff's, life and it wouldn't be that different from Holden Caulfield's. He wished in the worst way that he could talk to Salinger. Holden himself said in the book that he wished he could chat with the authors he admired, become their friend, which meant Salinger must understand that yearning, too, since he actually wrote it. And then Jeff fell into a dream of spinning carousels with horses that looked like the gargoyles on the parapet of Ponsonby Hall.

He woke up late, around ten in the morning, and shuffled out of his room in his pajamas. Evelyn was in the foyer, donning her sealskin coat.

"Good morning, Pussycat."

"Where are you going?"

"I've got a loose crown with Dr. Krajak," she said, the family dentist. "God help me. Then I have lunch with Betty Silver at Bergdorf's."

"Oh? Who's going to guard me here."

"Nobody. You're going to be an exceptionally good boy and stay on the premises like your father told you. Do you read me?"

"Yeah."

"Because if you don't, things could get a little hairy around here."

"What's that supposed to mean?" Jeff asked.

"I don't even want to tell you, Pussycat," Evelyn said, swooping in to kiss him on the cheek on her cloud of perfume and then spinning out the front door. "Toodleloo!"

Jeff took a bowl of Cheerios into the living room and turned on the TV. What came up was a roundtable discussion about the new Warren Commission to investigate the Kennedy assassination featuring Walter Cronkite, Douglas Edwards, and correspondents Roger Mudd and Eric Sevareid. They all agreed that the commission members were a stellar group of first-rate government men who, with the FBI behind them, were sure to unravel the loose ends of the tragic event. There was something about the newsmen's demeanor that seemed off to Jeff, but he couldn't put his finger on it, like they didn't quite mean it. He wondered if Salinger was watching the same program and what he thought.

In the meantime, in a separate compartment of his mind, Jeff ruminated over whether he should call up Kathy Kaine at her hotel, just to let her know he didn't mind that she threw up at the party and was still her friend, and looked forward to meeting up with her again when Christmas vacation started. And he wanted to apologize for not coming over to say goodbye in person, on account of being grounded.

First, though, he had an even more urgent brainstorm. He went into the den and dialed his father's law firm, Slather Bancroft Hooker & Feigenbaum.

"Can I speak to David Hodge, please?" he asked the receptionist.

"Who may I say is calling?"

"This is, uh, Walter Cronkite's secretary," Jeff said.

"Really? Mr. Cronkite wants to speak with Mr. Hodge?"

"Yes."

"In regard to . . ."

"About, uh, President Kennedy."

"Oh, dear. . . . Hold, please."

"This is Hodge. Is that you Mr. Cronkite? I must say, this is a shocker. What can I do for you?"

"This is Bob Greenaway's kid, Jeffrey."

"Whu . . . ?"

"Sorry about that. I had to get through pronto."

"Yeah, well, mission accomplished, kiddo. What's up?"

"Can I talk to you confidentially?"

"Sure. I guess. Is this some family problem or something, is Bob okay? I didn't see him around here to—"

"No, no, no. Nothing like that. But can I trust you?"

"Well, yeah. I guess so. Of course."

"Don't tell my dad we had this conversation."

"What the hell's going on, kiddo? You've really got me going."

"Promise me you won't tell."

"Okay, okay, I promise."

"Okay. I'm trying to contact this author, this J. D. Salinger guy. Dad says you represent the company that put out his book."

"Uh, Little, Brown, yeah."

"Who's the guy there?"

"What guy?"

"The guy you talk to at Little, Brown for lawyer stuff."

"Oh, Mr. Woodburn. Robert Woodburn."

"Can you give me his phone number?"

"Just a minute, kid. What do you want to talk to him for?"

"I told you. I want to get in touch with Salinger."

"Oh, for chrissake. How about I call him and see what I can dredge up?"

"Okay, I guess. Sure. Can you call him soon? Like, after we hang up?"

"Jeez kid. It'll have to wait. I have an appearance in the Appellate Division over on Madison in ten minutes and then I have lunch with a client. Maybe after that."

"It's Friday. You might not get hold of him before the weekend, this Woodson."

"Woodburn, like a fireplace. Yeah, so? What's the hurry?"

"I've got to go back to school on Sunday."

"You go to school out of town now?"

"Yeah, Ponsonby Hall, up in New Hampshire."

"Well, that's a coincidence. Salinger's up there, too, in New Hampshire. I saw in some magazine . . . *Time*, I think it was. They did a cover story on him."

"Yeah, we heard that he lives near our school. Everybody's reading his book."

"Catcher?"

"Yeah."

"Pretty good book. Story of my life. The early years, anyway."

"Do you happen to know what town, exactly?"

"Nope."

"Are you sure you can't give me Woodson's phone number?"

"Woodburn. Sorry, can't do it. I'll call him, tell him you want to drop in on old J.D.—"

"Don't say that! Just say I want to write him a fan letter."

"I can give you his address."

"Salinger's?"

"No, Woodburn's. Care of Little, Brown at Thirty-four Beacon Street, Boston, Mass. You can also try to send J.D. a letter in care of them, Little, Brown. I'm sure they forward his fan mail."

"Great, thanks."

"I've got to go. Can't be late for the judge."

"Hey, remember, don't tell my dad that I called—"

Dave Hodge had already hung up.

Jeff sat on the love seat there in the den, staring at the shelf across the room where his father displayed his collection of miniature liquor bottles. The sight of them prompted him to try to make that call to Kathy Kaine. He dialed the Bomoseen's front desk. They rang Kathy's room.

"It's me," Jeff said, when she picked up.

"Hello, you."

"How are you feeling?"

"Not so great. A little woozy. I just woke up a few minutes before you called."

"At least I didn't wake you up."

"I'm ashamed of myself."

"Don't be. You live and learn, I guess."

"I learned to never drink a goddam grasshopper ever again. Yccchhhh. They ought to call it the green death."

"Yeah, well. . . . Look, I would have come over to say goodbye in person, but I'm not allowed to leave the goddam apartment."

"Oh?"

"My parents grounded me."

"What for. What'd you do?"

Jeff explained about tossing the pumpkin off the terrace.

"You did that?"

"Afraid so."

"Well, maybe somebody ought to ground your dad, he's not such a prince himself."

"Huh? What'd he do?"

"He's a little pervy, turns out, like Viktor in the show. Remember him?"

"Pervy? How's he pervy?"

"Handsy."

"Handsy?"

"With me. Putting me to bed."

"How was he handsy?"

"Well, he made me take my dress off—"

"What!"

"Helped me take it off, anyway. To go to bed."

"Did he see you naked?"

"No, I had a slip on. But after I laid down, I thought I felt him touch me."

"What! Where?"

"You know."

"How would I know?"

"My, uh, little bosoms."

"No!"

"I think so. Things were spinning around pretty bad, but—"

"My dad wouldn't do that."

"Maybe I dreamed it. I dunno."

"My dad is not a perv."

"I thought he was a nice guy. But you can never really tell until—"

"I've got go, Kathy. Maybe I'll call you after the show."

He hung up.

*

Jeff's mind clouded over with a sensation of the greatest urgency, bordering on panic, roiling through an inchoate list of things he had to do seemingly all at once. He found himself rising off the love seat in the den as if on automatic pilot. Then, he was in his own room, stuffing some clean socks and underwear and a sweater in his old canvas rucksack from Camp Timahoe, along with the now dog-eared copy of Catcher in the Rye. He fetched the wad of his remaining money from where he'd hidden it in the closet inside one of his old galoshes, and then donned his now customary uniform of khakis, button-down shirt, green and red rep necktie, and Ponsonby blazer. Finally, he pasted on a new fake mustache from the disguise kit and stuck the rest of it in his rucksack. Then, he was out of the apartment.

He took the service elevator to the basement so as to avoid Anton the doorman in the front lobby. There was egress down there to the alley between his building and the next building west on 79th Street. Once out on the street, he hailed the first taxicab he saw with its roof light on.

"I want to go to Fifth Avenue and Fifty-first Street," Jeff told the driver. There, just up the block a little way, he knew, stood the renowned Donnell branch of the New York Public Library. This was the place that pupils in grade six of P.S. 6 had been encouraged to go to learn how to do research for their various reports on this-and-that. Jeff had been there many times. It was much more congenial than the venerable, but gigantic and overwhelming, Main Branch on 42nd Street, with the great stone lions out front. He knew, for instance, that Donnell had an excellent collection of all the popular magazines—and a great many more that were obscure and recondite. He had to find that issue of *Time* with the story about J. D. Salinger.

The driver turned south on Park Avenue, heading downtown, but after only a few blocks, at 72nd Street, there was a great clot of traffic where literally two minutes earlier a UPS truck had collided with a tiny Volkswagen sedan and sent it flying diagonally across the wide intersection into a fire hydrant, decapitating it so that a geyser of water was spraying a hundred feet in the air. Sirens wailed and police cruisers closed in on the scene with their lights flashing. All four lanes of traffic, both up and downtown, east and west, were closed off.

"Aw, shit," said the cabbie. "We'll never get outa here."

"I've got to get out of here," Jeff said. The meter read eighty cents. Jeff pulled out a dollar and held it out for the driver. "Keep the change."

The driver swiped it out of his hand. "Thanks, Bub," he said facetiously.

Jeff hopped out of the cab. He crossed 72nd and continued south on Park. The stream of traffic going south had stopped completely, of course, so there were no more taxis coming. Within a few more minutes, Jeff realized he was approaching a familiar landmark: the old Percy Rivington Pyne House on 68th Street, that is, the Russian Mission to the United Nations. As usual, two musclebound young security guards stood at either side of the front portico in their ill-tailored brown Soviet overcoats, plus sunglasses and black gloves.

Jeff slowed down, eyeballing them. He moved his rucksack to one shoulder, leaned against the iron pole of the "No Standing" sign at the curb, and fished his cigarette pack out of his blazer pocket. He stuck the brown filter tip in his mouth and attempted to light up. A wintry breeze was blowing down Park Avenue and it took him almost ten tries with his matches to figure out how to cup his hand and shield the flame. With his first drag, he noticed the Russian guards juddering with laughter inside their big coats.

"Either of you want one?" he inquired. "Nice American cigarette!" He wiggled the Marlboro pack at them.

The guard on the left patted his coat pocket, indicating he was all set for smokes.

The one on the right made a pistol of his gloved hand, pointed it at Jeff's head, went "Pew, pew!" as in the sound of gunshots, and then held his index finger to his mouth as if to blow the smoke out of his gun barrel.

"That was real funny, ha-ha-ha," Jeff said.

The guard smiled and shrugged.

"Who's the big cheese in there, anyway? Is Khrushchev around, by any chance?"

The guard on the left shook his head as in, No.

The guard on the right, who was quite an accomplished comic, made like a gunslinger itching to draw, and then mimed pulling the imaginary gun from his holster with more "pew, pew" gunshot noises. "Cowboy!" he barked.

"What? Who, me or you?" Jeff asked.

"Oswald from Texas. Ride 'em, cowboy! I remember you, malchick!" The guard pointed his pinky finger at his left eye. "You. Narushitel' spokoystviya!" (Troublemaker.)

"Mooski Toffski Offski to you, you moron."

The two guards cut a glance at each other.

Just then, the elegant Federal-period door between them swung open, revealing a capacious hallway within, yellow electric light gleaming from polished brass wall sconces and flowery wallpaper in contrast to the gray gloom of Park Avenue. A half dozen men in overcoats milled around in there. Another moment and a massive, black, Soviet-made ZIL-111 limousine pulled up to the curb right behind Jeff with a slight screech, making him jump. One of the men within the embassy came out and confabbed with the guard on the left, who pointed at Jeff, now standing in the middle of the sidewalk. Jeff recognized him. It was the suave attaché from the other day, not so recognizable now in an overcoat and his drumlike lambswool Astrakhan winter hat. He nodded his head and stepped over toward Jeff.

"You again," he said.

"Yeah, it's me again, you moron."

"I assure you I am not moron," the attaché said, regarding Jeff humorously. "I am graduate of Moscow State Institute of International Relations. Why you keep coming back here, bothering my men?"

"Because you bastards killed President Kennedy?"

"Where you are getting this bezumnyy idea?"

"A guy named Einstein."

"Einstein!" the attaché said. Affecting to be impressed, he nodded his head sagely. "You communicate with the dead?"

"It's a different Einstein, not the atom guy, and he's not dead. But he's still a genius."

"Yes, Einsteins are born every day here in Cowboyland. Must be all that milk and your wonderful cornflakes. Maybe you are Einstein, too, eh? Genius wisecracker. I tell you what."

"What?"

"I think you would enjoy to talk to boss here."

"Boss of what?"

"Boss of Soviet Mission to UN."

"Why would you think that? I don't need to talk to some head commie."

The attaché laughed demonstrably.

"You wait here a minute," he said. "He is just inside."

The attaché went back to the foyer within and had words with an older, shorter, white-headed gentleman. The older fellow nodded and then he strode out of the building with the attaché and another burly aide behind, right up to Jeff.

"Mr. Tootski," he said, extending his gloved hand. "I am Ambassador Zorin. It is so nice to meet you, redblooded American boy. We should talk."

Jeff reluctantly shook hands with him. He had a kindly, grandfatherly demeanor and a soothing diplomat's voice.

"Okay," Jeff said. "Go ahead, talk."

"Get in car, please."

"What?"

"We go to park, sit on bench, chitchat about your excellent President Kennedy, rest his soul."

"Are you trying to kidnap me?"

"Nyet, molodoy chelovek!" the ambassador chuckled. "No, young fellow. Do not fear. This is, how you say, on the level. Come. Get in."

Jeff hesitated a moment. The attaché climbed in the car.

"You now," the ambassador said and gestured to the open car door. Jeff took a deep breath and went in, with his rucksack on his lap. The rear compartment was even more spacious than a Checker cab The upholstery was plush like his mother's sealskin coat and the interior had a spicy aroma like exotic wood from a strange land. The ambassador got in next to Jeff, and finally the aide got in the front seat beside the driver. They drove down to 67th Street, then west to Fifth Avenue, and after a few blocks entered the park at 72nd. The flashing lights of the police cars at the scene of the traffic accident could still be seen two blocks east. Not far inside the park, the limousine pulled up to the edge of the curved drive and stopped.

"We are here," the ambassador said. "Hill of pilgrim. Come."

He got out and Jeff followed. Indeed, they were hard upon the statue of the Plymouth Bay pilgrim, by John Quincy Adams Ward, completed in 1885.

The ambassador ushered Jeff to a nearby bench and took a seat there.

"My favorite spot in all of park," the ambassador said. "Favorite bench. Please sit. I am not bear, will not bite you."

Jeff sat beside him. The drained Conservatory Pond could be seen a hundred yards down the hill, the magnificent wall of apartment buildings along Fifth Ave ranged behind it.

"So," the ambassador began, "I hear you have been hanging around embassy."

"I'm keeping my eyes on you."

"You are spy?"

"I'm a watcher."

"Who you are watching for?"

"Just me."

"Private detective?"

"That's right."

"That is excellent disguise you have, Tootski," the ambassador said. Jeff reached up and felt the fake mustache on his upper lip. He'd forgotten he had it on. "I would never know it was you."

Jeff was too busy feeling embarrassed to get the joke.

"This Kennedy busyness," the ambassador continued. "Terrible thing. We had nothing to do with it, I assure you."

"Yeah? I'm sure you tell everybody that."

"We like Kennedy, after unfortunate missile busyness with Cuba. He turn out to be straight shooter. Comrade Khrushchev is very fond of him now."

"Yeah, well, Kennedy's dead now, and I think you Russians bumped him off."

"Okay. But see it from our shoes. Relations between countries improving. Warming up. Now this! I tell you confidentially, young fellow, because you feel so deeply over terrible tragedy. I tell you, American government not always what it seems to be."

"What's that supposed to mean?"

"You think Soviet government is big evil d'yavol, devil, always doing secret dirty work?"

"Of course."

"American government not so, how you say, squeaky clean. You know CIA?"

"Sure. Our spy department. To fight your spies."

"Exactly! Like in *Mad* magazine! Spy versus spy!"

"You read *Mad* magazine?"

"Absolyutno! Yes! Best way to understand American mind. You read it?"

"Sure."

"Brilliant analysis of your crazy country!"

"We're not crazy like you. We have freedom. You can do what you want in America. You Russians push everyone around. Throw people in jail for nothing. You don't even have real stores where you can buy stuff. How crazy is that? You must love living here, in New York, where you just go around corner and buy a goddam sandwich if you feel like it."

"I like New York," the ambassador admitted. "I am lucky ducky. Sovetskiy has room for improvement. We know this. But back to point. CIA. You know the name Mr. Allen Dulles?"

"Dulles. . . . I heard of John Foster Dulles. He was secretary of state when Eisenhower was president."

"You remember this?"

"Sure, we get the *New York Times* at home."

"Ah, good! Your government's favorite news organ. You are well-informed boy!"

"Plus, the news on TV."

"Excellent! Huntley Brinkley. I watch every night! Allen Dulles is brother of this John Foster. Allen Dulles was chief Indian in CIA for many years, 1953 to 1961. But guess what?"

"Chief Indian?"

"Director. Head spy of USA."

"Okay. What about him?"

"I will tell you. President Kennedy was very upset with Mr. Allen Dulles. Bay of Pigs, Cuba. You have heard of that?"

"Yeah. Just after he became president."

"Exactly! Big embarrassment for John Kennedy. Fiasco. International joke. Only a few months after he is in White House, too. Bay of Pigs is CIA's baby, you see. Attempt to throw over Fidel Castro with little tiny army, pipsqueak invasion. Frankly, insane.

Kennedy was poorly informed of Operation Pluto—they call it. Castro saw it coming from thousand kilometers. Loose lips in Miami. We knew about it, too, of course. Anyhow, Cuban militia smashes invaders on the beach. Castro brings in tanks. American air cover, naval support, all is hopeless mess. End of story. When they meet at Vienna summit three months later in June, President Kennedy told Chairman Khrushchev operation was big mistake."

"Okay. So why are you telling me all this?"

"Oh, yes, ancient history. Well, you see, President Kennedy was very unhappy with CIA chief Indian, concocting insane operations behind back of president, lying to him. He kick Allen Dulles out of CIA. No more chief Indian. A lot of, how you say, bad blood between President Kennedy, Allen Dulles, and many friends of Dulles in CIA. President Kennedy told his people in White House he is planning to smash CIA into a million little pieces. Then, in the autumn of this year, Kennedy loses patience with next big CIA brainstorm. Vietnam. You know what is Vietnam?"

"Sure. It's on the news all the time these days. Some little country near China."

"I am telling you, big war is coming in Vietnam. If you are unlucky, maybe you get to fight in it. Die in miserable jungle. Okay now, here is big news for young private detective: CIA killed your President John Kennedy."

"You're a liar."

"I know, truth hurts."

"What about Oswald? He went to Russia for a whole year. You had a whole year to mess around with his brain."

"Oswald is just what he said he is in only public statement before mystery man Jack Ruby liquidate him."

"What did he say?"

"Said he was patsy. You know what patsy is?"

"Yeah, more or less. A guy who's set up to take the blame for something."

"Tochno! Precisely correct."

"What about the rifle and stuff they found up in the schoolbook building?"

"Props, like in movie."

"He didn't shoot Kennedy from up there?"

"Nyet. No."

"Then where did the shots come from?"

"Underpass in front. There is steel utility cabinet in underpass. Man climbs on top of steel cabinet and lies on stomach with rifle. Perfect line of fire to Kennedy in car. All happens in blink of eye. Chaos on street. Nobody sees man in underpass slip away."

"It's freezing out here," Jeff said. He was shivering. "Can we go back to the car? I need a ride across the park."

"Certainly. We can give you ride."

Jeff got up from the bench and so did Ambassador Zorin.

"Why did you tell me all this, anyway?"

"Well, you are very troubled boy. You know what is said, truth will set you free. I want to set you free. You are free now to hang around some other place besides Soviet Mission to UN."

"That's funny, coming from a communist."

"Yes. Relish the irony! You read Dostoevsky in school?"

"No, we're reading *Uncle Tom's Cabin*."

"Achhh. Very tedious book. At least in Russian translation."

"It's goddam tedious in English, too. Have you read *The Catcher in the Rye*, by any chance?"

"I don't know this book. Who catches what in rye?"

"I could never explain it in a million years," Jeff said. "So, what if I go and tell everybody what you told me? The newspapers. The FBI."

The ambassador shook his head and chuckled, then put his gloved hand on Jeff's shoulder.

"Boy, boy," he said. "What you tell everybody? Hmmm? You say Zorin takes you to bench in Central Park and tells you whole truth of Kennedy murder? They will never believe you."

He laughed all the way to the car, where the driver had come around and opened the rear door for them.

Even inside the warm car, Jeff's shivering only got worse.

"Alexi," the ambassador said to the attaché, "give boy your hat."

"No thanks," Jeff said. "I can't go around America in somebody's Russkie hat."

"This is finest hat, I assure you."

"Can you just drop me off at Seventy-first and Amsterdam Avenue over on the West Side?"

"You hear what boy say, Sergey?" the ambassador asked the driver.

"Da."

"Okay, step on it."

154

Chapter Eleven

He felt better immediately upon entering the Bomoseen Hotel's lobby with its now familiar elegant decor. A maintenance man on a ladder was stringing lights on a tall Christmas tree. Jeff did not bother going to the front desk and calling upstairs, but walked straight to the elevator and asked for the seventh floor, then a short journey to the end of the hall where he knocked on Kathy Kaine's door. He had to knock a second time and she eventually opened it, wearing a silk robe embroidered with Chinese dragons.

"Oh!" she said, surprised to find him there. "It's you!"

"Yeah, it's me."

"What's with the mustache?"

Jeff had forgotten about it again. "I'm undercover," he said.

"From what?"

"From the whole goddam world."

"Why didn't you call up from the front desk?"

"Why bother? I know where you live."

They stood there awkwardly in the doorway for a long moment.

"Can I come in for just a minute," Jeff asked. "I won't be long."

"Okay, I guess," Kathy said. "But you can't stick around."

"What'd I just say? I'm not sticking around."

"Okay."

Kathy backed up and went into the suite, and Jeff followed. Room service had delivered a breakfast tray on the coffee table. The scrambled eggs and toast looked barely nibbled at.

"You going to be in the show tonight?" Jeff asked.

"Of course."

"That's nice. I'm taking off."

"Huh? I thought you were grounded."

"Yeah, but I'm taking off anyway."

"Where are you going?"

"That's a state secret."

"What about your parents?"

"My parents? That's a good question. Let's start with my dad, huh?"

"What about him?"

"You still say he acted pervy and all last night?"

"I don't know . . ."

"Now you don't know? Really?"

"Well . . ."

"Then why would you say that?"

"Say what?"

"That he tried to feel you up."

"I dunno. I was awful sloshed. And then I was all hungover this morning."

"So now you're making excuses."

"Look, I was embarrassed," she retorted. She made a pouty face and a choking sound like she might cry. "I don't know why I said

that. I don't really know what happened after we came back here."
Then, the dam broke and her tears began to flow.

"He told me he just put you on your bed and sat out here for ten minutes until he thought you were asleep and left."

"Maybe it happened that way. I dunno."

"Why'd you say it, then?"

"I dunno. Look, I just can't be your girlfriend."

"I know that. You think I'm a moron?"

He let her cry for a minute, suspicious that she was merely acting.

"You're a very nice boy," she eventually said. "But you're a boy. You're not mature enough."

"Yeah, that's really mature of you, throwing up at a big party in front of a million people."

"You know what I mean."

Kathy wrapped her arms around herself and plopped into the wing chair.

"Are you going to eat that toast?" Jeff asked.

"No."

"Mind if I do? I'm starving."

"Go ahead. But I have to ask you to leave."

"I'll leave in a minute."

"I have to get dressed and all."

"Yeah? For what. The show's not until eight o'clock."

"That's not all I do all day. Sit around waiting for the show."

"Okay, I'm going." Jeff grabbed two more pieces of toast and jammed them into his blazer pocket. "Do you know where I just came from?"

"How would I know?"

"I had a meeting with the Russian ambassador to the UN."

"Really? Where?"

"In Central Park."

"You're taking this secret agent idea way too seriously, Jeff."

"You know what he told me?"

"I have no idea."

"He told me that the CIA killed President Kennedy."

"Why would they do that?"

"Because . . . well, it's goddam complicated. Bad blood."

"Bad blood?"

"Between Kennedy and the guy who ran the CIA."

"I don't believe that. Our own government?"

"He said no one would believe me."

"That's true. No one will believe you. That is, if it even really happened."

"Oh, it really happened. I'm not making it up, like you did about my dad."

"I'm sorry, Jeff. I really am. I was so ashamed of myself."

"Maybe you should stop hitting the booze."

"I know. I will, I promise. But I have to get dressed now, Jeff. Can we just say goodbye like friends? It's been really fun getting to know you."

"Sure, like friends. You know you really killed me when I first saw you onstage," he said, reaching for the door. "I couldn't believe I was able to meet you."

"I'll never forget you, either," Kathy said. "Maybe a few years from now when we're both more grown up, and I'm in another show, you can visit me backstage again and we can start over. But, please, go now. I have to change."

"I'm going. I'm going," he said, heading out the door. "Look, I'm gone!"

He waited for the elevator for barely ten seconds before the door opened and out strode the second baseman (and sometime left fielder) of the New York Mets baseball club, Todd Merritt.

"You!" Jeff said.

"You!" Todd Merritt said, pointing. "What are you doin' here?"

"None of your goddam business. I think I know what you're doing here."

"What's with the mustache?"

"I grew it last night."

"Ha ha. That's rich."

"You going to see Kathy?"

"Maybe I am. What of it?"

"You know, she's only thirteen goddam years old, don't you?"

"Naw, she told me she was seventeen."

"Well, she's not. She's a kid. If I was you, I'd lay off her."

"I'm just takin' her out for some lunch."

"Yeah, and then come back here and give her the time, right?"

"The time?"

"You know what I mean."

"I'm not giving her any time."

"Uh, going down, young man?" the elevator operator intervened.

"Yeah. Hold your horses," Jeff said and leaned in close to Merritt. "You better not knock her up. If I find out, I'll call the goddam Mets and tell them you gave the time to a thirteen-year-old girl, and you'll be selling cars instead of playing second base next year while the Mets lose a hundred games."

"Hey, watch what you say about the Mets," Merritt said.

"Uh, gentlemen . . . ," the elevator man said.

Jeff walked around Merritt and into the elevator.

Merritt started to take a step down the hall, but then he swiveled around with the catlike grace of an infielder and stepped back into the elevator instead.

"You goin' back down now, too, young man?" the elevator man asked the ballplayer.

"Just do your job and shut up, pal," Merritt said. As the car dropped, he mumbled, "I swear she told me she was seventeen. And, you know, she's gonna tell that to the next guy, too."

Jeff suspected that was true.

"Just don't be a moron," Jeff said when they arrived on the ground floor and debarked into the lobby.

"If you weren't a midget, I'd rearrange your face," Merritt said as they both made for the revolving door at the hotel's entrance. "Have a nice life, kid."

*

Jeff walked over to Broadway and caught a cab going downtown. He was in front of the New York Public Library's Donnell branch on 53rd Street in five minutes, and headed directly to the third floor where he knew all the magazines were kept. There, a stylish brunette around thirty, disturbingly wearing the same perfume as his mother's, reminded him where the *Reader's Guide to Periodical Literature* resided. He had used the reference once before when he was in Mrs. Snipes's sixth grade class at P.S. 6 to research his "report" on the Cuban Missile Crisis of 1962. He didn't know in which year to begin to look for the issue of *Time* with the story about Salinger. *The Reader's Guide* was a massive volume.

"I believe it might have coincided with the publication of *Franny and Zooey*," the stylish librarian said when he asked her. "Come over here a sec."

They went to her desk in the center of the big room, where she picked up her phone and dialed three numbers. The nameplate on her desk said "Miss Canavan."

"Say, Dinah, can you get me the pub date on *Franny and Zooey*? Yes, I'll hang on a sec." Then to Jeff: "My colleague down in the contemporary literature stacks. She knows everything. Have you read *Franny and Zooey*?"

"No," Jeff said. "I've been reading Catcher."

"In the Rye?" she added.

"Yeah, of course. I don't think there's any other Catcher by Salinger, is there—?"

"Excuse me . . . What's that, Dinah? September 1961? Thanks a bunch." She hung up. "I loved it," she said.

"What? Catcher?"

"No, *Franny and Zooey*."

"Maybe I'll pick it up. What's it about?"

"A family. The Glass family. Their various kids who are all brilliant and a little crazy."

"A family made of glass? Like, a fairy tale?"

"No, no, that's their name, Glass. Franny, Zooey, Seymour, Boo Boo, and Buddy Glass. And one more. Walker or Wakefield or something. I forget. He's hardly in it."

"Sounds complicated."

"It's deep. They've all been on a quiz show on the radio called *It's a Wise Child*. That must have been the thirties when Mr. Salinger happened to be a child himself. Only in the book it's years later. They're all adults now and Franny's having a nervous breakdown."

"Jeez. What from?"

"Some religious thing she's obsessed with. The 'fat lady.' It's sort of a crazy god figure the family has conjured up based on all the people out there who listen to the radio. It's a very eccentric family."

"He wrote that? Salinger?"

"Yes. It's brilliant. But nothing like *Catcher*, of course. Let's look it up," she said. "I'll come with you. Say, that's not a real mustache, is it."

"No," Jeff said, matter of factly.

"Just wondering," Miss Canavan said.

Jeff let the matter drop.

They found the *Time* article listed in the 1961 edition of the *Reader's Guide:* September 15. Miss Canavan told Jeff she'd be back in a jiff, and not two minutes later she stepped up to Jeff proudly holding the magazine, with an artist's rendering on the cover of Salinger from the shoulders up wearing a dress shirt and a necktie, like a businessman. Behind him is a field of grain, ostensibly rye, and in the far distance behind Salinger's left ear a cliff is depicted with the tiny figure of a boy standing at the edge of it. Salinger has a full head of dark hair, a touch of gray at the temples, and a curious demi-smile, as if he is withholding secrets. He's almost movie-star handsome, like Gregory Peck or Gary Cooper, though his nose is prominent. Jeff was surprised that Salinger looked so gravely serious and so grown up. He'd pictured him all week as impish, a man-child, not unlike his creation Holden Caulfield.

"Can I look at it?" Jeff said.

"Oh, certainly." Miss Canavan gave it to him. The magazine was well worn, as if many hands had leafed through it since 1961. "Just bring it back to my desk when you're done."

"Thanks a million," Jeff mumbled and started flipping through the pages. The article began with an epigraph taken from *The Catcher in the Rye*, Holden speaking:

I thought what I'd do was, I'd pretend I was one of those deaf-mutes. That way I wouldn't have to have any goddam stupid useless conversations with anybody. If anybody wanted to tell me something, they'd have to write it on a piece of paper and shove it over to me. I'd build me a little cabin somewhere with the dough I made. I'd build it right near the woods, but not right in them, because I'd want it to be sunny as hell all the time.

Then, exactly what he was looking for was right there in the first sentence of the article:

"It is sunny at the edge of the woods, but the tall man's face is drawn, and white. When he came to Cornish, N.H., nine years ago, he was friendly and talkative; now when he jeeps to town, he speaks only the few words necessary to buy food or newspapers. Outsiders trying to reach him are, in fact, reduced to passing notes or letters, to which there is usually no reply. Only a small group of friends has ever been inside his hilltop house . . ."

Cornish, New Hampshire. The name was vaguely familiar to Jeff after three months at Ponsonby Hall. Someone there had mentioned it in connection with something, he was sure. Perhaps Mrs. Dinsmoor, the school cook, or one of the masters. It was at least in the vicinity of Ponsonby and the town of Orcus. He went back to Miss Canavan's desk and asked for a pen and a sheet of paper, then retreated to a vacant table and jotted down pertinent nuggets from the lengthy *Time* article. Salinger's house, it said, was near the edge of the woods—so it wasn't right in the town proper, probably out in the country somewhere. It was painted barn red and it had a six-and-a-half-foot-high fence in front of it. That would help him find it.

The author was forty-two then, in 1961, so now he must be forty-four. Once, back in 1953, a sixteen-year-old high school girl in the town of Windsor, Vermont, across the Connecticut River from Cornish, wrote a story about Salinger for the school paper. But otherwise, he had avoided all attempts by reporters to be interviewed since. He refused to sell *The Catcher in the Rye* to Hollywood. Salinger grew up in Manhattan, like Jeff, only back in the 1920s and '30s. Salinger's father had a company that imported cheeses and hams from Europe. They were well-off and lived on Park Avenue. The author was called "Sonny" as a little boy and later on, when sent to a military school, preferred to be called "Jerry"—his actual given name being Jerome. Jerry was a lousy student. Before that, he flunked out of the McBurney School in New York (one of the schools Jeff's father had suggested sending him to, before the Thanksgiving debacle). After military school, sometime maybe in 1937 or '38, Jerry washed out at New York University after a few weeks of college. His father, Sol, made Jerry go on a business trip to Europe to purchase hams in Poland. But Jerry had no interest in the ham and cheese import business. He wanted to be a writer.

Salinger got drafted in 1942 and was sent off to the war in Europe. The article said little else about what happened to him there. After the war was over, he got married for a few months to a German girl who was a doctor, but they split up. He came back to the States in 1946 and stayed at his parents' house on Park Avenue, trying to write short stories for the popular magazines and working on his novel about a teenage boy—that is, Holden Caulfield—which would get published, finally, in 1951. Salinger left New York for good in 1953 and bought the country house in Cornish. Around the same time, he met a woman named Claire and got married. In his early years at Cornish, Salinger would go across the river to Windsor and hang around with teenagers for hours in a soda fountain called Nap's Lunch. By 1961, when the article was written, he'd quit doing that. Now he just worked on his writing from morning till night in a little concrete study building behind the house. He was working on several books about that Glass family, of which *Franny and Zooey* was the opener. With his wife Claire, he had produced two children, a boy named Matthew who would now be around three-years-old and a girl named Peggy, now seven.

That was an awful lot to know about J. D. Salinger, Jeff thought. It sounded like the fairly normal life of a family man who had just quit the rat race of New York to get some peace and quiet and raise his kids, Jeff concluded. After all, Holden himself mentioned more than once his desire to live off in the woods, and surely Holden was speaking from some part of Salinger's brain. Jeff was aware that he, himself, had developed a preference for rural life at Ponsonby Hall over the hubbub of Manhattan. He returned the magazine to Miss Canavan and asked her where he might find an atlas with maps of the U.S. states. She directed him to the second floor, where the encyclopedias and other reference books lived.

He found a 1962 edition of the Rand McNally road atlas and went directly to the page for New Hampshire, which included Vermont on the opposite page. The two states looked like twins lying down on the page like two mummies, foot to head. He found Windsor easily enough—the train home less than a week ago had passed through it south of White River Junction. On the page, Windsor appeared to be an actual town with a network of streets to it. Cornish, across the river, not so much. Rather, it was just a rural township with a few meandering roads and houses scattered around on them. For Jeff, that explained why Salinger was said to hang out with teenagers in Windsor. There were no places to hang out in Cornish. All this was good to know because Windsor, he realized, would be his destination.

Chapter Twelve

By now it was midafternoon. Jeff thought to catch a cab at 53rd Street and Fifth, but it being the first big shopping day after Thanksgiving the avenue with its many exclusive stores was clogged with people and there was not a cab with a lighted sign on its roof anywhere to be seen. The motor traffic in the roadway was hardly moving. So Jeff decided to walk the twelve blocks to Grand Central Station, first escaping to less-crowded Madison Avenue. Many of the shops on Madison had put up Christmas displays and the scene was palpable with festivity. The Salvation Army bell ringers manned their donation pots every few blocks. Manhattan's whole striving, struggling population labored under their burden of requisite holiday merriment—ignorant that their own CIA had bumped off President Kennedy, Jeff brooded. He couldn't wait to tell Salinger what he knew. The whole country had become more phony than Holden could ever comprehend.

At 45th Street Jeff found himself at the entrance of Abercrombie & Fitch, the renowned sporting outfitters. He had visited the emporium many times over the years with his school friends. The ground floor was a giant game room with elegant toys imported from England—skittles, tops, the Labyrinth Maze puzzle—and you could play with the display items as long as you liked. Having explored the entire store before, Jeff knew that the guns were upstairs on the fourth floor along with the hunting and expeditionary outfits. He went up there directly.

A well-mannered floor clerk not unlike the suave attaché at the Soviet Mission soon attached himself to Jeff.

"Can I help you, sir?" he asked, visibly nonplussed by Jeff's fake mustache.

"Have you got hunting hats here?"

"Certainly. Follow me." The floorman took Jeff to a cabinet with built-in drawers at the side of the large room and extracted a rabbit-skin hat with three flaps, two for the ears and a mystifying one in the front above the eyes, a fancier version of what the poor old chestnut vendor on 59th Street wore in cold weather.

"No, not that," Jeff said. "But, wait! I have to know. What's the front flap for? Why would you want to pull it down over your eyes?"

The floorman looked suddenly chagrined, as if he had never considered the question and examined the hat closely.

"Ah! See?" he said, showing Jeff up close. "That flap is sewn to the crown. You're not supposed to pull it down."

"Then why would they even sew it on?"

"Why . . . uh . . . for balance, I suppose."

"Do you have something more like a cap with a peak and ear flaps?"

The floorman opened another drawer in the wall unit and took out a red and black checkered cap with a bill and quilted black satin lining. He demonstrated how the flannel ear flaps were tucked inside the crown. The sight of it electrified Jeff.

"That's perfect!" he said.

"Try it on."

Jeff took the hat and put it on. There was a mirror nearby on a wooden pillar. He turned the hat around with the bill facing backward.

"Do you intend to wear it that way?" the floorman inquired.

"Maybe," Jeff said.

"It's meant to be worn with the bill forward."

"I know."

"Very well, young sir. The price is seventeen ninety-five."

"I'll take it."

"Is it a gift?"

"No. I'll just wear it out of here."

"Like that? Backward?"

"Yes, I think so."

"If you insist."

"If I pay for it, I can wear it any way I want, right?"

"That is correct. You will be the owner of it. Come this way then."

They completed the transaction at a register near the elevator. The floorman looked surprised by Jeff's wad of dollars, probably a bit more than his weekly salary.

"Enjoy your hat, sir," he said as Jeff stepped into the elevator.

Wearing the hat out on Madison had an immediate impact on Jeff's emotions, transporting him into the raucous melancholy that saturated Holden Caulfield's vantage of things, as if he could now fully comprehend the phoniness and pointlessness of everything around him. It thrilled him to feel he was entering Holden's actual world, becoming Holden, to some degree. Continuing his journey to

Grand Central, he forced himself to feel sorry for everyone he passed on the sidewalk along the way, making up one-sentence vignettes to explain why they were so pathetic—*just got fired from his job . . . was told he had a tumor . . . lives in a crummy apartment over a pet shop . . . got robbed down in the subway . . . boyfriend beats her up . . .* The last one got him thinking about Yvonne, the girl at the Dreamboat Landing dance hall who got beat up by her boyfriend and was taken to Bellevue Hospital two days ago. Old Yvonne, he thought . . . as Holden would surely refer to her. *I wonder how she's doing?*

By then, though, he had made it to the Vanderbilt Avenue entrance of Grand Central Station and he ventured within. The place was jammed with travelers and commuters at this hour on a Friday at holiday time. A Salvation Army band played carols slightly off key from a balcony over the Oyster Bar at the far end of the main hall. Jeff had considerable experience with trains. He went directly to the ornate information kiosk at the center of the enormous room where he had to wait behind five other people before his turn came.

"Do you have a train to Windsor, Vermont, from here?"

The wizard of timetables behind the brass grill said, "New Haven Line. You just missed the three-seventeen."

"What!"

"Sorry, bud."

"When's the next one?"

"Next one is seven-ten tomorrow morning. The Montrealer."

"Aw, for chrissakes!"

"Next! Move along, bud."

Jeff peeled away and trudged across the terminal's Great Hall to a concourse where he found the Chock full o'Nuts café. His rucksack weighed him down and he was hungry. He took a stool at the counter and ordered a hot cocoa and a cream cheese on date and nut bread sandwich, the establishment's specialty, with which he was well acquainted. As his spirits revived, a plan formulated in the jumbled forefront of his mind. He would go down to Bellevue and visit old Yvonne, see how she was doing . . . then go out for a nice dinner . . . then maybe take in a movie . . . then come back to Grand Central late and catch a few winks in the waiting room until the train to Windsor departed in the early morning.

He was aware that his father and mother would probably be worried about him in a few hours. He decided to call them later, around suppertime, and tell them he had returned to Ponsonby Hall a day early on his own, out of shame for what had happened at Uncle Ira's, and not to worry, he was fine. That would be sufficient, he told himself, not quite believing it, but he didn't want to think about it anymore. Having provisionally settled that sticky business in his mind, he joined the line at the New Haven Railroad ticket window and waited to buy a ticket for the morning train to Windsor. The ticket cost fifteen twenty-five, one way.

"Boarding is ten minutes before departure," the ticket agent reminded him upon payment.

He'd barely walked five steps when he serendipitously encountered a police foot patrolman on duty in the station.

"Say, officer, can you remind me where Bellevue Hospital is located?"

"Twenty-sixth and Foist Ave," the cop said. "Planning to check in?"

"No sir."

"Why don't you toin your hat around, then?"

"I'm the owner of this hat. I can wear it however I like."

"Yeah? Well, you look like cuckoo bird that way. I can call the boys down at the precinct and they'll escort you over there."

"No thanks. I'll get a cab."

The policeman seized the bill of Jeff's hat and turned it frontward. "There," he said. "Now you look like a model citizen. Except, what's with the fake mustache, kid?"

"I'm practicing at being a grown-up."

"Is that how it's done?"

"That's how I'm doing it."

"Yeah? Well, good luck."

Jeff put as much distance between himself and the cop as quickly as possible, navigating over to the station's Lexington Avenue exit, and caught a taxi there. It was a short ride, a dollar and a quarter with tip, to Bellevue.

In the late afternoon gloom, the grand and forbidding front entrance of the ancient hospital hinted at the institution's dark history of disease and madness. Inside the main lobby, a maintenance man on a ladder hung red and gold glass balls off a seventeen-foot-tall balsam pine. A matron of a certain age with a startlingly blue-colored bouffant hairdo and a kindly face sat behind an ornate semicircular art deco visitor check-in desk at the center of the room. Around and behind her, doctors, nurses, visitors, and patients on gurneys came and went, scurrying out of various portals and disappearing into others. There was no waiting line at this hour, so Jeff stepped up to the desk.

"I'm trying to visit somebody who I think is here," he began warily.

"You're not sure they're here?" the lady asked pleasantly.

"I was told. By a friend of hers."

"I see. And what would this person's name be?"

"She's known as Yvonne, but that's not her actual name, not the name she might be here under."

"That's unusual. Is she in show business?"

"Yes! Yes!," Jeff said, thrilled to be so easily understood. "Yvonne is her stage name."

"Hmmmm . . . Are you a relative?"

"Sort of. If I tell you what she looks like, do you think you might figure out if she's here?"

"I don't know what any of our patients look like. They're just names on a list. What sort of relative are you then?"

"I'm . . . uh . . . a long-lost nephew."

"Really? Does she know you?"

"She knows about me, I think. We met once."

The matron was not so much losing her patience as becoming bemusedly perplexed.

"This is most unusual, I must say."

"I know. It's odd. But it's really important for me to see her."

"Okay. I don't know how to even look her up without a name."

"Maybe if I told you why she's here."

"Yes, that might help narrow it down. Is she having a baby, by any chance? A surgery?"

"Her boyfriend threw her down a flight of stairs."

"No!"

"Yeah."

"That's atrocious!"

"I'll say. The guy's name is Angelo."

The blue-haired lady made a face. Her bemused perplexity was turning into consternation.

"You don't know your aunt's real name, but you know her rotten boyfriend is named Angelo?"

"I was told. I don't know this Angelo personally."

"Did she prefer charges against him with the police?"

"I don't know."

The matron glanced down at the visitors log in front of her.

"Well, what do you know! Would his full name be Angelo Muh . . . Muh . . . Mastronzo?"

"Yeah, it could be that. I think it is."

"But you don't know for sure?"

"Why? Has he been here?"

"Someone named Angelo Mastronzo was here."

"Well, how many Angelos come in here on the average day?" Jeff said.

The matron couldn't say. She looked back down at the visitors log.

"Apparently he's the only one, this Mastronzo," she reported. "It says he checked in at 2:17 this afternoon, and back out at 2:41,

visiting a patient in Pavilion B. My shift started at three o'clock, so
. . ."

"It's probably who I'm looking for?"

"How can we possibly know?"

"Because Angelo came to visit her."

"Why would she want to see him if he threw her down a flight of
stairs? I'da had the bum arrested."

"Maybe they made up."

"Hmmmph!"

"Her name must be down there in that book, too. What's it say?"

"The patient's name is Peggy Kangle."

"That's her, all right. Aunt Peggy!"

"Is that your mama's maiden name, Kangle?"

"Yes. Of course."

"How did you happen to become so long-lost?"

"She went into showbiz and the family disowned her."

"Are you in show business, too, young man?"

"No, I go to school."

The matron gave Jeff a long hard look, then hooked her index
finger to make him come closer as she leaned in on her side of the
desk.

"Why are you wearing a fake mustache?" she whispered.

"I like people to think I'm older than I am," Jeff whispered back.

"Really?"

"Yes."

"May I ask why?"

"It makes life much easier."

"I've never heard that before."

"Life is hard when you're a kid."

"It doesn't get a whole lot easier," she said, expelling a sigh.

"So, can you tell me how to get up to see Aunt Peggy?"

The matron eyeballed Jeff again, as if trying to decide.

"What is your name, child?"

"Uh, Holden Caulfield."

"Is that C-a-w or C-a-u?"

"C-a-u-l field."

Finally, she scribbled something on a notepad and handed the leaf to Jeff. It said: Pavilion B, third floor, 27-A.

"Go down that hall and take the elevator to the third floor. Visiting hours are over at five. I hope you have a nice visit."

*

He inquired at the nursing station, and was directed to room 27-A on the left side of the corridor. The door was just ajar. He knocked, but the reply within was muffled. He entered warily. He could tell at once by the color of her hair that it was Yvonne. But otherwise, her identity was well disguised by her injuries and their various dressings. A substantial bandage covered her nose. Her right ear was bandaged, too. Both of her eye sockets were purple. Her lips were bruised and enlarged. Her right leg was in a cast and suspended in traction from a ceiling-mounted pulley. To her left, on the window side, a curtain divided the room. Behind it, another patient groaned at regular five-second intervals.

"Yvonne?"

She turned her head slowly until a yelp of joy came out of her.

"You!" she said.

"Yeah, it's me," Jeff said.

"You've got a different mustache."

"Yeah, I've got a bunch of 'em."

"The other one was real bushy."

"Yeah, this one's more modest."

"You look like Ronald Colman in *Lost Horizon*."

"I don't think I ever saw that one."

"Except he wasn't a midget. Ow . . . it hurts to laugh. What are you doin' here, kid?"

"I was worried about you," Jeff said.

"How'd you know?"

"I stopped in to see you at the dance place. One of the other girls said you were here."

"Musta been Pearl."

"She had painted-on eyebrows. Kind of chubby."

"Yeah, that's Pearl awright. She's got snitchitis. Well, hey, it's great to see ya. Have a seat. There's a chair there."

Jeff fetched the chair and sat.

"I heard about what Angie did to you."

"It was my fault. Shouldn'ta opened my big yap."

"Nobody deserves this for just saying stuff."

"I called him a faggot. I guess it was a bridge too far."

"He is a faggot if he roughs up girls this bad. You should have called the police on him."

"Naw, he apologized and all. We're good now."

"Look what he did to you! How do you know he won't do it again?"

"I won't mouth off like that again. I learned my lesson. Hey, look what he gave me!"

Yvonne held out her left hand. There was a diamond the size of jelly bean on her ring finger.

"We're engaged! Ow . . . it hurts to smile."

"You should get a better boyfriend when you're out of this place and the bruises go away. You could. You're real pretty and a good dancer. You should dump that bum."

"Naw, he's not all bad, Angie. It comes with the territory. Speaking of which, here's the good news. We're moving to the country, over in Jersey. Angie got a big promotion. We're getting a real house with a picket fence and a yard and everything. I'm done with Dreamboat Landing. I'm gonna have a baby, maybe two or three babies. Be a homemaker."

"That's nice. But I'm worried about you."

"Aw, I'll be fine. Tell me what you been up to."

"I got mixed up with an actress," Jeff said. "They're nothing but trouble." He recounted the sad story of his brief romance with Kathy Kaine of Glen Oaks, Wisconsin, a star in the big musical hit *The Wayward Family Singers*, playing across 47th Street from Dreamboat Landing.

"Funny," Yvonne said. "It never occurred to me to see that show."

Jeff related further the multiple humiliations at Uncle Ira's Thanksgiving party.

"That's a tough break, kid," Yvonne said. "Forget about actresses. They're all nutso. When you're ready, you should find a nice homemaker."

"Also," Jeff said, "I had meeting with the Russian ambassador to the UN."

"Really? How'd you arrange that?"

"I staked out the joint at Sixty-eighth and Park until they couldn't stand it anymore. You wouldn't believe what the guy said."

"What?"

"He told me the CIA killed President Kennedy."

"No!"

"For real."

The patient on the other side of the curtain gave out an unearthly wail. Then, she returned to her regular interval of groans.

"The CIA," Yvonne said. "I mean, I heard of it. But what's it do, actually?"

"It's the government's spy service. The guy who ran it had it in for JFK."

"How come?"

"It's complicated. The Bay of Pigs and all."

"Well, that's not right. It's awful! What are you gonna do with this scuttlebutt?"

"I'm going to drop in on J. D. Salinger, who wrote that book you gave me. I'm going to ask him what to do. He'll know, I'm sure."

"You read it, that book?"

"You bet I read it. I read it twice so far. It's the best book ever written. And guess what. Old J.D. lives right up where my goddam school is in New Hampshire. Can you believe it?"

"What's he doing up there?"

"Just living. Writing more books. He's married to some homemaker having kids, like you want to do."

"I didn't know what to make of that book, frankly. I didn't understand the kid in it. He was a pill, always complaining about something or other. And I never got what the title was supposed to mean. Catcher of what?"

"*Catcher in the Rye*. He explains it, the kid, Holden Caulfield, later on in the book. You probably didn't get to that part. He dreams that he's standing under a cliff in a field of rye, catching all these young kids who stray over the cliff. Holden's *The Catcher in the Rye*. He saves kids like me."

"So, you think this J. D. Whatsisname is gonna save you?"

"Maybe."

"What from."

"From all the goddam phonies out there."

Yvonne laughed again. "Ow . . . Lookit, there will always be phonies, as long as there's a human race. That's a losing battle, kid. There's only one person out there who knows the score, if you can even call him a person, God. Maybe J.D. can write a book about him, The Watcher in the Sky."

"Yeah, maybe . . . Anyway, I'm going back up to the North Woods tomorrow. I already got my ticket for the morning train. Hey, you want to come out with me for a swell dinner before I go?"

"I can't leave here, kid. I'm a patient."

"I wish you could."

"Anyways, Angie's coming back any time now with some veal parm for me. Do you like veal parm? I could split it with you."

"I don't want to be anywhere near that bum."

"Don't say that. He's my fiancé."

Jeff rose out of the chair and hoisted up his rucksack.

"Well, congratulations on getting hitched, Yvonne," he said. "I hope you have a nice time over in New Jersey."

"Thanks for coming to see me. It means a lot."

"I won't forget you. I'm glad you didn't die. Oh, by the way. Do you know of any restaurants around here that I might go to for dinner. I'm loaded. Don't worry about that."

"Well, there's my all-time favorite joint, Lüchow's, on Fourteenth Street. It's grand."

"Lüchow's? Is it Chinese?"

Yvonne laughed again. "Ow . . . It's anything but. Go there. You'll never forget it."

"What avenue?"

"Off Lex."

"Okay, I'll try it, I swear. Rest up, Yvonne, and get well soon. See you around, maybe."

The elevator way down the hall opened just as Jeff stepped out of room 27-A. A man wearing a Chesterfield topcoat came out and strode down in Jeff's direction. His shoes made a bright tapping sound on the granite floor. As he came closer, Jeff could see he was strikingly handsome, with wavy black hair and a roman nose. His coat was impeccably cut. He had a brown paper bag in one hand and a big paper cone of flowers in the other. As they passed in the hallway Jeff croaked just barely under his breath: "Angie, you faggot . . ." He detected that Angie had stopped in his tracks. The aroma of marinara sauce hung in the air.

"Hey," Angie said. "You."

Jeff stopped and turned around. Angie was facing him.

"Who the hell are you?"

"Nobody," Jeff said.

"Maybe you should keep your big yap shut, Nobody."

"Maybe I will," Jeff said. "I'll think about it."

"Hey, stugots, you little prick. Get lost before I lose it on ya."

Angie swiveled around, muttering to himself as he continued down the hall. Jeff stepped into the elevator and banged the door close button.

*

Darkness had fallen. There was a cab line outside Bellevue's main entrance and Jeff got into the first one.

"Do you know where Lüchow's is on Fourteenth Street?" Jeff said.

"Yeah, Mac. It's on Fourteenth Street. That where you want to go?"

"What are you, a moron? Why do you think I asked?"

"Get outa my cab, ya jerk."

Jeff didn't have to be told twice. He realized that meeting up with Angie had put him in a very bad mood. He decided not to take a cab after all, but to walk instead, hoping the fresh air would calm him down. He went west on 26th Street and then downtown on Lexington. It was a quiet part of Manhattan, no Salvation Army bell ringers or sidewalk Santas to be seen. Lexington soon terminated at Gramercy Park. The park gate was locked, since it was privately owned and only the residents of the neighborhood had keys. Jeff walked all around it. On the downtown side, Lexington turned into Irving Place. It was as posh a street as Jeff's home territory on the Upper East Side.

At this hour, it occurred to him that his parents were probably on the verge of worrying about him. He resisted the temptation to catch a cab and go back uptown, reminding himself that he was supposed to be grounded and would surely be in for severe punishment if he walked in the apartment now. God knows what they'd do—tie him up and chain him to his bed perhaps.

Irving Place came to an end at 14th Street and there, on the far side, very prominently, stood Lüchow's restaurant, an ornate, eccentric, three-story building painted red with swags along the cornices, and yellow-gold Greco-Roman columns and balusters on an upper balcony, and a ground floor base of dark wood, and the red awning bearing its name proudly jutting up from the sidewalk at the entrance. The place looked both grand and enticingly homey. Jeff realized that he was ravenously hungry and jaywalked across the center of the block straight to Lüchow's door.

The interior was a vast wilderness of tables covered with white linen. Few of them were occupied at this early hour, which was just a few minutes after five o'clock. Waiters were still filling saltshakers and stacking breadbaskets. The Weber waltz *Aufforderung zum Tanz* (Op.

65) played lightly over the PA system. An enormous Christmas tree blazed with colored lights at the far end of the big room. Mounted heads of slain deer, elk, moose, and bighorn sheep ringed the room along the fascia overhead, beneath the high coffered ceiling and its great skylight at center.

A rotund, cheerful captain suddenly appeared before Jeff out of nowhere.

"Good evening, sir. Just yourself?" He was entirely professional but visibly suspicious.

"Yes, just me," Jeff said. "Don't worry, I'm loaded."

"We never ask," the captain said, placing a large menu under his arm. "This way, sir."

Jeff was given a small table against a wall between a wooden pillar and the Christmas tree.

"Your hat, sir," the captain said as Jeff settled into his chair.

"What about it?"

The captain leaned in and whispered, "You must take it off in here. This is a genteel establishment."

Jeff obeyed and put it on his lap.

"Sorry about that."

The menu was laid ceremoniously before him, its offerings a dazzling, incomprehensible universe of dishes, many with German-inflected overtones—"Bismarck herring," "Wurstplatte mit Kartoffelsalat," "Hausmacher Blut Schwarten Magen"—and some items downright disgusting—"eels in jelly," "pickled lamb's tongue," "calf's head en tortue." Soon, a waiter materialized, wearing a floor-length crisp white apron below his short black service jacket.

184

"Something to start with, sir?"

"Can I have a scotch and soda?"

"Absolutely not."

"Why not?"

"We do not serve alcohol to children."

"I have a mustache?"

"I can see that it is fake, sir. How about a nice Coca-Cola?"

"Make that a ginger ale."

"Ginger ale, then," he scribbled on his order pad. "We have some very nice appetizers."

"I won't be getting those eels in jelly, that's for sure."

"I understand. That is not a dish for the young."

"Who would even order such a thing?"

"You'd be surprised. There are people who like it. May I suggest the shrimp cocktail?"

"Sure. I'll have that."

"And for your entrée?"

"This menu is so huge. I don't understand what half these things are."

"All young people like the Wiener Schnitzel. That's a breaded veal cutlet. It comes with the lovely Kartoffelknödel, which are dumpling noodles."

"That sure sounds better than corned pig's knuckles. Must be all gristle and bones."

"It's an old-world favorite."

"No wonder the Nazis lost."

"The schnitzel then?"

"Sure. Yeah, I'll have that."

"Red cabbage or creamed spinach?"

"Red cabbage."

"I'll put your order right in, sir."

Couples and quartettes streamed into the big room now, taking their seats as a comforting murmur of conversation filled what had been a void garnished lightly with music. A busboy swooped in and deposited a large basket of bread and rolls before Jeff, along with a ramekin of butter. Jeff attacked them without hesitation. There were soft Butterbrezeln, crusty Brötchen, dark, dense slices of Pumpernickel, and flaky Hörnchen. The shrimp cocktail arrived along with a tall ginger ale. Four colossal shrimp were hooked around a tulip glass filled with the customary red cocktail sauce liberally seasoned with horseradish. The shrimp had the bold snap of freshness from the sea and the sauce just the right tang. By the time he finished his appetizer, the restaurant was filling up. Waiters and busboys whizzed around in a ballet of diligent service. The empty shrimp vessel was no sooner swept away than his Wiener Schnitzel landed. It was enormous, overhanging each side of the plate, decorated with lemon wedges and sprigs of dill. The side dishes were set down in separate bowls. He could eat only half the schnitzel.

Jeff watched the legion of black-and-white waiters tote giant trays around the big room as though they were weightless. Champagne corks popped. Well-dressed customers Jeff's parents' age laughed and toasted each other. A Strauss waltz played gaily in the background. But Jeff only grew restless taking it all in from his table in the corner.

And he fell so deep in thought that the waiter spooked him again, materializing out of nowhere.

"Some dessert, sir?"

"Huh . . . ?"

"I recommend the Pfannkuchen mit Preiselbeeren."

"What on earth is that?"

"Ah, I thought you might ask. It is a big, lovely pancake with lingonberry sauce."

"I couldn't possibly eat another thing. Say, could you put the rest of that schnitzel in some tinfoil. I've got to take a train tomorrow."

"Certainly. Where to?"

"The goddam North Woods."

"Oh, dear. I hope you have a delightful journey there, sir."

The waiter deposited a check on the table. It came to seven thirty-five. When he returned promptly with the schnitzel in foil, Jeff handed him a ten and told him to keep the change.

On his way out through the barroom, Jeff noticed a phone booth on the far side. He slipped into it and closed the door. A little light came on. He took a dime out of his pocket and held it in front of the coin slot at the top of the telephone box, but he could not bring himself to drop it in. Eventually, he just sat down on the little shelflike seat. The phone booth was upholstered on the inside for soundproofing. It felt like a cozy little world of its own. It even smelled good, as if some lady before him had left the scent of her perfume in it.

He stayed in there for a long time, weighing his predicament before deciding that he had to accept the fact he was now on the lam, a desperado, a no-goodnik, possibly even wanted by the police.

Somehow, he had to get through the rest of the night until his train left Grand Central just after seven in the morning.

He decided to spend the next few hours hiding out in the theater watching Kathy Kaine perform in *The Wayward Family Singers* one last time. He put his hunting hat back on, swung the peak around to the rear, and ventured out into the cold and the dark.

Chapter Thirteen

He caught a cab straight to the Barrymore on 47th Street. Since it was Friday after Thanksgiving, the house was nearly sold out. Jeff could only get a ticket in the farthest back corner of the upper balcony. It was quarter to seven and they would not be admitting the audience inside until seven-thirty for the eight o'clock performance.

Jeff went around to the alley and up the short flight of stairs to the stage door. Inside, he was greeted by the same old duffer with the battered fedora and the dangling cigarette who had let him in the first time.

"Remember me?" Jeff asked.

"No," the old guy said.

"Can you tell Kathy Kaine I'm here?"

"No."

"Why not?"

"Can't do it."

"You let me in last time."

"Well, for one thing, I don't remember any 'last time' with you. And the second thing is they don't allow no visits from any stage-door Johnnies before the show."

"You mean you won't even ask?"

"No."

"What if I had an important message from her family?"

"You can write it down and I'll bring it to her soon as the show's over. Here." He took a blank sheet of foolscap from under the other sheets on his clipboard and held it out for Jeff along with a pencil.

"I can't do that."

"Why not?"

"You might read it," Jeff said. "It's personal."

The duffer withdrew the clipboard.

"Look, you can't come in before the show. The management don't allow it. It rattles the actors. Come back here after, then we'll talk about it."

Jeff could see it was hopeless. He went back outside and up to Broadway to the Wonderland Skee-Ball parlor. There was a bank of Skee-Ball machines on one side of the entrance, but deeper within stood dozens of game machines. The establishment was populated at this hour by a motley collection of Puerto Rican teenagers, seedy-looking grown men of questionable occupation, a cross dresser, an off-duty sidewalk Santa, and some young couples out on dates.

Jeff got three dollars' worth of quarters and dimes from a booth at the center. He spent thirty-five cents right away on a fresh pack of Marlboros from the cigarette machine. As he lit up, he realized the smoke no longer made him dizzy but calmed him down. Back in the days before Ponsonby, Jeff spent many an after-school session in Wonderland. His favorite amusement was a machine that entailed firing a machine gun on a swivel at silhouettes of gangsters in fedoras who popped up mechanically in the windows of a mob-infested Victorian house. If you "hit" one of the gangsters, the console emitted morbid groans or the crudely recorded phrase, Aw, you got me! He played it repeatedly until he was plugging a gangster on every shot, and then it was no fun anymore.

He moved on to another that styled itself as "Indy-500!" The player took a steering wheel to control a small car on a swing arm inside the cabinet that followed a revolving drum of racetrack hazards. If you veered off the roadway, or hit another car, recorded crash sounds played and lights flashed. It quickly bored him so he migrated to another shooting game called "Safari," which was much like the gangster game, except African animals popped up from behind trees and rocks. But it failed to engage him so he moved on to a pinball machine tricked out like a baseball field. The object was to use the bat-shaped flipper to whack steel balls into slots at the top of the machine that denoted single, double, triple, and home run. Other slots and holes were for outs. He tired of that one after two plays. His wristwatch said ten minutes to eight and, impressed at having managed to kill an hour, he scurried back out and around the corner to the theater.

The orchestra was already tuning up as an usher at the entrance of the upper balcony inspected his ticket and pointed to the very last seat in the corner. When he got there and sat down, the stage looked so far away it might have been across the Hudson River in New Jersey. But it was warm and comfortable inside, and the seat was plush, and the lights dim, and barely had the first act begun in the Norwegian fjords when Jeff fell fast asleep. He woke up briefly at intermission as his fellow theatergoers squeezed by him coming and going, but slipped back into a dream that was like being inside the Wonderland gangster house game with all its gruesome alarms, and awoke sometime later with a sharp startle as the big finale played out onstage featuring a tap-dancing Franklin D. Roosevelt. He barely had time to catch a fleeting glimpse of Kathy Kaine when she exited stage right just as the curtain came down. Minutes later, with the curtain calls concluded, he was borne down the balcony steps on the wave of adult humanity making for the exits.

When he was free of the crowd, he slipped back down the alley to the stage door. Inside, a tall young man with a helmet of wavy blond hair and a tailored charcoal-gray overcoat had entered backstage ahead of him and was already checking in with the old duffer. After the briefest interrogation, the tall, blond young man headed deeper within, down the sea-green hallway.

"It's me again," Jeff said, swinging his rucksack onto his other shoulder.

"Yup, it's you," the duffer agreed.

"Can you tell Miss Kaine I'm here."

"Nope."

"What! Before the show you said I could get in to see her after the show."

"You have to wait. She's got company."

"Who?"

"Well, that fella who come in ahead of you."

"He went down to see Kathy?"

"That's who," the duffer said. "Look. I wrote it down here." He proffered his clipboard. "See?"

Jeff glanced at the clipboard but didn't really register anything.

"How long is he gonna be in there?"

"I don't know. There's no time limit. It's probably her date."

"Her date! He's old enough to . . . to be her . . . teacher, for godsake!"

"Yeah, he might teach her a thing or two."

"Do you know that Kathy Kaine is just thirteen years old?"

"Hey, kid, she's an actress. I've seen a million of 'em. They learn fast."

"How can you let them?"

"What do I look like, the Mother Superior? It's none of my business who they step out with. Anyways, if it wasn't the Johnnies, they'd meet some loverboy over at Sardi's."

"Okay, then let me go back there and tell the guy she's just a kid and lay off."

"You ain't doin' no such thing."

Jeff attempted to dart down the hall but the duffer spun around with surprising adroitness and caught the collar of Jeff's jacket.

"Let go of me!"

The duffer swung Jeff around and slammed him face-first against the rough brick wall beside the stage door. Jeff's rucksack went flying. Then the duffer rotated him face-front, grabbed a fistful of Jeff's shirt, and stuck his face inches from Jeff's. The cigarette was still plugged into his mouth. The force of all the manhandling had knocked Jeff's hat off.

"Don't play games with me, buster, or I'll pitch you headfirst down the stairs into the alley."

"Okay, okay!"

"And one more thing. What's with the fake mustache? You're a kid, obviously."

"Yeah? Well, someday I won't be."

"If I was you, I'd put it off as long as possible. Now scram, and stay scrammed!"

The duffer let go of Jeff and flung open the stage door. Jeff retrieved his rucksack and his hat and hurried out. He felt something warm and wet on his upper lip and realized his nose was bleeding from where it struck the wall. He had no handkerchief so he wiped the blood away with the sleeve of his Ponsonby blazer. He retreated across the street from the alley and lurked next to the entrance of an establishment called Augie's Chop House. After a few minutes, the blood stopped dripping from his right nostril. But it had loosened the adhesive on his mustache and the constant dabbing with his sleeve made it fall off. The temperature had dropped by this hour and Jeff tried to put the ear flaps down on his hat, but they didn't work wearing it backward so he had to turn the peak around.

Just then, he saw Kathy Kaine coming down the alley of the Barrymore Theater arm in arm with the tall, young, blonde-headed man.

"Kathy," he called out to her. "Hey, Kathy, it's me."

The couple stopped at the mouth of the alley and peered across the street. The young man bent to say something to Kathy but, with the din of passing cars, Jeff couldn't hear it, nor what she said back to him. He only saw her shake her head. Then, the two turned and walked up toward Broadway. Jeff followed them on the other side of

47th Street, only to see the young man open the door of a taxicab to let Kathy in, and moments later the cab sped away.

He stood there for a minute in the cacophonous chaos of blinking and flashing colored lights that was Times Square, wishing he could go home and hide in his room, but concluded it would be impossible under the circumstances. So he just plugged his way downtown along Seventh Avenue. At 44th Street, he came upon an establishment called the Fortuna Bar and Grill. It was still moderately busy at this hour, though he could tell that the clientele was a less fortunate class of people than, say, his parents' circle. A line of men past the midpoint in life occupied the bar, drinking with the intense concentration of those who had made a career of alcohol. Couples occupied some of the tables, but they, too, had a shabby, worn-out look, as if they had no better place to go at that hour. Jeff navigated past them all and found the men's room in the back.

Instead of individual urinals, there was a long enameled-steel trough with several men relieving themselves there. To allay his shy bladder, Jeff sought out a regular toilet stall. When he came out and stood before the mirror over a filthy sink, he was shocked to see the dried blood all over his right cheek and chin. He moistened a wad of paper towels and cleaned his face off, then rifled through his rucksack to find his disguise kit and selected a fresh mustache labeled "Casanova." He stuck it on and donned the fake eyeglasses. On his way out, he noticed the same three men standing at the urination trough as when he came in, their arms all strangely in motion, as if swatting flies away from their private parts.

To test his new mustache, Jeff found an empty spot at the bar and took a stool there. A bartender with a face of the most practiced utter blankness approached.

"What'll it be, pal?" he said for perhaps the three millionth time in twenty years on the job.

"Scotch and soda," Jeff said.

The bartender peeled away and in less than a minute set a highball glass before Jeff.

"Sixty-five," the bartender said. Jeff gave him a dollar and told him to keep the change. He sipped the drink at first, savoring the now familiar smoky taste, and then, noticing that he was actually quite thirsty, quaffed the rest. He began to observe the other people in the Fortuna intently, wondering what their stories were, imagining scenarios of woe and failure that had led them to this barroom. As the minutes ticked by, he enjoyed the spectacle more and more, thinking that he'd finally fallen into a circle of kindred spirits.

"'Nother round, pal?" the bartender said.

"Sure," Jeff said and forked over another dollar.

The drink went down smoothly. Jeff felt better and better. The world seemed soft and plush, so easy and pleasant to be in. But then there was the crash of glass breaking, and chairs falling over, and shouting as two middle-aged men, both bald and chubby, grappled with each other toward the back of the room while their girlfriends shrieked. The men were so tightly entwined that neither could get a punch off. Instead, they just spun around scattering the other patrons, knocking over their tables and chairs, with more glass crashing to the tile floor. Not a minute later, as if on cue in a Broadway show, two policemen entered the scene and set upon the brawlers to pull them apart. Even in his brain-softened state, Jeff realized that he did not want to be anywhere near any policemen. He hoisted his rucksack back up, scurried out of the place, and didn't slow down until he came to the corner of 42nd Street.

There, he turned west to what looked like an endless procession of movie marquees. Instinct prompted him toward them. The first theater he came to, the Gem, was showing a "Triple Crown Extravaganza" featuring *The Creation of the Humanoids*, *The Three Stooges Meet Hercules*, and *Posse from Hell*. Jeff noticed a man sitting behind the box-office grill.

"When do you close?" he asked the man, who had been reading a comic book.

"We're open all night," he said, listlessly.

"Maybe I'll come back, then." Jeff wondered if the other theaters ran all night, too. If so, he'll be looking for movies somewhat loftier in tone than these.

The next theater, the Adelphi, offered a "Triple-threat Triple Feature" with *Hand of Death*, *The Brain That Wouldn't Die*, and *The Premature Burial*. Someone was on duty in the freestanding kiosk that served as the ticket booth, but Jeff decided to walk on, still searching for more elevated fare.

The next theater, called the Little Odeon, advertised a "triple playbill" featuring *The Chapman Report*, *Birdman of Alcatraz*, and *Billy Budd*. These sounded quite serious and elevated to Jeff. He didn't have the slightest idea what *The Chapman Report* was a report on, but the word "report" itself had a consequential ring to it. He'd read about *Birdman of Alcatraz* in *Time* magazine some time ago and knew it was the story of a convict who kept wild birds as pets in his cell and became an expert on them. And he knew that *Billy Budd* was a Herman Melville story, the same author who wrote the great classic *Moby Dick*, which was on Ponsonby's spring reading list for the first form boys, so he was sure it was grave and substantial, probably set on the high seas a hundred years ago.

A gray-haired lady, with a severe downturned mouth that spoke of heartache and disappointment in life, sat in the ticket booth. She wasn't reading, just listening to the radio, WABC-AM disc jockey Scott Muni who presided in the late night slot. As Jeff approached the booth, the deejay was introducing number 5 on the pop charts, "Sugar Shack," by Jimmy Gilmer and the Fireballs. Jeff stepped up.

"Are you open all night too?"

"I'm afraid so," she said.

"What's on now?"

"Does it matter?"

"I was just wondering."

The ticket lady took a sheet from the shelf beside the radio, held it up to the overhead light and squinted.

"*Chapman Report*," she said. "Been on for half an hour."

"Do you happen to know what it's a report on?"

"Cough up a buck and a quarter and you can find out."

"That's the adult ticket price."

"You're an adult, aren't you?"

"I don't know."

"You don't know? You got a mustache."

"I'm in between."

"There is no in between price as far as tickets are concerned. You're either a kid or a grown-up. And you got a mustache so . . ."

Jeff gave her the money.

"Can you tell me now?"

"Tell you what?"

"What's The *Chapman Report* a report on? I'm going in in the middle."

"I don't have the slightest idea, and I couldn't care less. When you come out, maybe you can tell me."

Jeff discerned that this was a person with whom you could only get nowhere.

A little gray ticket squirted out of a steel slot behind the grill and she shoved it under at Jeff.

"Enjoy the show."

Inside, the theater had a rank odor rather like stepping into the open mouth of a giant with halitosis. Jeff looked for a seat in the farthest back row. He tried several partially broken ones until he came to a seat that didn't sag. Perhaps a dozen other seats were occupied, and from most of them smoke curled up toward the distant ceiling.

On-screen, a young woman (Jane Fonda) pleaded with her husband, who accused her of being *a woman of ice, that's you*! Jeff couldn't see anything that was wrong with her. Plus, she was throwing herself all over him. *That's what's known as being frigid,* the husband says, and storms out, leaving her shattered. Next, she wakes as from a painful memory, back in her father's living room, and falls weeping into his arms. Dissolve to another setting the next day: a clinical office. The same woman enters wearing a big floppy hat. A handsome man comes in another door and starts interviewing her from a desk behind a folding screen . . .

It was about her sex life, starting from being a teenager. Jeff tried to stay interested, but his brain pulled remorselessly in the direction of sleep, and before the end of the scene he succumbed. He woke sometime later to feel something nudging his left foot. He rapidly became conscious of another person sitting next to him, a pale man in his thirties with a combover that failed to conceal his baldness and several days of unshaven beard on his long, horsey face.

"Whaddaya want," Jeff said reflexively as he surfaced from the depths.

"Hi there, sleepyhead," the man whispered sibilantly. "Wanna have some fun?"

"Huh?" Jeff croaked, straightening out in his seat. He noticed that the man had a porkpie hat in his lap, and his other hand under the hat, which seemed to be moving around, making the hat jump up and down.

"Look," the man said. He lifted the hat with his other hand. Jeff's immediate impression was of the man trying to strangle a pink snake in his lap. It took Jeff another moment to put it together, and then he bolted out of his seat like a Jupiter-C missile launching astronaut Virgil I. ("Gus") Grissom off the launchpad at Cape Canaveral.

"You disgusting pig," he rebuked the man as he hoisted his rucksack and made for the door. He didn't even notice Burt Lancaster on-screen, being taken solemnly into his cell at Alcatraz. Outside, he went up to the woman in the box office. The hit song "Dominique" by the vocalist known as the Singing Nun played cheerfully on the radio.

"There's a guy in there being disgusting," Jeff told her.

"Really?" she said. "What a surprise."

"He was displaying his you-know-what."

"I'm shocked."

"You should throw guys like that out."

"If we did, nobody would come here."

Jeff was reminded that this was a woman with whom you will get nowhere. He looked at his wristwatch. It was 3:47 in the morning. He turned away and headed east down the sidewalk. Various women in garish costumes lurked in the shadows between all the movie theaters. He thought he heard one of them say, "Looking for a date, mister?" in an unusually low, gravelly voice as he passed by. He picked up his pace.

Traffic was light at this hour. One of a citywide chain of papaya drink stands was open on the far side of Broadway and 42nd. Jeff stopped and got a hot dog with sauerkraut, mustard, and onions and a piña colada combo drink. Assorted Times Square denizens stopped by for refreshments while Jeff worked on his hot dog. They uniformly looked like desperate characters—all men, mostly not young, unkempt, unbathed, unslept, itchy, jerky, furtive, eyes darting, limbs jangling. Jeff marveled that such a powerful and successful nation as the USA could produce such a large class of ne'er-do-wells. And, also, how oddly enterprising they were to still be up at such a late hour, so busy doing things that produced no improvement in their wretched lives. He wondered if he was destined to become one of them. The idea troubled him so sharply that he horsed down the remainder of his dog and vacated the place.

From there, as it began to drizzle, and the street grew slick and reflected the lights of cars, trucks, and successive storefronts with neon signs, he bustled as quickly as possible down 42nd, past Bryant Park and the big public library, with its noble twin lions guarding the grand stairway, and a block and a half later he arrived at the Vanderbilt Avenue entrance to Grand Central Station. A masonry eagle with wings spread roosted on a stone globe above the corner marquee to welcome travelers beginning their epic journeys. Jeff went inside.

Nothing was open at this hour, not the Oyster Bar, not the newsstands, the ticket windows, the information kiosk, nor anything else in and around the Great Hall or down the concourses that led to the dark underbelly of tracks and subways. He gravitated to the waiting room off the Great Hall with its rows of sturdy carved wooden benches, like church pews. A dozen people were scattered around on them in various postures, sitting, slumped, or lying down. Some were clearly asleep. Jeff took a seat in the farthest corner and checked the inside breast pocket of his Ponsonby blazer for his ticket to remind himself that his train was scheduled to depart at ten after seven, meaning they would probably board at seven. A big clock above the waiting room entrance said 4:30. Jeff turned his hunting hat around and pulled the brim down low so nobody would see anything on his face but his mustache. He crossed his arms and closed his eyes but he was dogged by the thought that he might sleep past seven and miss his train. And, anyway, he'd already slept quite a bit that night at two different theaters.

So he abandoned his sleeping posture, searched his rucksack, and pulled out both his paperback copy of *The Catcher in the Rye* and the remnant of his Wiener Schnitzel from Lüchow's. The hot dog had not quelled his hunger. He opened the book and began to read it all over again from the beginning while he nibbled on the cold veal cutlet: *If you really want to hear about it, the first thing you'll probably want to know is where I was born, and what my lousy childhood was like . . .* Holden explains. Soon, the reader is transported to Pencey Prep during the momentous day when Holden would eventually skip out to New York City and have his misadventures there. Jeff felt comfortable and secure reading about Pencey Prep. His three months at Ponsonby Hall had familiarized him with many of the same routines and shenanigans that defined prep school life, and he had come to enjoy being there terrifically, to use one of Holden's choice locutions. If there was one thing that still stood out in his memory, it was those pickup football games on the ball field after classes on fall afternoons, the grass still vividly green in October and nothing all around but a wall of forest blazing yellow, orange, and scarlet. And the feeling of fellowship with his classmates, no matter how much he liked them, or not, as individuals—and he'd come to like many of them—but even more, being part of a human tribe, like the kids in *The Lord of the Flies*, before everything went wrong for them.

Jeff wished that Holden wouldn't leave Pencey Prep, that he could just stay there through the whole book, but, of course, he already knew the story. What was different reading it this time around was that Holden's exploits, once he arrived in the city, no longer seemed as exhilarating as they had before. This time the events seemed depressing, just as Holden often said, and being depressed turned out to not be so much fun. Jeff knew many of the locales in the book, but he had his own locales in the New York of 1963, and after his week bouncing around from one place to another, and getting tangled in the lives of strangers, Jeff found the city to be rather garishly grubby and sordid. Holden noticed only the phonies and morons. Jeff saw that there were many other varieties of unappetizing humans: there were perverts, devious females, born losers of every imaginable description, criminals, mugs, goons, fools, and plenty of people who kept striving honestly and earnestly, only to be disappointed and give up on their petty hopes and dreams.

Jeff couldn't fail to notice that he was now sitting in one the very settings of the book, the waiting room of Grand Central, where Holden fled after he found his ex-teacher Mr. Antolini, he says, *sitting on the floor right next to the couch, in the dark and all, and he was sort of petting me or patting me on the goddam head*. In fact, Jeff realized, the man in the movie theater who woke him up with his hat jumping around in his lap was even more disgusting than Mr. Antolini had been. Holden had left some room to doubt whether Mr. Antolini had *made a flitty pass at him, or if maybe he just liked to pat guys on the head when they're asleep. I mean how can you tell about that stuff for sure? You can't . . .* Holden says. Jeff, on the other hand, was not so much in doubt about what the pervert in the movie theater was up to. Holden also said that being in the waiting room at Grand Central made him more depressed than anything in his whole life. Jeff understood completely.

But by now it was a few minutes after six o'clock in the morning. More travelers began to enter the waiting room. The sleepers stretched and yawned. Jeff grabbed his rucksack and went back out into the Great Hall. A little way down the Biltmore concourse that connected the station to the renowned hotel, he saw the orange and white colors of the Nedick's chain of coffee shops. They were just opening up. Jeff went in and ordered a hot chocolate with a cruller and a regular donut for backup. He ate them at the counter watching the station came to life.

He managed to kill another twenty minutes browsing the magazines in a newsstand and eventually bought a copy of *Time* to read on the train, featuring the new president, Lyndon B. Johnson, on the cover. He didn't know much about the big Texan and wanted to be better informed about who would be running the country now that JFK was gone.

One odd thing about *The Catcher in the Rye*, he paused to ponder. Holden never mentions who's president through the whole book, or anything else that might have been in the news at the time it takes place. It surely wasn't Eisenhower, since the book first came out in 1951, and Ike hadn't been elected yet. He doubted it was Harry Truman, either, because World War Two never comes up. Maybe the president in the time of the book was Franklin D. Roosevelt, but you'd never find out from listening to Holden.

Jeff had learned from the *Time* story at the library that Salinger, the author, was born in 1919, so if he was writing about anything like his own teenage time, it must have been the 1930s. Salinger would have been Holden's age, sixteen, in 1935. The Second World War hadn't even happened yet. But the Great Depression would have been on. Jeff knew that much. Odd that Holden never mentioned that either. Jeff's father and mother were born around the same time as J. D. Salinger, respectively in 1922 and 1924. Holden's teenage years were theirs, too, more or less. He couldn't help wondering what would have become of Holden Caulfield many years later. If he lived, Holden would be in his forties. Did he stay insane, locked up in a sanitarium somewhere for life? Or did he manage to recover? Did he get into the war, fighting the Nazis or the Japs? Did he survive it and get a job like anybody else, maybe even become a lawyer like Jeff's father, Bob Greenaway . . .

These musings alarmed Jeff as he was forced to remember he hadn't gone home last night and his parents would probably be out of their minds with worry. He briefly considered giving up his quest and heading back to 79th Street, apologizing, taking his punishment, whatever it was, and going back to normal life. What would Holden do, he asked himself? Holden's story was over, he realized. Holden would never get beyond that November day in the New York of the 1930s at the end of the book, sitting in the rain beside the carousel in Central Park, crying while his sister Phoebe rode around and around. Jeff realized, rather sharply, that he was in his own story now.

Chapter Fourteen

At quarter to seven, Jeff marched up to the information kiosk and found out what track the 7:10 Montrealer was leaving from. Track 12, he was told. A line of travelers had already assembled there and Jeff joined them at the gate. A policeman sauntered down the hall and Jeff watched him pass by the gate to Track 12 from under the peak of his hunting hat until the cop melted back into the crowd. Finally, the gate was thrown open and the line of travelers began to move like a single pulsating organism to the stairs, and down to the track level, a dim subterranean world of puffing steam, the noise of metal on metal, and the electric smell of ozone.

"All aboard," the conductor cried in a singsong voice, "for New Haven, Hartford, Springfield, Brattleboro, and points north to Montreal, Queeeee-bec, Canada!"

"Doesn't it stop at Windsor?" Jeff asked him.

"Yes, it does," the conductor said cheerfully. "That's one of the points north. But mind, there's two Windsors: first Windsor Locks, Connecticut, and farther up the line, Windsor, Vermont. Which one are you bound for?"

"Oh, the Vermont one."

"That's about an hour later, after Windsor Locks."

Reassured, Jeff boarded the car and found a window seat halfway up the aisle. The seat was so plush and comfortable, and the car so warm and cozy, that he immediately began to feel sleepy. He watched the parade of his fellow passengers stream up the aisle through half-closed eyes for a few minutes before succumbing to a dreamless slumber.

He woke up between New Rochelle and Stamford, with the conductor touching his shoulder.

"Ticket, fella?"

Jeff surfaced from the blank, dreamless depths with a startle as his frontal lobes lagged momentarily behind the limbic region of his brain. Shortly, he realized who he was and the basics of his situation: *myself . . . on a train . . . to Vermont*. He rummaged in the inside pocket of his blazer and produced the ticket.

"What time do we get to Windsor?"

"Eleven thirty-five," replied the conductor, briskly, punching his ticket and handing the stub back. "Refreshment car is two cars forward, restrooms in the rear of the car."

It was only then, reaching for the stub, that Jeff noticed the passenger sitting in the aisle seat next to him. He was a wizened, shriveled husk of a man with an impressive shock of white hair and plastic cannula under his nose secured by an elastic band behind his head. A plastic tube ran from the cannula down to a gray metal tank in a little wheeled caddy beside his bony legs, the outlines of which were visible through his worn gabardine pants. The man's eyes were open but he seemed to stare into eternity.

Jeff turned his attention out the window, to the suburban clutter passing by. Whole new housing developments were under construction. The new houses seemed as though they were trying to outdo each other for ugliness, Jeff thought. It was as if America had forgotten how to build a house that looked like a house. And in places where the tracks ran close to a highway, a whole new kind of shopping architecture was smearing itself over the landscape like a scrofulous infection. He couldn't wait to get to the end of it, and after the train finally pulled out of Stamford, the scenery softened to mostly woods and fields.

By that time, Jeff realized he was in need of the bathroom. He stole a glance at the old man next to him. He was still staring straight ahead, blankly. Jeff wondered whether the old guy was even alive. He was afraid to ask the man if he would mind letting him get by to the aisle. He tried pretending to cough, "ahem, ahem," but that did not get the man's attention. He knew that the situation in his bladder was only going to get worse. It crowded every other thought out of his head. Finally, he touched the old man's boney shoulder. The man's head slowly rotated toward him. Jeff didn't speak. He just pointed to himself and to the aisle.

"Go ahead," the man said in a voice full of broken reeds. He made an effort to scrunch deeper into his seat while Jeff managed to squeeze past the oxygen tank. He enjoyed visiting the restroom at the rear of the car, how cleverly all its stainless-steel appointments were designed for being in motion, and the spectacular noise that the toilet made when he pushed the flush button: a loud sucking sound followed by the clap of a valve shutting. Amazingly, hot water came out of the sink faucet. It was grand, he mused, to live in a country that afforded such luxury. On a Russian train, one probably peed through a hole in the floor, he thought.

He looked in the mirror above the sink and was rather surprised to discover that he was still wearing the fake mustache. It looked quite fake, indeed, he realized, and he decided to get rid of it. He was tired of pretending to be a grown-up. When he peeled both sides off, two red welts remained where the adhesive had stuck. It was not an attractive look, he thought, like one of those pitiful kids at camp with a horrible case of chapped lips. Plus, he had an abrasion on his nose where the old duffer at the stage door had flung him against the wall. But there was nothing to be done about any of that now, except wait for it to get better.

Next, he ventured in the other direction, forward to the refreshment car the conductor had mentioned. He enjoyed the rolling and rocking motion of the train and lingered for a while in one of the vestibules between cars where the air was cold and the sound of the wheels against the steel track was vividly rhythmical, like one of those Latin bands on the radio. But it felt good to reenter the warmth of the refreshment car. At center, a colored attendant in a smart white jacket and a clip-on bow tie took orders. There was a short line of two men and a woman. Jeff studied the menu. It was titled: Space Age Treats from the Rad-R-Range. It offered the Astro-dog, the Astro-burger (w/ cheez), and the Astro Cheez-melt. When his turn came Jeff ordered the burger with cheez and a can of ginger ale. The attendant put a cellophane-covered, preassembled burger into a steel box and twisted the dial. Two minutes later it was ready, placed in a cardboard tray with his soda can, two-twenty-five for the combo. Jeff left a quarter tip on the counter and ventured back to his own car.

It took the old man a minute to realize that Jeff was standing in the aisle, but then he scrunched up again and let Jeff through. Jeff put down the tray table for his meal and addressed the burger. The bun was mushy and the cheez's only contribution to the ensemble was an impressive saltiness. The meat itself was limp and gray, with a peculiar overtone of the stockyards. He ate it anyway, in such a rapture of animal satisfaction that he barely registered the old man trying to speak to him.

"Did you say something," Jeff asked.

The old man spoke very slowly and carefully, denoting the effort it took him. "What happened to your . . . mustache?"

"I didn't need it anymore."

"I thought maybe you was a midget."

"No. I'm a kid."

"What'd you need it for in the first place?"

"I was in disguise."

"What from?"

Jeff had to think about that.

"It would take me a million years to explain."

"I don't have a million years," the old man said. "Lucky if I got a coupla months."

Jeff didn't know what to say, considering the oxygen bottle. He addressed the rest of his limp burger.

"Where you going?" the old man asked.

"Nowhere."

"This train's goin' somewhere. Why are you on it then?"

"I just wanted to ride on the train."

"Is that so?"

"Yeah, I'm a nut for trains. I take 'em all the time."

"I expect this is my last time on a train."

"Oh? Where are you going?"

"I'm going home to die."

Jeff swallowed the last morsel of his burger with an audible gulp.

"Maybe you'll get better," he said.

"Naw, I'm done for. The docs give me a death sentence."

"What have you got?"

"I got the cancer."

"Jeez. That's . . . uh . . . uh . . . a tough break."

"Yeah, I guess," the old man said. "But I'll tell you a secret. We all got the same destination when all's said and done. The bone orchard. Even you, young fella. So I don't mind, see? I was young once, too. I had that already."

"I don't think about it so much," was all Jeff could say.

"Of course not. Kids never do. Want to know what it's like staring death in the face?"

"Not really."

"Okay. I don't blame you. Ask me about my life, then."

"I dunno . . ."

"Ask me if I had a good life."

"Did you have a good life?"

"It was all right. 'Bout average, I'd have to guess. Been here on earth since eighteen eighty-seven. We used to have horses everywhere when I was kid. I loved horses. Now you hardly ever see one."

"Yeah, the world was probably better with horses."

"A car's nice, but you get too many of them and they ruin everything. I worked thirty-eight years at Victor in Camden, New Jersey. Assembled radios. Floor manager the last eighteen. Radio was a wonder of the world when it come in around nineteen twenty. I started in 'twenty-two. Victor later become RCA. You know what Camden's motto is?"

"Its motto? I have no idea."

"*Camden makes, the world takes*. They made everything there. Fountain pens. Campbell made soup there. The whole city smelled like a different soup depending on the day of the week. Wednesday was tomato. Friday was chicken noodle. They built ships in Camden. I worked at the shipyard one year during the big war, nineteen and seventeen. They paid a bonus. Almost killed me. Everything you picked up weighed a ton. Wrecked my sacroiliac. Went back to the radio factory. Much lighter work. Retired in 'fifty-nine. Now it's all TV, the idiot box, they say. I don't mind it. It's all I do lately."

"I mostly read these days," Jeff said.

"Good boy. You'll go far in this world. Oh, almost forgot. I married a good woman. Ol' Jess. She passed away two years ago. She was a saucy gal, I'll tell you. I miss her. I'm going to Brattleboro where I was born and my people are from. We had a little summer house there after the war. Our son's in it now. I'm all wore out from telling my life story. Do me a favor and give me a heads-up when they call Brattleboro, next stop. Can you do that?"

"Sure. Don't worry."

"You're a good boy, all right."

The old man closed his eyes and his jaw quickly went slack. Jeff had to study him closely to make sure his chest was still going up and down. By now they were approaching Springfield, Massachusetts. Jeff noticed that snow was falling lightly.

*

Jeff tried reading his *Time* magazine, without much success. Everything about Lyndon Johnson—LBJ they were calling him—only made Jeff feel worse that JFK was gone. He sensed that something had changed in America far beyond any political personalities, that something dark had commenced in the nation's life and he would be growing up right into the teeth of whatever it was. He put down the magazine and resumed watching the landscape go by: woods interrupted by ranks of white, muslin-covered sheds in farm fields where the shade tobacco for cigar wrappers was grown. At times, he caught a glimpse of the winding Connecticut River. The train made stops in Holyoke, Northampton, and Greenfield, after which the cry Brattleboro, next stop rang through the car.

Jeff had to jostle the old man on his shoulder several times. It took him an alarmingly long time to wake up.

"Hey . . . hey, mister. Brattleboro's coming up."

"Are we there already?"

"No, they just announced it."

"Can you go tell the conductor I'll need some help getting' off."

"Sure."

He let Jeff squeeze by. Jeff found two conductors playing gin rummy at a little table in the snack car and gave the one he recognized the message.

"You tell him I'll be right along."

When the train finally stopped, the conductor preceded the old man down the aisle carefully pulling the oxygen bottle on its rolling caddy. It took several minutes until they emerged down on the platform. Jeff observed out the window as the conductor handed the old man off to a younger man and a woman there bundled in winter woolens. The younger man wore a red hunting hat not unlike the one Jeff had bought at Abercrombie & Fitch. For a moment, the thought crossed his mind that the man might be Holden Caulfield himself, all grown up now, married, and finally living in the North Woods of his heart's desire—until he remembered that in the book Holden says his father is a lawyer, not somebody who worked in a radio factory, like Lee Harvey Oswald in Russia. It only depressed him more to think about it and he looked away. The train chugged out of the station and soon got back up to speed.

Tobacco smoke curled above the other seats here and there in the car. Jeff remembered that he had a fresh pack of Marlboros in his pocket. He unwound the cellophane tear strip and proceeded to light up. The smoke filled a painfully empty space inside him and he relaxed back into the plush seat, enjoying the feel of the cigarette in his hand, the sense of being in command of . . . of something. The light snow outside was beginning to stick in the fields that raced by.

An hour later, the conductor called out Windsor–Mount Ascutney. A feeling of great excitement ran through Jeff as he reached his journey's end. He'd felt more comfortable that final hour on the train, alone in his seat, than at any time through all the days, a week ago, exactly, since Headmaster Stilgoe sent the boys home from Ponsonby.

Jeff was the only passenger to get off at Windsor. The cold air was a bit of a shock. He stopped a moment to behold his destination, as though it were a prize he had been awarded. The brick station with its handsome brackets and arched windows pleased him. He entered it to pass through to the street side. The interior walls were clad in varnished wood wainscoting, dark amber with age. He couldn't help wondering if he would have to sleep there that night, and whether they would even let him. A big clock over the ticket window said eleven thirty-five. As he stepped out through the street-side door, Jeff realized, all of a sudden, that he had no plan whatsoever.

Chapter Fifteen

It was a mere one-block hike uphill on Depot Street to where it met Main Street, which was a classic of the genre, with its stolid two-story redbrick buildings, each with a storefront at the ground floor. Several had Christmas decorations up in their windows, wreathes, apple-cheeked Santas, and candy canes, and one establishment, Mayer's Appliances, had twinkling Christmas lights arrayed around a Frigidaire. Jeff gazed up and down Main Street for a full minute, first one side (north) and then the other (south). Snow still fell lightly and was sticking to the parked cars.

Painfully conscious that he was not sure how to proceed, Jeff decided to stretch his legs and take a little tour of Windsor, thinking that some notion of a plan would arise as he set himself in motion. He pulled the peak of his hunting hat around, pulled the ear flaps down, hoisted his rucksack straps on both shoulders, and proceeded up State Street, past Distell's Machine Shop and Beloit's Custom Turnings to just beyond the classic redbrick and white-steepled Episcopal church where the street leveled off. Across from the church lay a small park, called the Village Green, with a bandstand at the near end. And just a little farther, on the other side of State, stood the village library, a foursquare redbrick building with massive limestone pillars holding up the entrance portico. The early outlines of a plan began to form in Jeff's mind. He decided to step inside.

Being Saturday around noon on a cold, wintry day, the place was busy, with many well-behaved children combing the stacks or seated at sturdy oak tables, reading peacefully. Jeff found his way to the fiction shelves and hunted under "S." There were several copies each of J. D. Salinger's latest books, *Franny and Zooey* and *Raise High the Roof Beam, Carpenters* but no copies of *The Catcher in the Rye*. Realizing that he had read neither of the first two books, Jeff grabbed one of each and retreated to an empty table by the window, thinking he might discover some additional clues about the author.

The circulation card in each showed that they had been taken out only by four and two readers, respectively, since their publication. Strange, Jeff thought, considering the author was a sort of local hero. He cracked *Franny and Zooey* and began to read. He quickly ascertained that there was no trace of the authorial voice that had captivated him so completely in *Catcher*. The main character, Franny Glass, a college girl on a weekend date, bore some circumstantial resemblance to Holden Caulfield. She was upset with everything in the society around her—apparently having a nervous breakdown over it. But Jeff could not figure out what was really bugging her. It seemed to involve a religious book she was carrying around with her called *The Way of a Pilgrim*, and a so-called Jesus Prayer that it recommends to people who are at loose ends. In other words, Jeff grasped that she was having some kind of religious crisis, a quandary that held little interest for him, having been raised in a religion-free household. The history of the Glass family and Franny's many siblings also bored him completely. In any case, he skipped to the end where Franny passes out in the bathroom of the restaurant where she went out on her date.

The Zooey part of *Franny and Zooey* involved a long conversation that Franny's actor brother Zooey is having with their mother Bessie in the bathroom of the family's New York City apartment. Zooey is in the bathtub for much of the story. Jeff skipped to the end where Zooey tried to calm Franny down over the telephone with a lot of talk about a mythical "Fat Lady" who makes up the audience of radio shows all over America. (The author does not acknowledge the existence of television, Jeff noticed, so the story, like Catcher, must take place before the war.) Zooey tries to put across the idea that the "Fat Lady" stands for Jesus Christ. Jeff could not follow the reasoning of that at all and he put down the book in abject frustration.

Raise High the Roof Beam, Carpenters was even more enigmatic and opaque to Jeff. The narrator sounds exactly like the sort of phony that Holden Caulfield detests, a verbose professor type who feels obliged to explain a million details that the reader couldn't care less about before coming to any point, which he hardly does. There's a big wedding set piece where the groom doesn't show up. Then a lot of boring business in a taxicab with the groom's brother and all the squabbling relatives. Jeff couldn't stand to continue. He just wondered what on earth had gotten into old J.D. that he had to write such a boring book. He was dying to ask the author about it. He didn't even venture to continue reading the companion piece, *Seymour, an Introduction* (Seymour being the groom who'd skipped out in the first story).

He left the books on the table and made for the front exit, but a librarian behind the front counter caught his eye. She was a plump woman about his mother's age with a beehive hairdo, a clingy cashmere sweater with much flesh to cling to, and a silk kerchief tied jauntily around her neck. She had just finished checking out a book for a younger schoolgirl. Jeff approached her warily.

"Can I help you?" she asked.

"I'm not sure."

"You're new here," she said. A statement, not a question.

"How do you know that?"

"I know all the boys and girls. Are you new in town?"

"Not exactly."

"Oh? Well, I'm Mrs. Codmann," she extended her hand and Jeff shook. "What's your name?"

"Ackley," Jeff said, referencing Holden's neighbor in the Pencey Prep dorm.

"Christian name?"

"Yeah, I guess."

"I mean, your first name, like John or George."

"Oh, it's . . . Robert."

"Bob? Bobby?"

"Sure, either way's fine."

"Well, Bobby, is there something I can find for you?"

Jeff leaned forward pushing up against the counter to whisper.

"Do you know Mr. J. D. Salinger, the writer?"

Mrs. Codmann appeared to blanche slightly.

"We're all sort of acquainted with him."

"I wonder if you can tell me where he lives around here."

Mrs. Codmann recoiled somewhat.

"Mr. Salinger's quite . . . private," she declared. "So it's said."

"I know. I read the article about him in *Time* magazine. Did you happen to see that?"

"Our copy disappeared from the stacks some time ago. Where did you find it?"

"In the library, where I used to live."

"Where was that?"

"New York."

"Is that where you live now?"

"Not exactly."

"Where do you live, exactly?"

"I can't tell you."

"I see," she said, not seeing at all and showing it. "Will you be staying with us in Windsor long?"

"Probably not."

Mrs. Codmann crossed her arms and took a long quizzical look at Jeff.

"Are you a little wanderer?" she asked.

"Just for now."

"Anyway, I couldn't tell you any address," she said with a sigh. "Across the river on the New Hampshire side somewhere, or so they say."

"Okay, thanks," Jeff said and abruptly peeled away. She was making him nervous. He was relieved to be back out in the brisk air, at large in Windsor, with the light snow falling so prettily over the quaint New England townscape. He trudged farther up State Street, past many handsome old houses and a school, quiet on Saturday, and took a left on Ascutney Street, then another left back downhill on Union Street until it came to T back at Main Street. Discerning that he had navigated a rectangular route, Jeff walked north back up to the heart of Main. There he came to an establishment called Nap's Lunch and, feeling quite chilled from his walk, went right in.

It was the very picture of a classic soda fountain, with booths, a long counter with revolving stools, and a complement of local high school kids. He could smell hamburgers grilling and hear them sizzle on the grill. A malted milk shake machine whirred. In the rear stood a jukebox glowing like a spaceship, which was just then playing the song "Please Please Me" by an up-and-coming band from England nobody had ever heard of. A teenage couple in the back were dancing the Mashed Potato to it. Jeff took a stool at the counter.

A young man in his twenties in an apron and a soda jerk's cap came over to take his order. Jeff was astounded by how corny it was. By now it was one-thirty in the afternoon and he was quite hungry.

"What'll ya have, kid?"

"A cheeseburger with fries?"

"No fries. Sorry. Chips and a pickle?"

"Okay. Can you make a chocolate malted?"

"You mean a frappe?"

"A frappe? What's that?"

"It's what we call a milkshake."

"I never heard of such a thing."

"You from out of town?"

"Yeah."

"I thought so."

"How'd you know?"

"Never saw you before. I know all the kids. Chocolate or vanilla?"

"Chocolate. Say, by any chance have you ever heard of this local character named J. D. Salinger?"

"Yeah, Salinger, the writer guy?"

"That's right."

"He's pretty famous."

"Do you know him?"

"Naw. He used to come in here a lot, they say. Years ago. He liked hanging out with the high schoolers. A little weird, if you ask me."

The soda jerk bustled away, slapped a raw burger on the grill, took off two that were done, and carried the plates over to a booth with a teen couple in it. "It's All Right" by the Impressions played silkily out of the jukebox.

Say it's all right (It's all right)
Say it's all right (It's all right)
It's all right, have a good time
'Cause it's all right, whoa, it's all right

Jeff watched the action in the place. He wouldn't mind being a teenager in a town like this, he thought. It was like a TV show about teens come to life, so much more normal than New York with all its troubled people and their complicated problems. Indeed, it seemed like having a good time was exactly what the teens here were doing. Soon, the soda jerk bustled back with Jeff's burger and frappe.

"Hey." Jeff caught his attention before he could bustle off again. "Do you have any idea where Salinger lives?"

"Across the river somewhere. That's New Hampshire on the other side."

"Did you ever read his book?"

"Salinger's? Actually no."

"You should read it. *Catcher in the Rye*. It's terrific."

"I'm not much of a reader. I like to fix cars in my spare time. Pardon me."

The soda jerk bustled off again to take orders from two more teens who came in out of the cold, shaking the snowflakes off their shoulders.

When he was done sliding another two burgers on the grill, the soda jerk came back and slapped a check in front of Jeff.

"Hey, wait," Jeff said. "Does Salinger ever come in here nowadays?"

"I don't think so. Not when I'm working the fountain, anyways. You might go see Buddy Wepper up the street. He's got the barbershop. He's a little older. He might remember Salinger."

"Okay. Thanks."

"Why are you looking for him, anyway?"

"He's my long-lost father."

"Really? Must be some story behind that."

"I don't feel like going into it, if you want to know the truth."

"Yeah, sure. Well, good luck, kid."

For a minute, to avoid going out in the cold again, Jeff watched the teens in the back do the twist to "Surfin' U.S.A." by the Beach Boys. But eventually he was back on the street, marching north in the light snow toward the revolving electric barber pole that hung slightly out over the sidewalk. Across Main Street, some younger boys were enjoying a snowball fight in front of the Ben Franklin five-and-dime store.

Old-timey sleighbells attached to the door of the barbershop clunked musically as Jeff stepped in. The establishment was barely twelve feet wide, with just two barber chairs and one barber at work. Two other men waited in seats along the wall leafing through magazines as they all joshed with the barber and his customer getting a haircut. One of waiting men had a long gray beard, like someone out of a photograph from the past century. The other man next to him wore a flannel shirt in the muted gray Munro tartan motif and smoked a fancy meerschaum pipe with a bowl shaped like a sultan with a turban. His Cavendish tobacco put out a highly aromatic smoke redolent of black currants.

Jeff took the one remaining seat thinking he might as well get a haircut so that the barber would have to talk to him. The pipe smoke inspired Jeff to light up one of his Marlboros. There was a metal stand-up ashtray between the seats, nearly overflowing with old butts.

"So, he says 'Ayuh, you can have that sow, but I think you'll learn she's more trouble than she's worth,'" the man in the barber chair said. It was apparently a comic punch line to a joke. Everyone guffawed before turning their attention to Jeff, and then they all clammed up, watching censoriously as he enjoyed his cigarette. The barber brushed off his customer's neck and shoulders and that one soon departed. The graybeard rotated into the barber's chair.

"Looks like we're in for a spell of the white stuff tonight," he said.

"How much?" the pipe smoker asked.

"Eight to twelve. First good 'un of the season."

"I could do without it, my age," the pipe smoker said.

"You just figure out this iddin' Florida?"

"Well, I don't like it."

"Hey, listen up!" the barber interjected. "A duck walks into a bar. He orders a beer and a ham sandwich. The bartender looks at him and says, 'Wait a minute. You're a duck.' . . ."

The joking and joshing continued apace and then the pipe smoker took his turn in the chair. When he was done and gone, it was Jeff's turn. He and the barber were alone in the shop, just the two of them. The prevailing mood of jollity had dissolved.

"You're a new 'un here, aren't you," the barber said, snapping the protective cape over Jeff, who left his hunting hat and his Ponsonby blazer back in the waiting chair.

"I'm just passing through," Jeff said.

"Where from?"

"New York."

"City boy?"

"I guess. But I hate it there."

"I've been once or twice, but not in some years. Nice place to visit and so forth. Just a reg'lar cut?"

"Yeah, but not too short. Just normal."

"That's what we specialize in here," the barber quipped. "Normal."

"Are you Buddy Wepper, by any chance?"

The barber put his scissors hand down.

"Do I know you? I don't think so."

"So, you are Buddy?"

"Yeah, I'm Buddy. Who are you?"

"Nobody," Jeff said. "The guy at the soda fountain told me to talk to you."

"Did he now? What do you want to talk about?"

"He said you might know the famous author Mr. Salinger."

The barber quickly went about his business with scissors and comb. It took him nearly a minute to reply.

"I know him," he said. "Knew him. It's been some years."

"I hear he used to hang out with the teenagers at the soda fountain down the street."

"Ayuh, he did."

"And you were one of the teenagers then."

"Ayuh, I was."

"What happened?"

Buddy stopped cutting and just looked at Jeff's reflection in the wall mirror from his position behind Jeff's head.

"He quit coming around. Say, who are you anyway, sonny, asking about all this."

"I'm his long-lost son from New York."

"Well, I'll be. . . . He never talked about any such son."

"He doesn't know about me."

Buddy resumed cutting silently for a while.

"I was going to drop in on him and say hello," Jeff said.

"Isn't that a fine thing. You going to surprise him?"

"Yeah. I'm trying to figure out where he lives around here."

"He's across the river on the Lang Road over in Cornish."

"Lang?"

"Ayuh. L-A-N-G. It's over by the Saint-Gaudens."

"What's that?"

"Famous American artist who made statues. Abe Lincoln especially. He had a summer place over there. Quite a mansion. They made it an official historic landmark coupla years ago."

"Is that where Salinger lives?"

"He's just a little ways past there."

"Did you ever go there?"

"The Saint-Gaudens?"

"No, Salinger's."

"Indeed, I did. He'd have a bunch of us over after a game. He was crazy for sports, Jerry. We called him Jerry. Boys and girls both, we'd pile into his Jeep and go over. He'd grill us up hot dogs, make popcorn, put records on the hi-fi. Only jazz. He didn't go for songs of the day, just jazz. We'd try dancing to it, but it was hard. Crazy music. I think Jerry was a little crazy."

"When was that?"

"'Bout 'fifty-four. Must've been. Year I graduated."

"Have you ever seen him since?"

"He came in here maybe around nineteen fifty-nine, one time after I took this joint over from Harry LaBountie. Didn't come back.

I guess he didn't like the haircut. 'Course, I'm a lot better at this now. Once in a while, you'll see him go into the post office. Must have a box there. So, who's your ma, anyways, sonny?"

"She was an actress. On Broadway," Jeff said.

"No kidding. Old Jerry and an actress, and here you are! Is she done acting?"

"She passed away."

"Oh, dear. I'm sorry to hear that."

"She was in that plane crash in New Jersey."

"Oh, gosh. I must of read about it in the papers."

"It was on TV."

"The reception here stinks," Buddy said. "We get one lousy station out of Lebanon. The mountains and all. I'm sorry about your ma. That's a sad story."

"It's all right. She probably didn't feel a thing, it hit so fast."

Buddy reached for the electric clipper to clean up the back of Jeff's neck.

"Poor thing," he muttered and switched on the clipper. "Were they married at some point, her and Jerry?"

"Nope. It was just a brief romance."

"Really? How do you know he's your dad?"

"She told me, just before she got on that plane. She said, if anything happens to me you go up to New Hampshire and find your father, J. D. Salinger. You can stay with him."

"Hmmm. They say Jerry can be pretty tart with people who come around. We hear about it in town. Reporters and snoops and like that. Magazine people. They come here. He gives them the brushoff. What if he just denies who he is?"

"He won't deny his own son, I'm sure," Jeff said.

"You part it here?" Buddy said.

"I'm part of what?"

"Your hair," Buddy said, pointing with his comb to a place on Jeff's hairline. "Is that where you part it?"

"I guess so. The thing is, Buddy, I was wondering if you could maybe give me ride up there, where Salinger lives."

He watched Buddy stare at him in the wall mirror, moving his blocky head slightly from one side to the other, as though he were thinking it over.

"I wouldn't feel so good about it, how Jerry is, an' all."

"Is there a taxicab in this town, by any chance?"

"No. Not anymore. Burleigh Lanier shut her down a few years back. Everybody's got a car now. Burleigh's in the home these days, over to White River."

"Well, would you give me a ride over there? To Salinger's?"

"What if he gives you the heave-ho?"

"His own flesh and blood?"

"I don't know. And, apparently, he don't know. You're just some kid, showing up on his doorstep."

"Look, if he's all mean like that you can just drive me back here and drop me at the train station and I'll catch the first train back to New York."

"It'll be night by then."

"That's okay. I can sleep in the waiting room. I've done that before."

Buddy reached for a hand mirror and showed Jeff how the back of his head looked.

"Thar she blows," Buddy said, and began unsnapping the cape and brushing off Jeff's shirt collar and shoulders. "You like?"

"Yeah, it's perfect," Jeff said. "Greatest haircut ever. What do you say?"

"I say, it's been a pleasure and that'll be a buck fifty."

Jeff slid out of the chair and took the remaining wad of bills out of his pocket. He handed Buddy two dollars and, being accustomed to tipping barbers back in New York, said, "Keep the change."

"Obliged," Buddy said.

"What do you say, then, about giving me a ride over to Jerry's?"

"I don't know. It's coming down pretty hard now."

Jeff glanced out the front window. Indeed, Main Street looked like one of those glass globes that you shake and great big snowflakes swirl around inside.

"It's supposed to keep up like this," Buddy said.

"Isn't it only a few miles over there to where he lives?"

"Ayuh."

"I'll give you another twenty bucks if you drive me."

Buddy made a face.

"Hey, look, I'm not going to take advantage of a child."

"I've got to get over there."

Buddy did that side-to-side thing again, thinking hard, as if it made his head hurt.

"Okay," he finally said. "Just this once. But you're not paying me any twenty bucks. We're good people here."

*

Buddy kept his 1957 Pontiac Chieftain in the alley behind Main Street. Jeff helped him brush the accumulated snow off the windows with his hands. It started right up and the engine purred.

"Three hundred and fifteen horses," Buddy remarked, "and runs like a top. You like cars?"

"Yeah, sure. Cars are great," Jeff said. He had no more to say on the subject.

Buddy switched on the radio. The trio Peter, Paul and Mary were singing "Blowin' in the Wind" out of WBZ, Boston.

"Damn folk singers," Buddy said.

"What wrong with them?"

"Fags and commies," Buddy said.

They drove south on Main Street a few blocks to Bridge Street and then down to the river.

"Wow," Jeff said. "It's a real old-timey covered bridge!"

"Longest one ever built," Buddy said. "At least, this sort of design. It's called lattice truss. Put up in 1866, and still goin' strong, ayuh."

An antique sign over the entrance read, Walk your horses or pay two dollar fine.

On the New Hampshire side, they headed north on Route 12-A. Jeff glanced at his watch. It was ten minutes after four. Buddy switched on his headlights in the gathering twilight. The road ran right next to the Connecticut River, but it was barely visible out the window and, with the lights on, the large snowflakes came at the car like antiaircraft flak.

"Hey, mind if I ask, where'd you live down there in the city with your mother gone and all?"

"I lived at the orphanage."

"Oh, dear."

"It was okay, for an orphanage."

They turned off 12-A onto the Saint-Gaudens Road, as it was called. The snowflakes drove against the windshield hypnotically.

"Here's the artist's place, Saint-Gaudens," Buddy said, as they passed the historic marker by the roadside.

"Where's Salinger's?"

"Just a little farther."

Two more left turns and Buddy pulled up alongside the edge of the narrow road. A snow-covered Jeep was parked in a little clearing across from the house. A plain fence of horizontal slats stood between the road and the house, but lights glowed above it from dormer windows on the upper floor.

"We're here, sonny. Looks like someone's home."

"He's married, I read, supposedly with two kids."

"How'd you find that out?"

"*Time* magazine."

"Ayuh. They'd know, I guess. Well, you'll have plenty of company in there, then. Say, what's your name, anyway? You never did say."

"It's Holden."

"That's an odd name."

"It's from one of Mr. Salinger's books. Did you happen to read any of them?"

"Never did," Buddy said. "He never pushed 'em on us either. Just wanted to hang around with us kids. A little odd, now that you mention it."

"Well, here goes, I guess. If he's home and all, I'll come back down and tell you it's okay to leave without me."

"Okay, if you say so. Good luck."

"Remember, don't take off until I say so."

"I heard you the first time. Go on. This snow's getting worse."

On the radio, Roy Orbison launched into his hit "In Dreams" to a cha-cha beat.

Jeff pulled the peak of his hunting hat forward to keep the snow off his face and stepped out of the car. It was coming down even harder now, with two inches already accumulated on the ground. Jeff found the gate through the fence and went in. About seventy-five feet ahead stood a modest dwelling with a gambrel roof and an addition with two lighted dormers. Two windows on the first floor also glowed dimly.

He trudged through the snow toward what appeared to be a small entrance deck there. His footsteps were the first to disturb the snow on it. Jeff glanced back to see Buddy's headlights through the slat fence, turned to address the door, found the doorbell, and pressed it. He was unsure whether he heard anything like a chime within. He waited half a minute and tried it again. His heart sank as he was forced to realize that possibly nobody was home after all. In a last desperate move, he opened the storm door and rapped vigorously on the window there. He was about to knock one last time when the door flew open to the inside and a huge figure loomed above him, his height exaggerated by the step up at the doorsill. Jeff almost fell against him but recovered his balance. The looming figure was dressed in a green utility jumpsuit, the kind worn by school janitors. Though his head was back lit, Jeff could tell the face was pretty much the same long, grave horsey face that was on the cover of *Time*, September 15, 1961.

"Oh, Christ!" a voice boomed. "Not the goddam hat! Who the hell are you?"

"Sorry," Jeff said. "I couldn't hear any bell ring, so I had to knock."

"Do you think that isn't obvious?" the figure said. "The bell's out of order. What do you want."

"You're Mr. J. D. Salinger, aren't you?"

"Possibly. Depends. Look, I can see there's a car over there out past the fence. You go out to whoever is waiting and back to where you came from." The giant figure stepped back within and closed the door firmly in Jeff's face. Jeff stood there for a minute, confounded, then dropped his rucksack on the deck, bustled back down the stairs, across the snowy lawn, and through the gate out to Buddy's waiting Pontiac. Buddy rolled down the window.

"By jeezum, that took long enough," he said.

"He's home," Jeff said. "You can take off."

"Did you tell him you're his long-lost son?"

"No. Not yet. I'll get around to it."

"I hope so. Well, if it turns out you end up living here and all, come around to the shop for another haircut sometime, and bring your dad with you. I wouldn't mind saying hello again after all this time."

"Sure, Buddy. I'll tell him. And thanks. For ride and the haircut."

Jeff stood in the road and watched Buddy execute a three-point turn to retrace his journey back to Windsor. When the taillights disappeared through the scrim of snow, he returned to the deck, opened the storm door, and rapped briskly on the window again. He had to knock three times between intervals (out of politeness), until the door was flung open.

"You again! Didn't I tell you to get lost?"

"I don't believe you put it that way, exactly."

"Well, that was the gist of it. Now, get lost!"

The door banged shut in Jeff's face again.

He could see what Buddy the barber meant about Salinger being tart with uninvited guests. The famous author's manner was like an icepick to the guts. Though the snow was coming down ever harder by the minute, the air temperature wasn't so bad, hovering around thirty. There was a built-in bench on the deck opposite the door. Jeff swept the snow off a patch of it, pulled the ear flaps down from inside his hat, and took a seat to figure out his next move. He quickly concluded that it would be unwise to try hoofing it back to town in this storm. He'd probably get lost on the maze of roads that brought him here and freeze to death. He decided to just keep knocking on the door until either Salinger let him in the house, or somebody else, his wife maybe, answered the door and took pity on him or made Salinger drive him back to town, or, a final possibility: he'd drive Salinger so crazy that the author of *The Catcher in the Rye* would have to kill him right there on the deck, which Jeff judged to be an extremely unlikely outcome. He returned to the door.

This time he had to knock five times at ten-second intervals before the door got flung open again.

"What's the matter with you?" Salinger boomed. "Have you no decency?"

"I'm decent," Jeff explained. "I just read your goddam book. It was the best book ever."

"Which book? I've got more than one."

"You know which."

"*Raise High the Roof Beam*? That one just came out. It's my latest."

"I read the beginning of that one in the town library just today."

"Failed to interest you, I suppose."

"It's a different kind of book."

"Ya think? As if I'm going to write the same goddam book over and over again, leaving another trail of cookie crumbs that deranged kids like you will follow to my door to ruin my peace and quiet on a winter night?"

"No."

"That book of mine you read is old stuff. Water over the dam, get it? Dead and buried."

"Holden's not dead."

"Sure he is. I killed him."

"Not in the book, you didn't. He was alive in a mental hospital somewhere when it ended."

"Yeah, well, I made him up and I can do what I want with him, and I say he's dead."

"I'm Holden. There are thousands of other Holdens out there now."

"Well, I'm sorry you feel that way, but Holden is no more. I've moved on. Now, how about you move on—Hey, where the hell's that goddam car you came up here in?"

"He's gone. I told him he could take off."

"You told him—Are you out of your ever lovin' mind? There's a snowstorm!"

"I told him it was okay, you were home."

"You're goddam right I'm home, and I'm alone for a goddam change, and I like I like it that way."

Salinger slammed the door shut in Jeff's face yet again.

This time, Jeff did not wait politely. He knocked and kept on knocking until the door flung open again.

"You're a goddam pest, you know that?" Salinger said.

"Are you going to leave me out here in a goddam snowstorm?"

"Might be good for you. You know how many nights I slept in a cold foxhole in the Hürtgen Forest?"

"I have no idea."

"Plenty, that's how many. And look on the bright side. Nobody's lobbing artillery rounds at you here. You could curl up under that bench and have yourself a nice peaceful little snooze and find your way back to wherever you came from when the sun comes up."

"Are you nuts? I'll freeze out here. Look, I came here because your book meant so much to me and I have something important to tell you."

"Yeah? You're probably Yama, the god of death. Like in the *Twilight Zone* episode a few weeks ago with Mickey Rooney living in a cheap hotel."

"For chrissake, Jerry, I'm just a kid. Can't you just cut the crap and let me in?"

"Who said you can call me Jerry? Who gave you permission?"

"When you used to hang out with the high schoolers, they called you Jerry. You told them to."

"Oh, I see now. Which one of that goddam troop of baboons was it that drove you here?"

"I'm not going to tell you."

"You better."

"You can't make me."

"Jesus Christ, this is getting so goddam juvenile."

"Then just let me inside and we can both act like normal human beings."

"I can't believe this is happening."

"It's not a *Twilight Zone* episode, Mr. Salinger. It's real life."

"Oh, for godsake. Come in, then. You're letting all the goddam heat out of the house. And call me Jerry. I hate formal crap."

Chapter Sixteen

"Please," J. D. Salinger said when they were both in the kitchen. "Take the goddam hat off, at least. I can't stand the hat. And have a goddam seat."

Salinger sat down, too, across the kitchen table.

"I got this hat at Abercrombie and Fitch," Jeff said. "It's a fine hat."

"You got gypped, I'm sure. You could buy the exact same hat at the army-navy store for half the price."

"I didn't see any army-navy stores around. I happened to be on Madison down in the forties somewhere, and Abercrombie's was right there. You know the place?"

"Yeah, sure, across from Brooks Brothers."

"That's right."

"You're a New York kid, though. I can tell."

"Yeah, and so were you, once upon a time."

"How would you know."

"Obviously Holden was you once."

"What I was once is none of your goddam business."

"Anyway, I read about your whole life in *Time* magazine."

"Oh, Jesus. Don't talk to me about that odious rag."

"It was a good article. It was very informative."

"Is there some magazine article I can read about you?"

"Not yet," Jeff said.

For the first time that evening, Salinger's demeanor changed. He actually cracked a smile and grudged up a slight laugh.

"You're piece of work, kid. What's your actual name?"

"They call me Ace."

"Ace, huh?" Salinger appeared impressed. "That's a name for a ballplayer or a tail gunner on a B-17."

"Don't talk to me about ballplayers," Jeff said. "My girlfriend was messing around with one."

"You have a girlfriend?"

"It was brief romance, but quite intense."

"That's rich. What are you eleven, twelve years old?"

"I'm twelve."

"Twelve-year-olds don't have girlfriends."

"You can if you try."

"Is that so?"

"She was older, though, thirteen."

"Aha! An older woman. A woman of the world!"

"She was an actress on Broadway."

"Get outa here!"

"No, for real. She plays one of the kids in *The Wayward Family Singers.* I saw the show and went backstage to meet her. Do you know that show?"

"Why wouldn't I?"

"Because you live up here in the North Woods a million miles from Broadway."

"They play that goddam song from it on the radio all the time. And I get down to New York quite frequently, for your information."

"But you haven't seen it in person."

"God no. Why would I go see such a meretricious piece of crap like that?"

"I don't know. You might have took your kids. It's been playing for a whole year. By the way, it said in *Time* that you were married and had two kids. Where is everybody?"

"If you mention the name of that goddam piece of trash again, I'll toss you back out in the snow."

"Okay, sorry. But where is everybody?"

"My wife took the kids to New York for the weekend."

"Why didn't you go with them?"

"Because I wanted a little peace and quiet for change, and now here I am jawing away the dwindling minutes of the afternoon with a twelve-year-old."

"I can shut up, if you want."

"I don't know what to do with you, frankly. I'd take you over to Windsor except there's already four or five inches on the ground and I neglected to put the goddam snow tires on the goddam Jeep and Claire took the other goddam car to New York."

"Does that mean I can stick around?"

"I don't see any alternative. So, as long as you're here, I guess I can catch up on doings in my old hometown. Dear little old New York."

Salinger seemed to have a faraway look in his eyes. To Jeff, the author seemed inexpressibly sad, as from an old irreparable injury.

"The same old things are there," Jeff said. "The duck pond in the park. The merry-go-round. The crummy joints in Times Square."

"I had a romance with a young actress once," Salinger said. "She was Eugene O'Neill's daughter."

"Who's that?"

"You don't know?"

"I might have heard his name, but . . ."

"He was only the most celebrated playwright on Broadway. Frankly, I didn't go for his stuff. It was overwrought and histrionic, but they gave him all the goddam prizes. His daughter, though, Oona, was a heavenly creature. We used to go to the Stork Club."

"That's still around, I think, the Stork Club."

"It's a pale shadow of itself. This was back when it was absolutely the place to be."

"Oona. That's a strange name."

"It's Gaelic. It means lamb. She broke my heart. Ran off and married Charlie Chaplin."

"What! From the silent movies, the Little Tramp?"

"Yup, that one."

"He must be a hundred years old."

"He was fifty-four then. But she was just eighteen. He was a goddam cradle robber. Married two other teenagers before her and dumped them both."

"How did he sneak onto the scene?"

"Oona was trying to be an actress out in Hollywood, the eighth circle of hell. The place is full of degenerate old bastards like Charlie. He bamboozled her."

"Jeez, that's a tough break, Jerry. What'd you do?"

"The war was happening."

"Were you in it?"

"Yeah, I was in it."

"Did you fight the Nazis or the Japs?"

"Didn't I already say I was in a foxhole in the goddam Hürtgen Forest?"

"I don't know where that is."

"It's in Germany, just over the line from Belgium."

"Did you shoot any Nazis?"

"Let's not talk about that, if you don't mind, kid."

Salinger got up and went to the refrigerator and took out a pitcher of filtered water, poured two glasses, and brought them back to the table.

"Water?" Jeff said.

"Well, it's not gin."

"Don't you have a Coke or something?"

"Soda's poison. You know how many teaspoons of sugar there are in a Coke?"

"I don't know."

"Guess."

"Three, four?"

"Ten."

"You're kidding."

"I wouldn't kid you about it. That crap'll kill you. Take ten years off your life, anyway. This is good clean mountain spring water, with additional filtration. Your body will thank you."

"How about a hot chocolate?"

"What do you think this is, Schrafft's? Drink your water!"

Jeff followed Salinger's instructions.

"You should tell your wife to take the kids to see *The Wayward Family Singers*," Jeff said.

"I doubt they could stay awake long enough to sit through a Broadway show. They're going to the zoo, more likely. Maybe to the Museum of Natural History to see the shrunken heads and the whale."

"I love the shrunken heads!" Jeff said. "How do you know about them?"

"They had 'em when I was a kid, too."

"They look so peaceful, with their lips sewn up and all. Anyway, the girl in the show was Kathy Kaine. She's a terrific singer."

"Your so-called girlfriend?"

"Yeah. She plays the middle daughter. The one who ends up on Franklin D. Roosevelt's lap in the grand finale."

"Cute. So how'd you get to meet her?"

"I went backstage and asked."

"That was cheeky."

"It was the night before Thanksgiving."

"Where were your parents?"

"They weren't around."

"You go to Broadway shows by yourself?"

"Yeah, sure. Didn't you?"

"It was a long time ago. I mean, I went to shows. Maybe *The Boys from Syracuse*. Rodgers and Hart. Great music in that one!"

"I had some money, and I was down there, so I bought a ticket to the matinee."

"That's right. Wednesday is the matinee day."

"And there was no evening show that night because of the holiday, next day. So I asked her to go out for dinner."

"You're quite the gentleman!"

"You have no idea how beautiful she is. She killed me."

"I know the feeling."

"She lives at the Bomoseen Hotel on Seventy-first up on the West Side."

"I know the place well. Used to take girls there to the Champlain Bar."

"We had drinks in her suite."

"Get outa here! Drinks? Who are you Nick and Nora Charles?"

"Who are they?"

"*The Thin Man*."

"Oh, like the TV show."

"No, the original movie. Much better than the TV show. Nineteen thirty-four. William Powell and Myrna Low. Superb together. Sparkling dialogue! I have it here."

"The movie? You have a projector and all?"

"I've got dozens of movies. Maybe I'll show you one, if it'll get you to shut up."

"Really? You can go to the movies right in your own house?"

"It beats the idiot box. No commercials. So how the hell did she get drinks in her hotel room, this so-called girlfriend of yours?"

"The elevator man would get it for her. She had him under her spell."

"Figures. There's always some little creep like that on the scene in a New York hotel. Did the two of you get bombed?"

"Not exactly. But it was the first time I really tried booze. I could feel it, all right. She wanted to go to her favorite restaurant, the Gay Hussar, on Amsterdam, around Seventy-fourth—"

"I know that joint! Grand place. I took girls there myself in the old days."

"And the waiter knew her because she ate there a lot. He gave her more drinks."

"You say she was thirteen?"

"She could make herself look older. She's somewhat developed, too. They wouldn't give me any booze drinks, though. She got bombed and almost tossed her cookies on the way back to the hotel."

"Mmmmph. Some way to start a romance."

"Anyway, she was all sad because she couldn't go back home to Milwaukee for Thanksgiving. Her parents were split up and her dad was out of the picture and her mom had this crummy boyfriend, and she had to be onstage Friday night for the show . . . so I invited her to my family's Thanksgiving, which turned out to be a huge mess because it was a big fancy party at my Uncle Ira's penthouse and . . ."

Jeff went on to explain how Kathy got all dolled up for the occasion, and several grown-up young men had plied her with drinks, including that infielder for the New York Mets, and how he, Jeff, was getting so annoyed that he tossed the pumpkin off the terrace, and how that went, and finally how Kathy was singing show tunes with a guy playing the piano but then tossed her cookies all over Uncle Ira's oriental rug. And how he, Jeff, encountered the same ballplayer in the hallway of Kathy's floor of the Bomoseen coming out of the elevator the next day when he, Jeff, went to see her one last time.

"I don't think I'll be seeing old Kathy Kaine again," Jeff said with a deep sigh.

"Sounds like a bestseller someone could write: *Babycakes on Broadway.*"

"You could, Jerry."

"Are you kidding? I've got other fish to fry," Salinger said. "Speaking of fried fish, I suppose you want some dinner."

"I'm pretty goddam hungry," Jeff admitted.

"Hey, do me a favor, Ace. Can you quit saying 'goddam' every other word?"

"That's how you talk."

"Okay, I set a bad example. Stipulated. But please, clean it up a little, okay? Anyway, it's getting on five-thirty and we generally eat early around here. Better for your digestion and for sleep. So I'll get cracking on that, if you don't mind."

"Sure, Jerry. Have you got a bathroom?"

"What do you think we are, Aborigines? Far side of the living room, that way, by the kids' rooms." Salinger pointed through the kitchen door to the dim interstices of the house. "Don't forget to put up the seat."

*

Salinger was bustling around the kitchen when Jeff returned. He'd put something in the oven and was prepping up carrot sticks and celery. A loaf of very dense brown bread was already sitting on a cutting board on the table with several slices carved out and then cut in half. Jeff sat down again.

"Do you mind if I have some of this bread?"

"That's what it's there for."

"Got any butter, by any chance?"

"This is better for you." Salinger brought over a bowl of some brown mush with a spreader jammed in it.

"What is it?"

"Hummus. Mashed chickpeas with sesame paste and olive oil."

Jeff tried a bit on a piece of bread.

"You like it?" Salinger asked.

"It's okay. The bread's quite good."

"Not like that fluffy white garbage they sell at the supermarket."

"This is very chewy, all right. What have you got against butter, though?"

"It gets into your blood vessels and sticks to the lining and by the time you're forty-three you can drop dead of a heart attack."

"You must be around that age, Jerry."

"You're goddam right, and I intend to see ninety."

Jerry returned to the stove and took two lumps of meat out of the oven on a small metal pan. He plated them, along with the carrot and celery sticks, with some frozen green peas that had barely been in hot water long enough to defrost them and brought them to table.

"Dinner is served," he said.

"This meat is still a little pink on the outside," Jeff observed.

"I cook it to only a hundred and fifty degrees. Preserves all its nutritional value. Those char-broiled hockey pucks you get everywhere are pure death. We overcook everything in this moronic country."

Jeff poked at the grayish-pink lump.

"What kind of meat is this, anyway?"

"It's organic ground lamb. I get it from the health food store up in Hanover where Dartmouth College is. I know the fellow who raises the sheep."

"Have you got any ketchup, by any chance?"

"Now you're really out of order, Ace. Do you know how much sugar there is in a bottle of ketchup? How many teaspoons?"

"Five?"

"Guess again."

"I dunno. Ten?"

"Keep going."

"Twenty?"

"Nope. Twenty-four."

"Twenty-four, Jeezus!"

"Yeah, I'll say. Pure poison. I daresay, ounce for ounce, it's worse for you than goddam ice cream."

"Funny, though, you don't think of ketchup as putting sugar on your hamburger. It's more like a . . . a tangy taste."

"That's the vinegar. Gives it that edge. Hides the sugar. The wizards at the Heinz factory figured it all out long ago. There's some salt next to the napkin rack, by the way."

Jeff shook quite a bit out on the meat.

"Hey, easy there, pardner! That stuff'll kill you, too."

He watched Jeff struggle to choke down a forkful.

"Good, huh?"

"It's a little undercooked," Jeff said.

"What'd I just tell you about cooking?"

"Okay. But how come people all over the world cook their food? And probably have since the caveman days?"

"Science as we know it barely existed until a hundred years ago. Less, really. In some places, it still doesn't exist. Now we can measure everything. We know what food does to the body. Ice cream, for instance, will form a bolus of fat and milk solids and start putrefying in your upper intestine, and it'll make the whole, long journey to the . . . the other end . . . in this putrid mass, emitting poisons all the way down through the lining into your bloodstream where it travels to every organ in your body."

"That's disgusting."

"You're goddam right it's disgusting. It's a crime to get the whole population of the USA hooked on this stuff. You might as well get 'em all on dope. They're sugar addicts! And I'll tell you something else. That fluffy white bread everybody eats is no better than the sugar. Here, try some of this hummus on a carrot stick or some celery. You'll think you're in the faculty lounge of an Ivy League college."

Salinger addressed his own plate with what looked like actorish delectation, admiring the meat on each forkful before popping it in his mouth. Jeff horsed down his lump as quickly as possible to get it over with, then made short work of the peas. This allowed him to enjoy two more slices of the bread, which actually tasted like something a person would want to eat, chewy and nutty.

"When all is said and done," Salinger resumed, "eating is little more than an inescapable imposition on everything else in one's day."

"I like food," Jeff said. "I've been eating hamburgers and ice cream my whole life and I'm perfectly okay."

"You're a child. Your body can take the punishment now. But believe me, day by day, bite by bite, America is destroying itself. If we get to the year 2000 without blowing up the whole goddam works, this country is going to be a land of three-hundred-pound slobs—and I'm just talking about the girls! Put your plate up there on the counter by the sink and we'll wash them tomorrow. All this talk about dear little old New York has put me in the mood for a movie. Let's go in there."

Salinger dipped his large head in the direction of the living room. He got up and Jeff followed.

Jeff took a seat on a very plush blue velvet sectional sofa while Salinger rummaged through a pile of film cans on the floor until he found what he wanted and proceeded to load the projector. Then he fetched a portable screen that resided in a corner beside a bookshelf, and he stood it up on the far side of a coffee table stacked with New Yorker magazines and books.

"What are you putting on?"

"You'll love it, I'm sure."

"What's it say there on the can?"

"*Swing Time*, with Fred Astaire and Ginger Rogers."

"Uccchhh."

"You're in no position to be picky. I bet you don't even know who Fred Astaire is."

"Sure I do. He wears a goddam top hat and dances like maniac."

"So, you're a film buff, huh?"

"I've seen a million movies."

Salinger rolled the projector and switched off a lamp on a side table. Jeff endured about ten minutes of the preposterous story that was only an excuse for the dance numbers.

"I'm sure I've seen this before," Jeff said. "*The Million Dollar Movie*, on channel nine. They show everything."

"It's worth seeing again. Fred Astaire's a great artist. Underappreciated, I might add. Look how graceful they are up there."

"You must have the movie around here that Holden was so crazy about, *The 39 Steps*."

"Please, not Holden again."

"Why do you hate him so much?"

"I don't hate him. I'm just tired of hearing about him."

"We don't have to talk about him. It must be a great movie, though, the way he went on about it."

"He didn't go on about it. He just mentions he went to see it with his little sister Phoebe. That passage is about Phoebe, not the goddam movie so much."

"Yeah, but he tells you part of the plot."

"Only the bit about the guy missing the tip of his finger."

"Doesn't that kind of give away the story?"

"Hey, Ace. I wrote the goddam book, you know. I remember how it goes. I happen to get a lot of mail from readers and nobody ever complained about me ruining the movie for them."

"Do you happen to have it here, *The 39 Steps*? You must have it."

"Yeah, it's around here somewhere."

"I never saw it. It must be a hell of movie."

"It's quite good," Salinger agreed.

"Do me a favor and put it on. I'd like to see it."

"Aw, for chrissake. If you insist."

Salinger turned on the light, got *Swing Time* on rewind, and rummaged around the dozens of film cans on the floor.

"I got it," he said at the same moment that *Swing Time* stopped rewinding with a flap-flap-flapping noise. He switched the reels efficiently and *The 39 Steps* came on the screen.

"The master," Salinger declared.

"Who?"

"Hitchcock. The director."

"Oh, the same guy who made *Psycho*. Did you see that?"

"Yeah. It lacked the subtlety of his earlier films."

"It scared the living shit out of me," Jeff said. "When you go down to the cellar and the chair swings around and you see that Anthony Perkins's mother is a mummified corpse. Jeezus!"

"Hey, shut up and pay attention since you asked for this. And in case you can't tell, it takes place in jolly old England," Salinger said as the credits dissolved into the opening music hall scene where "Mr.

Memory" is doing his act, answering miscellaneous questions from the audience.

"Hey this is really old," Jeff said. "Looks like the nineteen thirties."

"That's not so long ago."

"It is to me."

"Button it, will you?"

By the time the melee in the music hall was over, and Robert Donat, playing the Canadian Richard Hannay, returned to his London flat with the mysterious foreign lady, Jeff had fallen fast asleep.

Chapter Seventeen

When Jeff woke up, his shoes were off and there was a wool blanket over him. He heard Salinger banging around in the kitchen and quickly apprehended where he was. He pulled himself up, flung the blanket off, and padded into the kitchen. A radio was playing lowly in the background.

"Hey, it's still snowing out," Jeff observed.

"Yeah, I've noticed," Salinger said. He was back in his workingman's jumpsuit.

"I guess I conked out before the movie barely got going. Sorry."

"Your loss."

"I'll see the rest of it someday, I'm sure."

"On the *Million Dollar Movie*, no doubt."

"Probably. Hey, what day is it? I've lost track."

"Sunday."

"Oh, jeez. Everybody'll be going back today."

"Going back where?"

"To school."

"What school is that?"

"Ponsonby Hall."

"You're a Ponsonby kid?"

"Yeah. I got sent there last September. For being a screwup. It's a school for screwups, you know."

"Hmmmph. I should have guessed. It's over in Orcus, right?"

"Yeah, Orcus is the nearest town. You weren't sent there as a kid, were you, by any chance?"

"Gawd no. I wasn't that much of a screwup. That headmaster of yours, Stilgoe, self-important prick, came to our town meeting and tried to lecture us about the archaeology of the Abenaki Indians when we were trying to just put up a new firehouse."

"Yeah, he's a fiend for Indians. Wrote several books about 'em."

"Yes, he told us all about them. Seriously, If I had to go back to that school, I might entertain committing suicide," Salinger said.

"I kind of like it, being away from New York, having the woods all around. There's even a lake. I'm going out for the junior rowing crew in the spring."

"That's grand."

"Did you get sent away to school or go to one in the city?"

"Away. Valley Forge Academy, a military school."

"So, not Pencey Prep, then?"

"Pencey Prep is a made-up place. But Valley Forge happens to be in Pennsylvania."

"Did you like it there?"

"It was all right. I got along with the guys."

"You get the feeling in the book that Holden secretly liked Pencey Prep quite a bit since he took his time leaving the place. Several chapters, actually."

"Did I fail to make it clear? We're not talking about him."

"I'm just saying—"

"Find something else to say."

"Okay." Jeff took a seat at the kitchen table. "Have you got any cereal around, by any chance?"

"No."

"You have kids and you don't have cereal in the house?"

"Claire feeds the kids. I don't know what she gives them."

"Really? How about we rummage around and see what's in there."

"There will be no rummaging. You can have what I'm having."

"What are you having?"

"Lovely peas and brown bread and some apple."

"Goddam peas! For breakfast! Who eats peas for—"

"Shut up!"

"—break—"

"Shaddup!" Salinger lunged for the radio and turned up the volume. "Weather report's on," he said. "Be still!"

". . . Fourteen inches at the Lebanon airport, sixteen inches at Claremont," the radio said, "and fifteen reported at Thetford. The storm is expected to move through the area entirely by eleven o'clock today. We'll see a high of thirty-three here in Hanover with a little sunshine breaking out late in the day . . ."

"Goddam it," Salinger said.

"Hey, it's going to be all over in a few hours."

"The goddam town doesn't even start plowing until after the last goddam snowflake falls, and they don't get to these back roads up here until after they clean up the highways. Which means, I'm probably stuck with you until then. Do your parents have any idea where you are?"

"Probably not."

"Don't you think they're kind of worried?"

"Yeah, I suppose."

"Maybe you should call them up."

"I prefer not to."

"They're probably out of their goddam minds with worry. Go ahead, call them. There's a phone right on the wall over there."

"I prefer not to."

Salinger glared at Jeff.

"Who do think you are? Bartleby the goddam scrivener?"

"You know that book?"

"Of course. I'm a goddam professional writer."

"We read it at school in October. I loved how he kept saying that, I prefer not to, until he drove everybody else in the story nuts."

"Yeah, Melville. He kills me. Sonofabitch could write," Salinger said with a faraway look, which he quickly snapped out of. "Look, I'm driving you up to that goddam school of yours as soon as the road is clear. Got that?"

"Yeah, that would great. How come you haven't called the police, if you don't mind me asking?"

"Do you want me to call the police?"

"No."

"Because that's all I need. Police crawling all over the house. You think I could keep that out of the papers?"

"I don't know."

"Well, let me assure you, I couldn't. Next thing you know, every goddam newspaper and magazine in New York would send some moron reporter up here and I'd be accused of harboring a fugitive minor. Acchhh. I can't even stand to think about it! Let's put it this way. At the first opportunity I'm driving you up to Orcus without any goddam fanfare and dropping you off at that school for juvenile delinquents, and that'll be the end of this horrible episode. And you better keep your trap shut about ever being here with me. Now, let's just have a peaceful breakfast, if you don't mind."

Salinger put the block of frozen peas in the now boiling water to blanche, sliced up what remained of last night's bread, and brought it to the table with apples cored and cut into eight slices each, plus a jar of honey. Then he brought Jeff a small glass of milk. A minute later, he drained the peas and served them in two saucers.

"Peas for breakfast," Jeff shook his head. "That's the weirdest thing I've ever seen."

"You think? Want to know the weirdest thing I've ever seen?"

"Sure."

"Guy hanging sixty feet up in a pine tree from a parachute with his head blown clean off."

"Jeezus. Where'd you see that?"

"Where do you think?"

"That's pretty terrible. Did you have to shoot anybody there?"

"That subject is closed."

"You brought it up."

"Well, I'm shutting it back down. Try the peas. They're delightful."

"Delightful! That's a riot."

They proceeded to eat in silence. Jeff choked down a few spoonfuls of the peas, then slathered honey on two slices of bread, and topped them off with some apple slices.

"This isn't too bad," he remarked. "But the milk tastes funny."

"It's goat's milk."

Jeff put the glass down as if it were a live hand grenade.

"Goat's milk, for chrissake!"

"Much better for you than that pasteurized crap from the supermarket."

"Don't you do anything like a normal person, Jerry?"

Salinger appeared stung.

"What's your idea of normal?" he said.

"Pancakes for breakfast."

"Let the morons out in normal land have their pancakes. I'll stick with what I eat. You know what your problem is, Ace?"

"Yeah, I'm a screwup, apparently."

"You can get over that. That's easy. Your problem is you're too attached to the things of this world."

"Attached? What's that supposed to mean? Sounds like you really think I should commit suicide."

"Not at all. I'll explain later. I have to do my morning meditation practice now. I'll be back in about an hour."

Salinger got up, traipsed through the living room to a staircase deeper within the house, and vanished.

*

When he was quite sure that Salinger was gone and out of earshot, Jeff got up and began peeking into the cabinets above the kitchen counters. They contained many boxes, glass jars, and sacks of things he was unfamiliar with: lentils, chickpeas, nuts, seeds, desiccated strips that looked like mummies of fruit. But in one cabinet beside the refrigerator he discovered a box of Kellogg's Rice Krispies. He had to wonder whether Salinger had been lying, or if he was so dissociated from the things of his own household that he didn't know his wife kept a box of the reviled breakfast cereal there.

He took the box out. It seemed pretty light. In another cabinet near the sink he found a stack of china bowls and he poured what turned out to be the remaining contents of the Rice Krispies box into it. The refrigerator was a wilderness of things in covered dishes, wax paper bundles, and glass jars that he could not identify. The goat's milk he'd been served was one of them, but he had not even finished what he was given, and he did not want to put the stuff, redolent of a barnyard, on his Rice Krispies. Finally, there was nothing else to do but put on a few gobs of honey, and so the cereal ended up being a sticky mass that was barely manageable with a spoon—but actually quite tasty.

Jeff was careful to put the empty Rice Krispies box back where he found it, dogged a little by the thought Salinger's wife would eventually be perplexed by it. He was, at least, no longer hungry. After washing the bowl and carefully putting it back, he repaired to the living room and found an Admiral-brand console TV with a deluxe-sized twenty-three-inch screen in a moderne-style cabinet behind the movie screen Salinger had set up. Jeff moved the movie screen aside and turned on the TV. A game show on NBC called *Word for Word* was underway, hosted by a personable young fellow named Merv Griffin. The contestants had to decipher word puzzles. The reception was poor. Reception of the other two national networks on the dial, CBS and ABC, was even worse, like watching TV in exactly the sort of blizzard that had hit New Hampshire overnight. Yet, for all that, Jeff managed to lose himself in Merv's shenanigans with words, and by the time the next show came on—*The Price Is Right*—Salinger appeared back in the doorway to the living room.

"I'm crazy about that show," he declared. "They really manage to get perfect morons every day, day after day."

"Do you actually watch this show?"

"I catch it now and then, for laughs."

"You watch daytime TV?"

"Occasionally, yeah. Any sign of the goddam snowplow?"

"I don't think so. It's been real quiet out there."

Salinger strode into the kitchen and went to the window.

"Yeah, the road is still pristine. Looks like the snow's finally letting up, though, thank God."

He returned to the living room, switched off the TV, and took a seat on the side of the sectional sofa that curved around.

"I thought you wanted to watch it?" Jeff said.

Salinger merely cocked his head slightly and smiled as though he were enjoying an inside joke with himself.

"How was . . . whatever that thing is you did?" Jeff asked.

"Mediation. It was . . . nothing."

"Then why do you do it?"

"Aha!" Salinger said, snapping a finger. "Exactly!"

"Huh?"

"You got it!"

"What'd I get?"

"Zen."

"What's Zen?"

"It's a school of Buddhism."

"That'. . . what? Some Chinese religion?"

"Japanese mainly. And not strictly a religion. More like a practice. It emphasizes meditation for achieving enlightenment."

"Okay. So what's enlightenment?"

"Serene detachment from the things of this world."

"Oh, what you said before in the kitchen. I'm too attached."

"Correct. Now, Zen uses little riddles or tales as a way to provoke insight and cleanse the mind of clichés, habitual thoughts, and other useless mental garbage. Often, they're posed as short questions and short answers, like we just did moments ago."

"What was that?"

"I said, 'Mediation was nothing' and you replied, 'Then why do you do it?' See?"

"Not really."

"Okay. The object of meditation is to clear the crap out of your head, so it's really about getting into a mental state of nothing. You see now? That was a paradoxical question and answer. Meditation is about getting to a place of nothing in the mind. That's why you do it."

"Are you saying you can't stand your thoughts?"

"Most people are quite discontented with the crap flowing through their brains."

"I don't mind the crap in mine," Jeff said.

"You'd be surprised. Or maybe you're just too young to have noticed. Believe me, after a while it gets to be a terrific burden, like Jacob Marley, the ghost in Dickens's *Christmas Carol* who wanders around limbo wearing those heavy chains of guilt and regret that dog his mind. You know A *Christmas Carol*, right?"

"Oh sure. They play it on *The Million Dollar Movie* for a whole week at Christmastime every year. I remember old Jacob Marley. I'm crazy about the ending when old Scrooge finally breaks down and goes to his nephew's house on Christmas morning and asks everyone to forgive him, and they play this beautiful old English song—"

"'Barbara Allen.' Yes, that that's the 1951 version of the story, with Alastair Sim as Scrooge. It's the best one"

"It kills me, that part. Every time I see it. It almost makes you cry."

"Yes . . . Well, anyway, if you like Christmas, which I'm not crazy about—"

"How can you not like Christmas, for chrissake?"

"Two words," Salinger said. "The Ardennes Forest."

"That's three words."

"The 'the' doesn't count."

"Okay. What about it?"

"You don't want to know."

"How do you know what I want to know?"

"It's a figure of speech, Ace. Translation: don't ask," Salinger said and shifted in his seat as if suddenly he couldn't get comfortable.

"We've strayed from the subject, haven't we, which is letting go of the things of this world."

"I don't want to let go of the things of this world. Well, maybe some of them. I'd probably let go of studying Latin, if they let me. I'd gladly let go of peas for breakfast—"

"Uh, uh, uh . . . Don't start in on the peas!"

"Just saying."

"You're always just saying. You should try just listening."

"Okay, I'll listen. Really. Go ahead."

"Anyway, Zen isn't the point here really. I've ventured beyond that into the original source of Buddhism, the spiritual and philosophical traditions of India, specifically as influenced by the Vedic line, which later evolved into Hinduism."

"I don't know anything about that."

"Which is exactly why we're having this conversation. Would you like to learn?"

"Okay, I'll give it a try."

"If you're searching for tranquillity of the mind, you might consider reading *The Gospel of Sri Ramakrishna* and Paramhansa Yogananda's *Autobiography of a Yogi*. A yogi, in India, is a holy man. A spiritual guide. You must study them. The goal is to manifest divinity inside yourself by controlling your own place in nature, through mental discipline. You must help all who are trying to do good, practice patience, purity, and perseverance. Faith in the divine calls out the divinity within. You achieve this through diligent meditation."

"I had no idea you were so religious, Jerry."

"You could call it that. But not religious in the usual way."

"If you want to know the truth, this sounds like stuff for old people in the hospital near death. I'm only just starting out in life."

"Ramana Maharshi was seven when he experienced his upanayana, his spiritual awakening, the initiation of the three upper varnas into Brahmanical learning and the knowledge of the self."

"I don't think I'm cut out for that. I'll be happy if I can just get on the junior rowing crew."

"So you want to grow up into a standard American moron?"

"You think everyone's a moron. There are plenty of people who know what the hell they're doing."

"Name one."

"I dunno . . . Yogi Berra, since you're so crazy about yogis."

"Yogi Berra's a major moron. You know what he said about El Morocco?"

"No. What?"

"He said, 'Nobody goes there anymore. It's too crowded.'"

"That sounds like one of those riddles the Japs make up."

"Yeah, well maybe the Buddha, or Jesus Christ, or the Brahman could be lurking inside old Yogi Berra. You never know."

"He's just a catcher who hits good. I'm sure he's not trying to be God, for godsake."

"Forget about Yogi, Ace. I'm sorry I brought him up. I'm curious, why did you come here to see me, anyway?"

"Because your goddam book, which you refuse to even talk about, meant a lot to me. And because I wanted to tell you about President Kennedy."

Salinger flinched. A pained look washed over his long face.

"That was pretty goddam horrible, wasn't it?" he said. "Jeezus, that goddam Oswald."

"I talked to the Russians about it."

"You what? You talked to the Russians?"

"Yeah. In New York."

"Which Russians? Some old bastards on the Upper West Side buying sturgeon and rugelach at Zabar's?"

"No. The guy who's ambassador to the UN."

"Really," Salinger said, cracking a slight smile, skeptical yet interested. "How'd you get in to see him? What are you? Some child prodigy secret agent?"

"He came out to see me."

"How'd you arrange that?"

"I staked out the place. You know that building they've got on Sixty-eighth and Park, the Russkies? I was hanging out there trying to drive the guards crazy. He came out and stuffed me into this big limousine and took me for a ride into Central Park. We went over to a park bench on Pilgrim Hill and he told me what happened."

"What got you all wound up about the Russians that you had to stake them out?"

"This kid at Ponsonby they call Einstein. He's a genius. He does everybody's math homework if you pay him. The day Kennedy got shot, he told me the Russians and the Cubans were behind it. What'd you think, Jerry, when you heard that Kennedy got shot?"

"Me? I was just stunned, I guess."

"Sure. But didn't you wonder if it was just Oswald, this lone nut, or some plot?"

"Well, the mind does swerve over to plots in something like that."

"You know what the Russian ambassador told me?"

"I don't know. What?"

"He told me the CIA killed Kennedy."

Salinger goggled at Jeff.

"The CIA?" he said. "Our own guys?"

"Yeah, our own guys."

"Why? That doesn't make any goddam sense."

"He said the guy who ran the CIA hated Kennedy's guts."

Salinger sank deeper into the sofa and his brow furrowed.

"A lot of those guys came out of the OSS," he eventually said. "My generation. Guys like me who were in the war, like Kennedy. He was a goddam war hero. PT One-oh-nine. We wouldn't kill Jack Kennedy, one of our own."

"What if they did?"

Salinger retreated somewhere back inside himself again.

"Well?" Jeff pressed him.

"I'd be pretty nervous about what's going on in this country," he finally mumbled. "But why did he pick you, some kid, to tell this to?"

"I happened to be there, I guess. He said no one would ever believe me."

"I'm not so sure I believe you."

"Believe me. He really said all that."

"That's a pretty crazy story, Ace."

"Yeah, but I'm not crazy. I'm not Holden Caulfield."

"That's for sure," Salinger muttered. He got off the sofa and dragged the movie screen back in front of the TV set. "Let's just watch the rest of the goddam movie, if you don't mind, okay? Since it's all cued up on the projector."

"Sure."

"Do you want some popcorn with that?"

"Is it allowed around here?"

"Popcorn? Sure. Why, it's the healthiest snack there is. I'll go make some."

*

They were just at the part late in the story where Richard Hannay (Robert Donat) and the blonde, Pamela, he is handcuffed to (Madeleine Carroll) have just escaped the spies who are after them on the Scottish moor and have taken refuge at a quaint country inn, when both Jeff and Jerry heard the loud, rough scrape of the town snowplow clearing the road outside.

"Is that what I think it is?" Salinger said. He bolted up and darted into the kitchen. "Halle-goddam-lujah," he cried from in there. "Put your shoes on and grab that knapsack of yours. We've been liberated!"

"Can't we just watch the end of the movie?"

"No."

"Jeez, Jerry, there's just a few inches left on the reel."

"I don't give a good goddam. I've seen it fifty times."

"But this is my first time."

"There's an important life lesson for you. The first time for everything doesn't always work out so well. Shake a leg, kid! Chop

chop! Get a move on. It's three o'clock. I want to get back here before dark."

Jeff did as he was told, found his Ponsonby blazer on a peg in the kitchen and his red hunting hat, and threw his muffler around his neck. Salinger was already bundled into his L.L.Bean storm parka and a pair of calf-high rubber boots and led the way out of the house. They waded out to the road and the little clearing across it where the Jeep was parked, grill facing out, humped under its cap of deep snow. Salinger extracted a snow shovel from the back seat and a long-handled snow brush, which he handed to Jeff.

"Clear the windows off while I shovel the front end out," he said. Salinger had a system, apparently, for clearing two paths for the front tires the ten feet or so to the road. It didn't take him long. "Go on, get in."

Salinger turned the key and the engine started right up.

"Good job, Ace. Now pray we can get there without killing ourselves on these tires."

Chapter Eighteen

The storm clouds had broken up into scattered sundry clots. The sun peeked through them and was so low lying that it flashed through the bare trees with an annoying stroboscopic effect. Salinger put on a pair of aviator's sunglasses and still had to cup his left hand around his head to shield his eyes.

"I'm pretty sure I know how to get to this joint. Are you going to call your parents when you get there?"

"I suppose."

"Just do me a favor, will you? Don't tell them you dropped in on me."

"I won't say a thing."

"Didn't you say your father's a lawyer?"

"Yes, I guess I did mention it."

"See, I really don't need trouble."

"Okay. I'll tell them I just ran away back to school."

"I can't spend thousands of dollars on some pain-in-the-ass lawsuit."

"He's not like that."

"They're all like that. And I'm pretty sure you have no idea how pissed off they're going to be at you."

"Relax, Jerry. Nobody will ever know."

"Yeah, well, this time it's me just saying."

"You want me to sew up my lips like the shrunken heads in the museum?"

"Sure. That's a great idea," Salinger said. "You'll get ahead in life a lot better that way, I'm sure." He turned and flashed a smile at Jeff. "You're not a bad kid, actually. I've known a lot worse."

"I'm sorry I didn't get to meet your wife and kids," Jeff said.

"You didn't miss anything."

Salinger reached for the radio knob and turned it on. A young man with a nasal voice was singing a song about being spurned in love above a catchy fingerpicked guitar.

"This is Dartmouth College FM radio WFRD in Hanover, New Hampshire, and that was Mr. Bob Dylan with 'Don't Think Twice, It's All Right,' off his album, released earlier this year, *The Freewheelin' Bob Dylan*," a disc jockey said in a hushed, reverent tone. "Lots of good tracks on that one."

"Goddam folk singers," Salinger said.

"Why does everybody hate folk singers?"

"Hey, Ace, we're shooting astronauts into space. This isn't the land of the goddam pioneers anymore."

"That song could come from any age. It's a goddam good song."

"If you say so. Usually, they play jazz on this station."

"I guess the times are changing," Jeff said.

"Life is just a bowl of cherries. Don't take it serious, it's too mysterious," Salinger sang. "Nobody writes lyrics like that anymore."

"How much is that doggie in the window?" Jeff sang. "I bet that's your idea of a real song."

"No. My idea is Lena Horne singing 'Stormy Weather.'"

"I don't know that one. I'll tell you a good one. 'Be My Baby' by the Ronettes. That song's deep."

"Rock and roll . . . deep, huh? Don't make me laugh."

"Did you ever hear it?"

"I don't know. Maybe when I took the car down to the Windsor garage. They're always playing that crap around the lube pit."

"Oh, Denise, shoobie-doo is another great one, by the way. It kills me."

"That's not Gershwin, is it?"

"No, Randy and the Rainbows."

"You really listen to that garbage?"

"It's what's on the radio now, Jerry."

"Sheesh."

They drove silently as twilight gathered over the landscape. Then, around a bend on Route 120, to the left, Ponsonby Hall appeared distantly on the shoulder of Linton Hill in all its Romanesque splendor, dozens of windows lighted up on this day of the scholars' return.

"There it is!" Jeff cried. "Turn here!"

Salinger swerved onto the entrance drive, which switchbacked dramatically going up the steep hill.

"One thing I've got to ask you," Salinger said, slowing the Jeep down on the first curve. "That Broadway cutie you got mixed up with, did you give her the time?"

"Me? Are you kidding?"

"I'm not kidding. Did you give her the time or not, you little bastard?"

"No."

"You didn't even try to put the moves on her?"

"Not really. She kissed me a couple of times. But it was like . . . how you kiss your dog."

"I bet you wanted to, though. Didn't you want to give her the time?"

"If you mean what I think, it didn't occur to me."

"Didn't occur to you! You're a liar."

"No, I'm not."

"You said she was pretty developed."

"Yeah, so . . . ?"

"Doesn't that tell you anything?"

"What do you think, I'm a moron?"

"But it didn't occur to you to give her the time. It's possible you're a homo and you don't even know it."

"Jeezus, Jerry. I'm pretty sure I'm not a homo."

"Then why didn't you put the moves on what's-her-name?"

"Kathy Kaine. I only went on two dates with her, and the second one, on Thanksgiving, ended up a complete goddam disaster."

"Didn't you say other guys were flirting her up? Older guys. Grown men."

"Yeah, she seemed to like the attention. And they were feeding her drinks. Well, so was I, actually."

"Really?" Salinger looked impressed. "How'd you manage that?"

"I told the bartender my mom was in a wheelchair in the other room and couldn't get to him."

"Hmm. Clever. Well, you know, sooner or later one of those men chasing her is going to give her the time. You know that, don't you?"

"I told you, the girl she replaced in the cast got knocked up. Kathy said she would never let that happen to her. She's already getting offers for Hollywood movies."

"That'll surely wreck her. By the way, you know how that works, don't you? Getting knocked up?"

"Yeah, it so happens I do."

"You have to give a girl the time."

"Well, I didn't, Jerry. It just worked out that way."

There were two cars in the capacious porte cochere of the Great Hall and several behind them out in the open driveway. Salinger pulled up in line with a slight screech of his tires.

"Okay, you can get out," he said. "And remember to keep your trap shut about ever being in my house. Come on! Chop chop! I need to get the hell out of here before anyone sees me."

"Can I just say one thing, Jerry?" Jeff said, reaching into the back seat for his rucksack.

"Go ahead."

"You're a miserable sonofabitch. I'm sorry I read your goddam book."

Salinger recoiled.

"Yeah? Well, believe me, I'm sorry I wrote it," he muttered.

Jeff took off his red hunting hat and tossed it in Salinger's lap.

"Here. You take it. You need it more than I do."

He darted out of the Jeep and dashed through the porte cochere to the big arched double door that led inside. Salinger frantically executed a sloppy three-point turn, just missing the bumper of a Cadillac ahead of him, and sped away down the hill.

*

Most of the Ponsonby scholars had already returned on the train out of New York to White River Junction, but Dr. Stilgoe was still greeting late-arriving boys and their parents who had driven them back. He commanded the spacious entrance lobby of the Great Hall like a demigod with its displays of American Indian art and several fine framed paintings of the Indian life by Remington and Bierstadt. Dr. Stilgoe happened, at that moment, to be chatting up the parents of Clarence ("Dash") Fortenbaugh, up from Ridgefield, Connecticut, when the headmaster locked eyes with Jeff scurrying toward the west wing, where his room was on the second floor. Stilgoe's fierce glance came with a forced, weak, altogether dubious smile, but he did not stray from his social duties with the Fortenbaughs and Jeff was soon up the big stairway.

Next came a happy surprise. His roommate Axel ("Stench") Knudsen was gone, replaced by a mild-looking boy with a mop of yellow hair, neatly dressed, lounging on Stench's former bed, which was neatly made too, even with hospital corners, the making of which Stench had been utterly incapable. When Jeff stepped in, the new boy was reading the liner notes on a record album that was spinning on his Decca portable record player. The song playing was the very number he'd just heard in Salinger's Jeep, "Don't Think Twice, It's All Right."

"Hey," Jeff greeted him. "Who are you?"

The boy got up briskly and took the needle off the record.

"Teddy Vincent," he said and stuck out his hand.

"Jeff Greenaway. They were just playing that song on the radio in the car I drove up in."

"Yeah, he's something else."

"So, that's the record?"

"It's really good."

"Are you my new roommate?"

"Yeah, I was assigned here. Hope you don't mind."

"I'm awful glad you have a record player. Wow, he really must be gone, then, old Stench," Jeff said. "The guy was the worst slob you ever saw in your life. He really stunk up a room. I wonder what happened to him."

"I don't know," Teddy said. "They just told me to come here. I'm pretty neat and clean."

"I wonder if they just moved him, or kicked him out of the joint, or if he got into some kind of trouble. I guess we'll find out. Anyway, where are you from?"

"Lexington, Massachusetts. It's outside of Boston."

"Why'd you get sent here?"

"I got caught with a gun in my room at Exeter around Halloween."

"Jeezus!"

"Don't worry, they confiscated it from me."

"How'd you get a gun?"

"I paid this janitor ten bucks to buy it for me. You can buy them in a hardware store there."

"What kind of gun was it?"

"Double-barreled derringer. High Standard brand. It was a beauty."

"Why'd you want a gun?"

"Everybody loves guns," Teddy said.

"Yeah? Well, I guess. Were you going to plug somebody?"

"No. I just liked having it around. Made me feel good to know it was there."

"If I'd had a gun last October I might have plugged someone," Jeff said, and then he proceeded to recount his ordeal with Jack Hannon and the bullying Ancients.

"Every school has goons like that," Teddy said. "At Exeter it was Darrel Swinty and his gang."

Three blasts rang out on the bell in the hallway, signifying that supper was ready.

"Time for chow," Jeff said. "Come with me. I'll introduce you around to the guys."

*

The featured entrée on the menu this evening of return to school was the ever popular cheese bombers and bacon (grilled cheese with a savory surprise inside), accompanied by tater puffs and Mrs. Dinsmoor's creamy coleslaw. Dessert was carrot cake with cream cheese frosting. Under the circumstances, every boy was a member of the clean plate club, and the mood in the dining hall was buoyant, considering the last time they were all there together was the dismal night after President Kennedy was murdered.

Teddy Vincent melded in easily with the likes of "Dash," "Useless," "Bones," "Tiny," "Monk", "Sparky," and "Eightball." The nickname "Bear" was conferred upon him. When all that was concluded, the gang went upstairs and piled into Sparky and Monk's room where, Sparky Veach said, "a great event awaited."

His father, an executive with Mobil Oil, had returned from London just before the tragic doings in Dallas and brought home with him an item he thought would interest his son, who was crazy for rock and roll music: a 45 rpm single of "I Want to Hold Your Hand," by a new band called the Beatles, which had been blasting out of every shopfront on Oxford Street, and would not be released in the USA until Christmastime. "It's like some kind of social mania I've never seen before," Walter Veach had told Sparky. "These boys are driving England crazy."

They played the Beatles record five times, and then the new boy, Teddy Vincent, went and fetched his copy of *The Freewheelin' Bob Dylan*, which evoked such reverent awe among them that they immediately played it all the way through a second time.

"Where'd this guy come from?" Bones asked.

"Greenwich Village, apparently," Teddy said.

"A Hard Rain's a-Gonna Fall," Monk said. "Feels like it already is."

"He's for real, anyway," Dash summed it up, "not one of those phonies."

By that time, the single blast from the hall bell signaled it was time to return to their rooms and prepare for lights-out. Jeff and Teddy went back to Two-West-Twenty-two. There, in the dark, Jeff recounted his romantic adventure with the Broadway star Kathy Kaine, including all the blunders and misfortunes it entailed. As he told it now, he could hardly believe it ever really happened. Most of all, he was overjoyed to be restored to the world of Ponsonby Hall, its reassuring routines, its fellowship, and even the old-wood smell of its ancient rooms.

*

Breakfast had just about concluded the next morning when Mrs. Dinsmoor notified Jeff that he was wanted in the headmaster's office and to come straightaway without dawdling. Jeff was truly stunned to enter the sanctum and discover Bob and Evelyn seated in matching club chairs next to the crackling fireplace.

"What are you doing here?" he croaked.

"What do you think?" Bob said dryly.

"Where the hell have you been?" Evelyn shrieked, half rising out of her seat.

"Sit down, son," Doc Stilgoe said steering Jeff to one end of the love seat opposite his parents. Doc sat at the other end.

"Well?" Evelyn pressed him.

"Your mother's quite upset," Bob explained.

"I could murder you," she said. "Are you just going to sit there?"

"Go on, son," Doc said.

"I ran away," Jeff said.

"We're aware of that," Bob said.

"He's done it before," Evelyn appealed to Doc Stilgoe. "He runs away. It's what he does."

"Is there any question of . . . mistreatment?" Doc asked. "At home?" he added.

"Are you out of your mind?" Evelyn said.

"Really!" Bob said.

"We're loving parents," Evelyn said.

"There's something wrong with him," Bob said. "The way his brain is wired."

"There's nothing wrong with my brain," Jeff said.

"Where the hell were you?" Bob said.

"I took a train up here."

"Where did you spend the night Friday and Saturday?"

"Friday, I went to Lüchow's—"

"Lüchow's restaurant?" Evelyn said. "For godsake!"

"Yeah, for dinner—"

"Where do you get the money for all this?"

"Evidently, he won it playing poker," Bob said, "before the . . . you know . . . what happened last week. You let them play poker for money, Professor?"

"Of course not," he replied. "Gambling is forbidden here, but—"

"But what?"

"Boys are very resourceful," he said. "It is a known fact the world over. The young warriors of the Elkhart Potawatomi, for instance, engaged in a practice of secret marriage with older women of the tribe—"

"This is not an Indian thing, Professor. Our boy is out of control."

"He's proven to be quite well behaved here. And his grades are outstanding. Of course, I'm not defending this running away business . . ."

"Where did you spend Saturday night?" Evelyn pressed him.

"In the train station in Windsor," Jeff said.

"I bet that was glorious."

"It was all right."

"I hear you called my colleague Dave Hodge, trying to get Salinger's address."

"He told you that? The rat!"

"Did you go to Windsor looking for J. D. Salinger?" Bob said.

"I thought about it," Jeff said.

"Is that why you went there?"

"I guess."

"Did you find him?"

"No."

"Did you go looking for him?"

"Only a little. Nobody knows anything over there. They all clam up."

"I wonder if that bum knows how many kids' lives he's wrecking with that damn book of his," Bob said.

"He wouldn't give a damn," Jeff said.

"How would you know?"

"I'm just saying."

"Well, here's what I'm saying," Bob said, clearing his throat. "We've been in touch with a place down in Lenox, Massachusetts, called MacLaren Park. They're holding a bed there for you."

"A bed? I just got up a little while ago."

"It means, a place for you to stay, Pussycat," Evelyn said with the rage finally drained from her voice.

"I've got a perfectly good bed here!"

"Yes, but you're going to stay at this other place for a while."

"Stay there? What is that place?"

"It's a facility," Evelyn said. "MacLaren Park."

"It's a nuthouse, you mean. You're putting me in a nuthouse."

"It's a place for kids with problems," Bob explained. "It has an excellent reputation."

"I don't want to go."

"You're going, Ace."

"I'm not crazy."

"Maybe not. We're going to find out."

"Jesus Christ!"

"Er . . . son!" Doc Stilgoe said.

"Are you going to let them do this?" Jeff appealed to Doc.

"They are your parents, son."

"I can't believe you're doing this!"

"It's best for all concerned," Evelyn said.

"All concerned?" Jeff snapped. "You won't be concerned. You'll be back on Seventy-ninth Street going out for lunch at the museum with your pals. I'm the one who's going to the nuthouse."

"I wish you'd stop calling it that," Evelyn said. "And by the way. That's a very cruel thing for you to say to me. As if I'm not concerned about you."

Jeff took his time saying, "Sorry about that," and then the conversation came to a sort of natural conclusion. Bob went up to room Two-West-Twenty-two with Jeff to help him pack up his things, and by ten o'clock they were on the road in their rented Chevy Impala, headed south to Massachusetts. They stopped at a Howard Johnson's restaurant in Pittsfield where Jeff had one of their signature "frankfurters" (not a hot dog, though it was most assuredly a hot dog) and was permitted to take a double-dip cone of fudge ripple and butter crunch into the car for the last leg of the journey.

MacLaren Park was eerily like Ponsonby Hall as it was also a great rambling mansion on a hill, only in the Queen Anne style, with an even larger modern wing, a three-story, flat-roofed box featuring turquoise enameled steel panels between the windows, as if to make it architecturally interesting. Jeff's bed was in this building. After a preliminary interview with one Doctor Braden, the director of pediatric psychiatry, a kindly gentleman with frizzy gray hair, laughing eyes, and a pipe, Jeff said goodbye to Bob and Evelyn and was taken within.

Chapter Nineteen

Jeff Greenaway remained at MacLaren Park through the Christmas holiday that year and a little beyond. His ward housed eleven other children under fourteen. Of these, Jeff became friends with two: Susie Planchette, daughter of the Yale physicist Hector Planchette. Susie, thirteen, had attempted to kill herself after a romance with a Yale graduate student ended badly. She had been in MacLaren for two months. A dark-haired beauty with a wicked sense of humor, she found Jeff "amusing" and became his mealtime buddy, along with Dicky Templesman, twelve, from Pound Ridge, New York, who had been stealing his mother's sleeping pills, Seconals, and developed an addiction. His withdrawal had been a hideous affair, requiring the better part of a week's stay in the specially upholstered room at MacLaren reserved for such episodes. They called themselves the Three Musketeers and the smaller kids idolized them.

Jeff was assigned to a young headshrinker named Dr. Andrew Twachtman—didn't Susie P. have sport with that!—to whom he told the whole truth about his escapades the week after Thanksgiving, including his sojourn at the home of J. D. Salinger. Dr. Twachtman, at first skeptical, believed that Jeff was making it all up—he'd seen sundry boys who had become slightly delusional after exposure to *The Catcher in the Rye*, confusing themselves with Holden Caulfield—but the details Jeff conveyed about the Salinger household, and about the author himself, were too compelling to dismiss, including his morbid fear of lawsuits. Nor did the doctor discern anything pathological in Jeff's romantic adventure with Kathy Kaine. Eventually, their therapeutic discourse was reduced to the practical matter that Dr. Twachtman called *learning how to make good decisions*.

Though, Jeff did spend the Christmas holiday in MacLaren, Bob and Evelyn came up on Christmas Eve, bringing with them a copy of *The Freewheelin' Bob Dylan* that Jeff had asked for.

"Looks like this is the new Holden Caulfield," Bob cracked, examining the album cover front and back.

"Holden Caulfield is dead," Jeff retorted. "He committed suicide."

Bob and Evelyn pretended to laugh.

They took Jeff, on a hospital pass, to dinner at their lodgings, Lenox's venerable Curtis Hotel, which served the traditional holiday meal clear down to flaming plum pudding for dessert.

Two days later, Dr. Twachtman recommended discharge for Jeff. There was simply not enough abnormal, disturbed, or unhappy about him to warrant further in-patient treatment at five hundred dollars a week. And so, on Sunday, January 5, 1964, Jeff said goodbye to Susie and Dicky, and returned to the Ponsonby Hall school in Orcus, New Hampshire, to commence the spring semester of his first form year.

On January 20, the record album *Meet the Beatles* was released in the United States. On February 10, Columbia Records released Bob Dylan's third record album, *The Times They Are a-Changin'*. In April Jeff Greenaway would try out for the junior rowing crew and be accepted onto the team. It was all a boy in his situation could ask for. Despite Doc Stilgoe's prohibition on card playing for money, the Knights of the Round Casino resumed their occasional games in a new location, the old abandoned dairy where the school's Holstein herd once mooed and brooded. Sometimes Jeff won and sometimes Jeff lost, but he had become preternaturally careful about making good decisions in life and knew when to fold 'em.

In May 1964, Kathy Kaine turned up pregnant and was replaced in *The Wayward Family Singers* by one Janine Keltner, of Fort Myers, Florida. Jeff did not hear from Kathy Kaine ever again. But he never let go of her memory.

THE END

www.ingramcontent.com/pod-product-compliance
Lightning Source LLC
Chambersburg PA
CBHW011132190726
48289CB00012B/3008